He kissed her enthusiastically, caressing her shoulders. Then, when she pressed even closer, he slipped the shoulder straps of her camisole down her arms.

When the camisole slithered around her waist he gulped and flushed slightly, bending down to take one milk-chocolate-coloured nipple into his mouth. His tongue felt red hot against her cool skin and Liz felt pleasantly languorous as she tipped her head back and enjoyed the sensation.

The ground seemed to be slipping away underneath her and she realised he'd picked her up and was carrying her over to the bed. Placing her on the blue satin bedspread he undressed her, kissing each bit of her skin as he uncovered it . . .

Also available from Headline Delta

Exposed
Love Italian Style
Ecstasy Italian Style
Rapture Italian Style
Amorous Liaisons
Lustful Liaisons
Saucy Habits
Eroticon Dreams
Eroticon Desires
The Sensual Mirror
French Frolics
Claudine
Wild Abandon
After Hours
French Thrills
In The Mood
A Slave To Love
Amorous Appetites
The Blue Lantern
Sex and Mrs Saxon
Fondle On Top
Fondle In Flagrante
Fondle All Over
Kiss Of Death
The Phallus Of Osiris
High Jinks Hall
The Delicious Daughter
Three Women
Passion in Paradise
Ménage à Trois

Indecent

Felice Ash

Copyright © 1994 Felice Ash

The right of Felice Ash to be identified as the Author of the Work has been asserted by her in accordance with the Copyright, Designs and Patents Act 1988.

First published in 1994
by HEADLINE BOOK PUBLISHING PLC

A HEADLINE DELTA paperback

10 9 8 7 6 5 4 3 2 1

All rights reserved. No part of this publication may be reproduced, stored in a retrieval system, or transmitted, in any form or by any means without the prior written permission of the publisher, nor be otherwise circulated in any form of binding or cover other than that in which it is published and without a similar condition being imposed on the subsequent purchaser.

All characters in this publication are fictitious and any resemblance to real persons, living or dead, is purely coincidental.

ISBN 0 7472 4269 0

Typeset by Avon Dataset Ltd, Bidford-on-Avon

Printed and bound in Great Britain by
HarperCollins Manufacturing, Glasgow

HEADLINE BOOK PUBLISHING PLC
Headline House
79 Great Titchfield Street
London W1P 7FN

Indecent

CHAPTER ONE

In the offices of the *Daily News*, mayhem reigned as usual.

Picking her way to her desk through the chaos, Ellen reflected that if anyone needed peace and quiet to turn in good copy, they just weren't cut out for journalism.

The phone on her desk was ringing but she ignored its imperious summons and slipped off her jacket, hanging it over the back of her chair. Just to her left through the open door of one of the outer offices she could hear the sound of raised voices. A few seconds later one of her fellow journalists stormed out, stumbled over her wastepaper bin and kicked it bad-temperedly across the room.

Going over to the drinks machine, Ellen got herself a cup of coffee and returned to her desk. Thankfully the phone had stopped ringing. Sinking gratefully into her chair, she leant back and sipped her coffee, long stocking-clad legs stretched out in front of her.

At twenty-two Ellen was the youngest journalist on the *Daily News*. It was a job she'd won against strong competition and one which she was extremely good at. One look at her petite but provocatively curvaceous body and previously taciturn men began spilling the beans in answer to her questions. Her round blue eyes would widen as she hung breathlessly on their every word, pushing back her dark curls from her face as she listened avidly.

Her general air of ingenuousness helped lull people into a false sense of security and they would become careless and indiscreet, willingly giving her information that other journalists had to use devious methods to obtain.

As she drank her coffee Ellen thought that it was a good thing she liked her job, as there was very little else in her life she was happy with at the moment.

Sighing to herself, she wondered again why her boyfriend, Simon, seemed to have gone off sex so completely.

She'd woken up next to him that morning after a particularly vivid erotic dream. She'd been lying in a garden next to a glittering turquoise swimming pool. The garden was full of sweet-scented exotic flowers and the day was very hot — she could feel the sun beating down on her naked body as she lay there.

A faceless and unknown man began to massage sun oil into her body, paying particular attention to her breasts and buttocks, until all her curves were gleaming in the sunshine. The massage had aroused her and she pulled him down beside her on the grass where he began to kiss her. She felt the hardness of his cock and she opened her legs and guided him in. He felt so good inside her, filling her completely and moving in a way which left her weak and trembling with lust.

Waking suddenly from her dream, Ellen willed

herself to go back to sleep and pick up where she'd left off, but it was no good — she was wide awake and very aroused.

Simon was stirring beside her so, reaching out, she'd taken hold of his cock and stroked it, revelling in the silken hardness of his early-morning erection. Taking his hand she guided it to the slippery wetness between her legs, parting them and moaning with pleasure as his fingers made contact with her pulsating flesh.

Her pleasure was short-lived.

Jerking his hand away, he climbed out of bed and stood glaring furiously down at her.

'What on earth's the matter with you, Ellen? You've been behaving very oddly recently and I'm getting tired of it.'

'What's so odd about wanting sex occasionally?' she asked, confused and frustrated.

'Occasionally!' he snapped. 'More like constantly! Is sex all you can think about? I blame your job; working for a low-life tabloid has changed you — and not for the better I might add.'

Turning on his heel he strode off to the bathroom, leaving Ellen feeling edgy and miserable. It was so long since they'd had sex that she'd been in danger of forgetting what it was like — until her erotic dream had reminded her.

After showering and dressing she went into the kitchen to find Simon hunched gloweringly over a dish of cereal, reading *The Times*. Glancing up, he eyed her clothes with distaste.

'And why do you have to dress so tartily?'

Ellen felt completely bewildered.

Felice Ash

'You used to like the way I dress,' she reminded him. 'Anyway – what's wrong with this outfit?'

'Your skirt's much too short – and tight,' he told her. 'And I really don't see why you have to draw so much attention to your breasts.'

She was wearing a scoop-necked red and white striped top which moulded itself to the generous contours of her breasts. A short black skirt, black stockings and a pair of high-heeled shoes completed her outfit.

It was no good talking to Simon while he was in this mood. Picking up her bag and jacket Ellen said, 'I'm unlikely to be back before nine. Shall I get us a takeaway on the way home?'

'Suit yourself,' replied Simon grumpily. 'I may already have eaten.'

Now, sitting at her desk, Ellen gave herself a mental shake. There was really no point worrying about it – she'd pick up a couple of bottles of wine later, and after a few drinks perhaps she could get Simon to tell her what was wrong.

After ringing the doorbell Jon arranged his features into an expression of sympathetic concern and mentally geared himself up to be ready with the right approach.

The woman he was about to try and interview was the wife of a prominent High Court judge, who had been arrested late last night for kerb crawling. The *Daily News* had received information that she was hiding out at the house of a friend in Beckenham, while the press besieged the family home in Primrose Hill.

INDECENT

Hoping he wasn't on a wild goose chase, Jon rang the bell again. Then a noise above his head made him step backwards and look up. Mrs Haydon was peering nervously out of a bedroom window.

'Who are you?' she asked.

'Jon Wright from the *Daily News*,' he called. 'Mrs Haydon, I think you owe it to yourself to set the record straight about your husband. May I come in and ask you a few questions?'

'I've been told not to speak to anyone,' she replied stiffly.

'Who told you that, your husband?'

She nodded, her thick blonde hair falling forward over her face. Jon hoped that at the very least he could keep her at the window long enough for the *Daily News* photographer – hiding in the bushes at the bottom of the drive – to get a few decent shots with a telephoto lens.

'Well, that's not very fair to you is it? Please let me come in for just a few minutes. I give you my word that I'll leave as soon as you ask me to, but you may find it a help just to talk to someone.' He smiled up at her, raking his fingers through his dark hair.

At twenty-eight Jon was possessed of the sort of charm and boyish good looks that women of all ages, but particularly middle-aged women, found irresistible.

Now Mrs Haydon hesitated. Then, as he increased the wattage of his smile, she said slowly, 'Alright. But only for a couple of minutes.'

She vanished from the window and Jon glanced behind him, giving a brief signal to the hidden photographer. A minute later she appeared at the door and he went in, being careful to take his time over it to give his colleague another photo opportunity.

Mrs Haydon was in her mid-forties and had a ripe, curvaceous figure which was only partially concealed by the peach satin robe she was wearing. Following her into the sitting room Jon admired the sway of her well-rounded backside. He could see the outline of a slip and a pair of pale-coloured, lacy pants under the robe and he noted with interest that she wasn't wearing a bra.

Sitting down on the sofa, he produced a notebook and pen. They were completely superfluous as there was a miniature tape recorder in his pocket already running, but he knew that they inspired confidence in anyone he was interviewing. It was as if anything said was off the record if he didn't actually write it down, a misapprehension he never corrected.

'I know it's early but I think I'm going to have a drink,' murmured Mrs Haydon. 'Will you join me?'

He smiled at her. 'You know, I think I will. Please allow me — what will you have?' He moved in the direction of the drinks tray as he spoke, this was going better than he'd anticipated. He poured her the vodka and tonic she requested, making it good and strong, then poured his own much weaker one.

After a few general and sympathetic questions it became obvious that Mrs Haydon was a woman with a grievance. Jon prompted her with several more solicitous enquiries until she suddenly burst out, 'It wasn't the first time you know, but they managed to hush it up last time! The humiliation of it! He never gives a thought to me or the children — we're just

INDECENT

trotted out every once in a while whenever he wants to play at being the family man. How are the children going to face their friends now? Or me mine, knowing that everyone knows.'

She took another gulp of her drink before continuing. 'He's always been obsessed by prostitutes, goodness knows why. I haven't let him near me since he gave me VD three years ago and I found out about them. He tried denying it at first, saying *I* must have been with someone else, but I hadn't and he knew it — he admitted it in the end. Why would a man want to pay for it with some disease-ridden slut when he's married?'

Looking her in the eye, Jon said in his sincerest voice, 'Beats me Mrs Haydon, particularly when he's married to a woman as attractive as you.'

She dabbed at her eyes, then smiled at him. 'Well, thank you for that. I know I'm on the wrong side of forty, but I was considered very attractive when I was younger.' She crossed her legs as she spoke and the peach satin robe fell apart, revealing a pair of firm milky thighs.

Jon allowed his glance to linger on them briefly but appreciatively before he raised his eyes to her face again.

'You're still a lovely woman, Mrs Haydon, and I know there must be a lot of other men out there who think so too. When did your husband first go with a prostitute do you think?'

Taking another pull of her drink, she said, 'It's certainly a few years ago.'

'And did he always pick them up by kerb crawling?'

'I'm not sure. At one time I think he had a regular one, but I can't be certain.'

Mrs Haydon downed two more vodka and tonics as she told Jon about her husband's indiscretions. Outwardly he was all sympathetic concern, inwardly he was jubilant. What a story this would make. What luck that he'd caught her at just the right moment.

It wasn't altogether a surprise when she moved to sit next to him on the sofa.

'You're a very nice man,' she told him, in a voice slightly thickened by drink. 'Do you have a girlfriend?'

'Not at the moment Mrs Haydon, my last relationship ended unhappily and I haven't really picked up the pieces yet.' He didn't add that he did, however, have an extremely satisfying sex life with Dana, an aerobics instructress at a plush health club.

'That's a pity,' she said, moving closer and nestling against him. 'Please, call me Susan.'

She placed her hand on his thigh and began to stroke it slowly, saying, 'In all these years I've never been unfaithful to my husband and I'm beginning to suspect I've wasted a lot of opportunities. I think after all I've been through I'm entitled to a life of my own — don't you?'

Her hand moved further upwards and came to rest on the hard bulge of his cock through his trousers.

'No one could blame you,' he agreed, turning towards her and sliding his hand into the gaping neckline of her satin robe. Her large, unsupported breast was heavy in his palm and he savoured the weight of it for a moment before his hand closed firmly over it.

Jon was facing the window and a sudden movement outside caused him to withdraw his hand and disentangle himself.

'I'll just close the curtains,' he murmured, crossing the room. Just as he'd suspected, Ernie the photographer was crouched in the shrubbery, camera as always at the ready. Closing the curtains Jon grinned and ignored his colleague's rude gesture.

Returning to the sofa, he pulled Mrs Haydon into his arms and kissed her. Her lips felt soft and pulpy beneath his own and she smelt of shampoo and talcum powder.

She had a great body, he thought — soft, yielding and voluptuous without being overweight. He slipped her dressing gown down to her waist, taking her slip with it. Her nipples were large and coral coloured and he fastened his mouth over one and sucked hard. She leaned back against the sofa and let him suck, lick and kiss his way over her breasts, moaning faintly with pleasure.

Jon was in no hurry — he intended to enjoy himself and to see that she did too, but when he slipped a hand between her thighs she suddenly went wild.

Pushing him onto his back, she knelt astride him and unzipped his trousers. Taking out his cock, she slid it into her mouth and wrapped her tongue around it, exploring it eagerly. He wound his fingers into her wavy blonde hair exhaling with pleasure, gasping at the sensations caused by her warm, wet mouth as she sucked him further in. With the tip of her tongue she began to strum the underside of his cock, working her way along the full length of it.

Adjusting her position, she rubbed the tip of it against her clit, then thrust herself downwards until he'd penetrated her deeply. She rode him frantically in a way which indicated just how hungry she'd been for a man inside her again. Her pleasure was so tangible that Jon redoubled his efforts, his hands on her breasts, thrusting upwards to meet her in a mutually enjoyable rhythm.

Two hours later when he emerged from the house Jon was a happy man.

Not only did he have a great story but he'd just enjoyed a sexual encounter which had left him aching, exhausted and completely satisfied.

Mrs Haydon had also confided a few of her husband's more esoteric sexual requests during the course of their marriage. One of her revelations had turned him on to such an extent that he'd managed to get it up for a third, and as far as his aching cock was concerned, final time.

He found Ernie behind the wheel of the car parked a hundred yards down the road, eating a bacon sandwich.

'You jammy bastard,' he greeted Jon sourly. 'I don't suppose that while you were comforting the betrayed wife you gave a thought to me stuck here in the car — you might at least have left the curtains open. Or suggested that if she was in the mood for being comforted, that you had a friend who'd be only too happy to oblige as well.'

Ernie finished his sandwich, disposed of the

INDECENT

wrapper by the simple expedient of throwing it out of the window, and put the car into gear.

'Good, was it?' he enquired after a brief pause.

Jon grinned at him.

'Mind your own business. Or better still get a life of your own rather than taking such a prurient interest in mine.'

Ernie overtook a white Ford Escort, taking his eyes off the road to gaze lustfully at the attractive girl driving it, just missing a cyclist in the process.

'That's easy for you to say. I'm always the one crawling round in the bushes or hanging around for hours on end while you bang some bint you're supposed to be interviewing. I chose the wrong career,' he added gloomily. 'I should have become a journalist then I'd have the endless supply of willing pussy instead of you.'

Jon had heard this diatribe many times before and had long ago grown tired of pointing out that his colleague's lack of success with women had more to do with his total dearth of charm, unprepossessing appearance and foul personal habits than it did with his chosen career. Instead he settled down in his seat and began mentally to write his story.

When Liz strode determinedly into his office, Vernon Rees, the editor of the *Daily News*, had to repress a slight tremor of erotic sensation which was half anticipation and half fear.

Liz Peters was the paper's leading columnist, a hard-edged, strong-willed journalist with a legendary sexual appetite. Tall and striking, with a mass of glossy chestnut hair, she was reputed to be able to bend Vernon to her will by the judicious manipulation of his more bizarre sexual preferences.

No one had any proof of this, but the fact that anyone who came up against Liz came off worst, and that Vernon always did back her, made for a lot of gleeful speculation.

'Hello Liz,' he greeted her cautiously. 'What can I do for you?'

'You can get me a new secretary,' she told him decisively. 'This one is even worse than the last one — if that's possible.'

Vernon suppressed a sigh. Liz got through secretaries the way other journalists got through cups of coffee. There had been five so far this year alone. The main problem, as far as he could gather, was that none of them had been gifted with the sort of psychic powers which would have enabled them to anticipate and prepare for Liz's unpredictable and wide-ranging demands.

Now, as she flung herself elegantly into the chair facing his desk and crossed her long slim legs, Vernon licked his dry lips and tried to placate her.

'I'll have Hannah phone the agency,' he assured her. 'See if they've got anyone more suitable.'

'Suitable!' she snorted. 'Anyone with an IQ higher than their body temperature would be more suitable than this dimwit. The stupid little bitch doesn't even know how to mix a Screwdriver.'

Presented with this example of the unfortunate girl's unsuitability for the position of Liz's secretary, Vernon made no attempt to reason with her. Instead he spoke briefly into the intercom which connected him with Hannah, his own secretary, and relayed

INDECENT

Liz's request. Then he unwound his tall, slightly stooped form from his chair, went over to the drinks cupboard, unlocked it and fixed her a drink.

This was a courtesy almost never extended to any of the other journalists and one which confirmed her position in the hierarchy.

'You're looking gorgeous today Liz,' he ventured. 'That colour really suits you.'

Liz was wearing a figure-hugging pale yellow dress and Vernon's eyes fixed lecherously on her breasts. He swallowed, wondering if he dare suggest a rendezvous later. It was unlikely she'd agree. Liz was a woman who liked to call the shots herself and she usually only accommodated him when she wanted something.

Regrettably, getting her a new secretary didn't qualify for the sort of sexual gratification only she could provide.

Still it was worth a shot.

'Liz?'

'What?'

Her terse reply wasn't very encouraging.

'I was wondering if you were doing anything tonight.'

'I have a date.'

'Who with?'

As soon as the words were out of his mouth Vernon regretted them. He knew Liz would resent the question.

'With someone half your age and with twice your stamina,' she hissed, standing up and slamming her empty glass down on his desk. 'And I'll need Hannah for the rest of the afternoon,' she added, turning on her heel and leaving him staring helplessly after her.

Ellen had finished work for the day by six o'clock, even though she'd not anticipated being ready to leave much before eight-thirty.

After touching up her make-up and spraying herself lavishly with perfume she left the *Daily News* building. She went straight into a nearby wine merchants where she bought a couple of bottles of white wine before heading for the tube station.

She decided not to bother with a takeaway until she'd seen Simon. If she bought Chinese he'd be sure to complain that he felt like a pizza and if she bought a pizza he'd undoubtedly say she should have opted for Indian.

Letting herself into the flat, she was just removing her jacket in the hallway when she heard a low moaning sound coming from the bedroom.

Her heart pounding, she pushed open the door to see Simon energetically screwing a fair-haired woman, and doing so with more enthusiasm than Ellen had seen him exhibit in months. For a few moments his buttocks continued to rise and fall until a strangled cry from his partner, as she caught sight of Ellen, made him stop and turn his head.

Suddenly everything fell into place. Ellen recognised the other woman as Charlotte Benning, the new solicitor Simon's legal firm had recently taken on and the daughter of the senior partner.

Stunned, Ellen sank onto the edge of a chair and stared blankly at the two of them. Simon climbed sheepishly off Charlotte and tried to pull the sheet up. Unfortunately it was tangled beneath them so Ellen had plenty of time to examine the other woman's naked body. She was stick thin and her ribs protruded like railway sleepers.

'Ellen – I can explain...' Simon began, but Charlotte interrupted him.

'How dare you just walk in here!' she exclaimed agitatedly. 'You may be Simon's flatmate, but surely he's entitled to some privacy.'

Astonished, Ellen looked at Simon but he refused to meet her eyes.

'Actually,' she said, 'until now I was under the impression I was Simon's girlfriend. Obviously I've been labouring under a misapprehension. You absolute shit, Simon – how could you?'

'We've been nothing but flatmates for months now, as well you know,' he asserted belligerently. 'I only let you continue to live here because I felt sorry for you.'

Ellen's jaw dropped.

'You miserable, lying bastard!' she flung at him. 'Well don't worry, I'm leaving now. Incidentally, Charlotte, have you had a look around the flat? This is the only bedroom.'

With that she went over to the wardrobe and dragged out two large suitcases, then she began to pull out clothes and throw them in, saying furiously, 'I think you've just become Simon's new flatmate, Charlotte – until the next one. Although as your father *is* the senior partner and Simon *is* very ambitious you may last longer. I'll be back for the rest of my stuff as soon as I've found somewhere else to live.'

Slamming the lids of the suitcases – regardless of the fact that half her clothes were hanging out – she grabbed them and staggered out of the flat, walking around the corner and out of sight before stopping to wait for a taxi to flag down.

As she waited she fumed.

How dare Simon deny her sex when all the time he was fucking another woman? She'd turned down all offers from other men (and there had been plenty) since moving in with him and she was already bitterly regretting it.

And as for Charlotte Benning, Ellen had met her a couple of times and had been chilled by the other woman's cool demeanour, supercilious air and perfect grooming. Charlotte was always dressed in dark suits with discreet knee-skimming skirts, worn over prim little blouses. Ellen's wardrobe was colourful and chaotic and somehow her stockings always seemed to have runs in them and her clothes buttons missing.

It was bad enough that Simon had either fallen for Charlotte or had decided to further his career by fixing his interest on her, but bringing her back to the flat and screwing her in their bed was unforgivable.

Particularly since she hadn't been able to get him to screw her in weeks.

Well, from now on she was going to make up for lost time as far as men were concerned.

Switching off her computer and pushing back her dark blonde hair, Kate stretched voluptuously and glanced at her watch. Seven-thirty. Good, just time for a quick drink before going to meet James.

She was pulling on her jacket when Ellen appeared at the end of the office burdened by two large, badly packed suitcases.

Kate was the *Daily News* political journalist with whom Ellen was on fairly friendly terms. Regarding the suitcases quizzically she asked, 'What's up?'

'Nothing really,' said Ellen, 'if you don't count the fact that I've nowhere to live, no man in my life and I haven't had anything to eat since a Mars bar at eleven o'clock.'

'Sounds bad,' returned Kate, 'how about a drink?'

'That's the best suggestion I've had all day,' said Ellen, pushing her cases against the wall beside her desk.

The two women wound up in the Vine, a pub frequented primarily by journalists. Once ensconced at a corner table with their drinks — and in Ellen's case a plate of lasagne and two scotch eggs — Kate asked, 'So what happened?'

With her mouth full Ellen said, 'I went back to the flat earlier than Simon was expecting and found him in bed with someone else.'

Kate said nothing as Ellen continued, 'Do you know Kate, he hasn't screwed me in weeks. He kept saying that I was oversexed — and all the time he's been sleeping with that supercilious cow whose daddy just happens to be the senior partner in the firm Simon works for.'

Viciously, Ellen pronged another wedge of lasagne and forked it into her mouth. 'It wouldn't be quite such a disaster except that it's Simon's flat. Now I'm going to have to book into a hotel for the night and spend goodness knows how long looking for somewhere else to live.' She finished her pasta and downed the rest of her drink. 'Another?' she asked.

'Sure.'

When she returned to the table Ellen bit into a scotch egg and continued, 'That's it for me – at least for now. No more long-term relationships, just lots and lots of lovely men. I've got a fairly lengthy period of abstention to make up for.'

Kate looked amused. 'Well, that's one way of looking at the situation. Aren't you upset at all?'

Putting her head on one side Ellen pursed her rosebud mouth.

'Kind of, but I'm half relieved, too. I was beginning to think there must be something wrong with me. Anyway, I was fed up of his constant criticism. Do you know what he said this morning?'

'What?'

'That I dressed tartily.'

Looking across at her younger colleague, Kate burst out laughing. Sitting there with her dark curls dishevelled, her creased short skirt stretched tightly around her thighs and a massive hole in the knee of one stocking where she'd caught it on her case, Ellen did look, if not exactly tarty, certainly endearingly sluttish.

Glancing downwards, Ellen said grudgingly, 'Alright – I know I wouldn't win any prizes for immaculate grooming at the moment. Here, I'll put some lipstick on.' She proceeded to apply a clear red gloss to her lips which made her look as if she'd just sucked a strawberry lollipop. In fact, her pouting mouth, round blue eyes and helpless air often

INDECENT

combined to give the impression that she was much younger than her real age − her nickname in the editorial offices of the *Daily News* was 'Lolita'.

Rummaging around in her bag, Kate produced a key and tossed it across the table.

'Well, I can help you with your homelessness problem, but you're on your own as far as men are concerned − that's the key to my flat.' Scribbling something on a piece of paper she added, 'Here's the address. Just go round when you're ready, I'll be back later. I'm afraid the spare room is only about the size of the average wardrobe, but you can stay for a few days while you find somewhere else.'

'Thanks, Kate,' said Ellen, much relieved. Hotels in London were so astronomically expensive that even a few nights in residence would make a big dent in her salary, though her job paid quite well.

'See you later,' replied Kate. 'Help yourself to something to eat if the lasagne and scotch eggs weren't enough.' Then, threading her way through the crowded pub she vanished from view.

Kate was on her way to a rendezvous with her current lover, a cabinet minister. He kept a small flat a few minutes walk from Westminster where they met regularly. Letting herself in, Kate went straight into the bedroom where James, wearing only a dressing gown, was propped up against the pillows drinking whisky and reading a report.

He didn't speak, merely laid the papers on the bedside table, removed his glasses and watched her.

Slowly she shrugged off her jacket, tossing it carelessly aside. Her scarlet dress had buttons down the front which she undid at a leisurely pace, revealing first the swell of her generous breasts and a deep cleavage, then her lacy cream silk slip.

Kate was extremely attractive with her dark blonde hair and deep brown eyes. Standing there in her slip, suspender belt, stockings and high-heeled shoes she let her lover's eyes roam over her as she waited for him to speak.

'Bend over the chair,' James told her hoarsely. Obediently, hips swaying, she walked over to the chair and gripping the arms, bent over it. Her slip was very short and when she leant forward it rode up over the creamy curves of her backside, exposing the moist pink folds of her sex. She'd dispensed with her panties before leaving work.

'Open your legs.'

Kate did as she was told.

She could feel his gaze on her and knew that he was devouring her with his eyes. Internally she could feel herself beginning to cream. So when he said, 'Touch yourself,' and she obeyed, her fingers slid easily over her slippery wetness. Languidly she caressed her own clit, feeling it swell and become more sensitive as she increased the pressure.

She heard a rustling sound as he shed his dressing gown. Then she felt his hands on her, running over the smooth skin of her buttocks. She removed her own hand and braced herself slightly. With a delicate touch he felt between her legs, first rubbing the side of her clit for a while until the pressure began to build, then pushing two fingers inside her.

She squirmed, bearing down against the exploring fingers giving her so much pleasure. A few moments later he removed them and she felt the head of his cock pushing between her legs.

He began to move it backwards and forwards, sometimes entering her a short way then withdrawing. At last, unable to bear it any longer, she moaned softly and ground her rear into his groin. Seizing her by the waist he thrust deeply into her and commenced a vigorous pumping, her buttocks making a slapping sound against his thighs.

Still holding onto the chair, Kate moaned as the rhythm increased. Reaching between her legs from the front he rubbed her clit to the same tempo, until she let out a muffled cry and came, arching back against him as her body enjoyed the shuddering release of orgasm.

James slid his hands inside her slip and over her breasts, holding her clasped tightly to his chest. He continued to thrust away until he too groaned and ejaculated with a force which left him, at least temporarily, spent.

They moved over to the bed, still holding onto each other, and sank onto the quilt panting.

'You were late,' he muttered a while later, idly caressing her left breast, rubbing the palm of his hand over one stiff, puckered nipple.

'Mmm,' she returned, gliding her long fingernails over his cock and registering a perceptible stiffening. 'Something came up.' Then as she closed her hand firmly over him, she added, 'Feels like something else is coming up now.'

'You could be right,' he agreed, sitting up and peeling off her slip, leaving her clad only in her suspender belt, stockings and high-heeled shoes.

Rolling onto his back he pulled her astride him. 'The question is, how far up?'

'Oh, all the way,' she told him, raising herself long enough to get the head of his dick against the yielding entrance to her pussy. Lowering herself onto him in a fluid movement she bore downwards until he was completely inside her.

Holding him in place with her internal muscles she began to rock slowly backwards and forwards while his hands found her breasts again and fondled them. When the unhurried rhythm of her movements became too much for him, James slipped his hands under her backside, pushing her upwards then pulling her down hard. Kate rose and fell above him, sometimes moving upwards so far that he nearly slipped out. Silently he urged her on to greater efforts, holding onto her hips.

Her head fell backwards and her eyes closed as she felt herself on the brink of orgasm. With a deep sigh she thrust down hard again, then cried out loudly as she felt the hot spurting of his release. She came herself a few seconds later.

CHAPTER TWO

Reclining on the sofa in the living room of Kate's flat, Ellen was munching her way through a family-sized bag of crisps and watching a mini-series on TV, when she heard the sound of the front door opening.

'I'm in here,' she called, swinging her legs onto the floor and turning towards the door.

Kate came in. Ellen took one look at her and knew immediately that her colleague had only recently got out of bed; she gave off the unmistakable glow of a sexually satisfied woman.

Retying the belt of her old kimono style dressing gown Ellen said enviously, 'Well, I don't need to ask if you've had a good evening — you look like a cat that's just lapped up a whole bowl of double cream. Anyone I've met?'

Kate shook her head, smiling.

'I don't think so.' She stretched contentedly then added, 'Did you find everything you need?'

'Yes. I took some sheets out of the airing cupboard to make up the bed and I've had a shower — is that okay?'

'Mmm? Oh yes. Well I think I'll have one too, then I'll turn in. I'll see you tomorrow — hope the bed isn't too uncomfortable.'

Yawning, Kate left the room, leaving Ellen feeling

she must be the only woman in the world without a sex life.

Climbing in between the crisp, cool sheets of Kate's spare bed a few minutes later, she wondered how difficult it was going to be to find herself a satisfying sex life.

Not *too* difficult, she hoped.

Rising early the following morning, Ellen made herself a cup of coffee then ate two apples, a bowl of muesli and several chocolate biscuits. Sitting at the kitchen table wearing only an oversized tee shirt and a pair of black lace panties, she was just wondering where to begin her search for a new flat when Kate came in.

Kate's dark blonde hair was wet and she was rubbing at it vigorously with a towel.

'Morning,' she greeted Ellen, moving over to the kettle and switching it back on. 'How did you sleep?'

'Fine, the bed was really quite comfortable. How about you?' Ellen didn't add that she'd spent what seemed like hours trying to get off to sleep while wild sexual fantasies kept flitting across her brain.

'Oh, I slept well as usual.' Kate was wearing a filmy, knee-length dressing gown of oyster coloured silk through which Ellen could see her breasts and pubic hair quite clearly.

Trying not to stare, but fascinated nevertheless, Ellen compared Kate's slender body to her own more curvaceous one. If she were a man would she fancy Kate? Watching the front of her colleague's dressing gown separate to reveal a pair of firm creamy breasts as she reached for milk, Ellen decided she would.

The two women sat in silence for a few minutes, Kate leafing through the morning's post and Ellen in her usual early morning daze, until glancing at the clock Kate said, 'Better get moving I suppose. Want to share my minicab?'

Ellen had a meeting scheduled with the *Daily News* editor at eleven o'clock.

Vernon Rees smiled wolfishly at her across his oversized desk, his eyes on her breasts. Her dress was tight, stretchy and black and for a few moments he forgot the purpose of their meeting as he thought how much he'd like to pull down the front of her dress and fasten his mouth over one of her pert nipples.

Ellen cleared her throat and smiled enquiringly at him. She knew a man in the grip of lust when she saw one, but even in her current frame of mind she didn't want to start anything with anyone at work. Gossip spread like wild fire through the *Daily News* offices and she didn't relish the rest of the staff saying that she held down her job by virtue of her sexual availability.

Getting a grip on himself Vernon asked her, 'Well, Ellen, what ideas did you come up with for the series of articles we discussed?'

Ellen had spent a lot of time thinking up several ideas and was ready to present them, when suddenly she was struck by a completely new one.

They were interrupted by Hannah bringing in coffee and Ellen took the opportunity to rapidly consider her flash of inspiration. She continued to consider it while presenting her other suggestions and then when she'd finished, took a deep breath and said, 'My final idea is that I should do a series on lonely hearts columns.'

Vernon hadn't seemed particularly thrilled by anything he'd heard so far, but suddenly he looked interested.

'Go on,' he encouraged her, running his hand over his greying hair. Ellen swiftly outlined her proposal.

'I thought I could place ads in the lonely hearts columns of several different publications and arrange to meet some of the men who reply. I could write about the different types and whether they're what I'd have expected from their letters. I'd go on to describe the actual dates, where they took me, whether they expected sex — that sort of thing.'

Vernon nodded and scribbled a couple of notes on a notepad, pursing his lips thoughtfully. Ellen, meanwhile, was thinking how great it would be to kill two birds with one stone. She could simultaneously research a series of articles *and* find herself a varied new sex life.

Crossing her legs and pressing her thighs together she prayed Vernon would go for it. At last he looked up and said, 'Yes, I like it. Okay — draft your ad and get it in, say, three different publications. Let me know when you've had any replies.'

Rising gleefully to her feet Ellen smoothed her clinging dress down over her thighs.

'I'll get onto it right away,' she assured him.

As the lift rose silently towards the eighth floor,

INDECENT

Liz examined her reflection in the mirrored walls. Her chestnut hair hung down over her shoulders in glossy curls, making a perfect frame for her beautiful, predatory face. Smiling at her reflection she licked her red lips and smoothed the close-fitting jacket of her sea-green silk suit over her breasts. The matching skirt was also tight and stopped several inches above her knees. Black seamed stockings and spike heeled shoes completed her striking ensemble.

Arriving at the door of one of the hotel's most luxurious suites, Liz was looking forward to the scheduled interview.

Ledd Lomas was the lead singer in Sledgehammer — the hottest, dirtiest, raunchiest heavy metal band to ever make it big. Nineteen years old and with the face of a fallen angel, he exuded the type of animal sexuality which made Liz squirm in her silk knickers.

He opened the door himself and gave her the sort of openly appraising look that many women found offensive, but which Liz merely returned with interest. She allowed his gaze to travel the length of her lush body and when eventually his eyes met hers, she looked coolly back at him saying, 'Liz Peters. We have an interview arranged for two o'clock.'

He was wearing a pair of the black leather trousers which had become his trademark, even though he must know there was no photographic session planned. Didn't he find them just a bit hot and uncomfortable on such a warm afternoon? she wondered. She made a mental note to ask him.

'Come on in,' he mumbled at last. 'Drink?'

'Champagne,' she replied, noting with annoyance the presence of some underling hovering in the background. Liz always made it part of her arrangements that she should conduct her interviews on a one-to-one basis.

'What is he doing here?' she demanded crisply. 'I thought that my secretary had agreed with your publicist that only the two of us would be present.'

She glanced at his leather-covered crotch as she spoke, before lowering herself onto the sofa and crossing her legs sexily.

'Malcolm — open a bottle of champagne for the lady then piss off,' muttered Ledd over his shoulder. He sat down opposite her and stared openly at her legs.

He was even better looking than his photos, Liz decided. He oozed the sort of sexuality which made her want to grab his head and thrust it between her thighs, holding it there until she was ready for him to replace it with something else.

Still, plenty of time for that later, better get the interview done first before allowing herself to be distracted.

Malcolm put her glass of champagne on a small table next to the sofa and then, at a nod from his employer, left the room.

'You're one sexy-looking lady,' Ledd told her suddenly, leering at her breasts. 'Wanna fuck?'

Liz winced slightly, more at his bad attempt at an American accent than at the crude question. She got the definite impression he said the same thing to all women he came into contact with — he had his super stud image to maintain after all.

'Thank you, but not right now,' she said, her tone politely dismissive. She could tell that Ledd was slightly thrown off balance by her reply — presumably she was supposed to be either shocked or flattered. She lit up a cigarette and took her time about setting up the tape recorder, taking several pulls of her drink and ignoring him completely.

At last she was ready.

She started by asking him about his band's latest album and forthcoming tour, leaning back against the sofa cushions and dragging her cigarette smoke deep into her lungs while he replied.

God, he was sexy, she thought while he talked. Sexy and barely articulate. But then, he didn't sell albums because he was a witty raconteur. He sold albums because teenage girls wanted to go to bed with him and teenage boys wanted to be him.

She allowed him to wander off the point, narrowing her eyes as she looked again at his leather-clad crotch. Well, he certainly seemed to have something packed away in there. The question was did he know how to use it to give a woman the maximum pleasure?

She realised he'd stopped talking and prompted him with another question, this time about his personal life and a recent paternity suit. She'd already decided to do a hatchet job on him, because that, after all, was what she was famous for and anyone prepared to be interviewed by her knew it.

She'd long ago stopped being surprised that people still lined up to appear in her column — keeping in the public eye was what it was all about.

Half an hour later, when the urgent pulsing between her legs was getting unbearable, she leant forward and switched the tape recorder off while he was still speaking.

'Here! I haven't finished,' he protested.

'Oh, I've more than enough material here for an article,' she assured him.

'What are you going to write?' he asked her. Then, without giving her time to reply, 'Make sure you give the album a good plug — remind me to get Malcolm to give you a complimentary copy before you leave. Which magazine is it you write for again? *Teentime?*'

He stretched his well-muscled leather-clad legs out in front of him and looked at her so complacently that she couldn't help but stare at him in astonishment.

Did he really think she worked for a pop magazine?

Where had he been all these years?

She hardly kept a low profile. Not only did she have her own column in Britain's most popular tabloid, but she made regular appearances on chat shows where she could always be relied upon to say something good and bitchy.

Putting her tape recorder in her bag, she zipped it up and then leant forward, pouring herself another glass of champagne — she'd die of thirst if she waited for him to do it.

Crossing her legs seductively and allowing her skirt to ride up so that the tops of her stockings were visible, she smiled at him and waited.

He looked at her uncertainly. Liz sighed to herself,

INDECENT

what did she have to do, go over there and unzip his trousers?

'I'm ready to take you up on your earlier offer now,' she told him. He sat and stared at her, looking puzzled.

Rising to her feet and reaching up beneath her skirt she pulled her pale green satin camiknickers down over her hips and let them slither to the floor.

'What's going on?' he asked, taken aback, as Liz sat back down on the sofa, opening her legs and pulling her skirt up around her waist.

'Make an educated guess,' she told him. Then, as his cock visibly swelled under the tight-fitting leather, she added, 'I think your dick's way ahead of you on this one. Come here.'

Having an affair with a cabinet minister suited Kate perfectly — she now had her own inside line to the corridors of power, which gave her the edge over most political journalists.

She also had a sex life which could be fitted in around her professional life. The long and often erratic hours she worked had led to the break-up of several previous affairs and it was a relief to be sleeping with someone who didn't expect her to be automatically available every evening and weekend. James worked equally erratic hours and their rendezvous were as likely to take place at lunchtime or mid-afternoon as in the evening.

Kate thrived on the intrigue, backbiting and power struggles which took place on a daily basis within the environs of Westminster. She knew James only told her what he wanted her to know, but she was adept at reading between the lines and drawing the correct conclusions.

Sometimes she wondered which she enjoyed most, the slightly kinky sex James went in for, or their conversations afterwards. Either on its own would have been pretty good, but one after the other was an unbeatable combination.

Initially, Kate had been unhappy about beginning an affair with a married man – life was quite complicated enough without that – but to date it had worked out very well.

The phone on her desk rang at that moment.

'Hello, Kate Owen,' she said briskly, tucking the receiver under her chin so she could continue sorting through a pile of papers on her desk.

'Hello, darling.' James's voice was always instantly recognisable, dark and rich with a resonance which made him such an effective speaker in the House of Commons. 'How are you today?'

'I'm fine. How did the meeting go?'

'Not entirely the way I would have wished, but not a total disaster either. Will you be free for a couple of hours around five? I'll have to be back at the House sometime before eight.'

Kate flipped open her diary.

'No, I'm having a drink with someone at six, then I'll need to come back here to finish something off.'

'Hmm, pity. How about lunch tomorrow?'

'Yes, if we could make it around twelve. I've an interview scheduled for two-thirty.'

'Okay, twelve will be fine. Would you like to come here? I'll have something sent in.'

When they met in public it was usually in a quiet

bar or restaurant where they were unlikely to be seen, or in James's flat. He didn't want his liaison with the political journalist of a tabloid to become public knowledge, not only because he was married, but also because of the security aspect.

However, they would occasionally meet in his office or for a drink in the Members' bar, as a certain amount of professional contact between them wouldn't give rise to any comment. Giving interviews to journalists was all part of his job.

'Yes, your office at twelve would be fine,' she told him, making a note in her diary.

'And Kate . . .'

'Yes?'

James spent the next few minutes telling her in explicit detail what they would do in his office, while Kate's breathing became more and more erratic and a warm flush of arousal spread inexorably through her body, leaving her with pink cheeks and damp panties.

Ledd tried to remove his head from between Liz's thighs – he had after all been there for some time – but her legs were locked around his back and when he tried to move she dug the spike heel of her shoe into his shoulder.

She'd already come twice, but she intended to make it three times before releasing him. Ledd for his part was keen to move onto the next stage of the action. It wasn't that he hadn't enjoyed pushing his tongue into her warm, musky pussy, but he'd been ready to jam his cock into her for the last half hour. And these leather keks were killing him, threatening to cut off the blood supply to his hard-on.

He felt her shudder as she came again and took advantage of her slightly relaxed grip to pull himself free and strip off his trousers.

He bent over her and undid her jacket, tearing off a couple of the buttons in his haste. Sod it, he'd already made her come three times and hadn't even seen her tits.

She was naked under the jacket, her small breasts jutting provocatively outwards, high and firm with nipples the colour of milk chocolate. Greedily he fastened his mouth over one hard nipple and his hand over the other.

This was more like it, he thought as she grasped his cock and began to squeeze it firmly, before fluttering her fingers over his balls in a way which made him groan.

The tip of his dick nudged against the entrance to her honeypot and he thrust into her, sliding easily in up to the hilt because she was so wet and slippery after his previous ministrations. He began to move in and out fast, wanting an urgent release.

He'd felt horny since seeing her standing at the door to his suite. She was a bit older and classier than the type he usually went for, but he wasn't complaining. Even though he'd automatically propositioned her he hadn't really thought he'd get anywhere – teenage groupies were more his style.

And banging a woman who was wearing stockings and a suspender belt was a real turn-on, most of his encounters were with girls in ripped tee shirts, jeans and grubby nylon knickers.

INDECENT

His climax was approaching fast, when suddenly she twisted out from underneath him, caught the tip of his dick between her finger and thumb and squeezed hard.

He let out a howl — partially frustration and partly pain.

'What did you do that for?' he demanded.

Rising to her feet and undoing the zip at the back of her skirt she let it slip to the floor and stepped out of it. It had been bunched up between them while he screwed her and now she left it in a crumpled heap on the carpet.

'You were going to come too soon,' she told him, stepping back over to the sofa and kneeling above him.

'No I wasn't,' he returned aggrievedly, then gasped as she lowered herself onto him and began to ride him with the skill and muscle control of a woman who'd spent her early years on horseback.

After a fruitless day trying to interview the recently jilted fiancée of a TV soap opera star, Jon decided to go to the luxurious health club where Dana worked and do a few laps of the pool while he waited for her to finish.

Having ascertained her whereabouts from the receptionist, he went down to the gym to let her know he was here.

She was taking an aerobics class, her spectacular body clad in a fondant-pink leotard and matching leg warmers. When he entered the gym he was treated to the sight of about twenty female backsides turned in his direction as the women obediently bent forward from the waist, then from side to side to the thumping beat of the disco music Dana liked to work out to.

Folding his arms, Jon leant back against the wall and watched contentedly while Dana led the women through a gruelling programme of exercises. Her back was still to him so she hadn't seen him yet, which was probably just as well because she insisted that his presence in one of her classes distracted her.

Dana's body was undoubtedly the best in the room, but several of the other women were also in excellent shape and Jon spent a pleasurable few minutes imagining himself in bed with three of them. They would still be in their leotards, perhaps even a little sweaty, and one by one he'd peel the tight-fitting garments from their gorgeous bodies and lick the perspiration from their cleavages . . .

He came back to earth with a start as he became aware that the music had stopped and all the women were looking at him, while Dana stood with her hands on her hips and her head on one side.

'I see we have a new class member,' she said brightly. 'Shall we put him through his paces ladies?'

Jon grinned at her and made for the door.

'Just letting you know I was here. I'll be in the pool when you've finished.'

Jon loved visiting the club. Dana had negotiated a much-reduced membership fee for him and he spent a lot of his leisure time there. He wasn't all that keen on exercise, but he like being surrounded by well-heeled, well-groomed women in skimpy clothing.

Expensive and exclusive, the club had a lot of prominent people as members and more than once Jon had picked up some gossip there which had led to a story. His occupation according to the membership files was technical writer — the club protected its members' privacy and journalists weren't eligible to join.

The pool was fairly empty and Jon dived in and swam several not very energetic lengths before climbing out and sitting at one of the poolside tables. A waitress came and asked him if he wanted to order a drink, but as the bar served only soft drinks he refused.

A natural voyeur, he passed the next half hour watching the women in and around the pool. He was just covertly admiring a blonde in a pink and white striped bikini, when Dana arrived. Taking his eyes reluctantly off the blonde's prominent nipples, Jon kissed her and ran his hands caressingly over her hips. Dana was wearing a black swimming costume cut high in the legs and swooping down low at the front and back — so low that the sight of her cleavage brought Jon out in a sweat.

'Shall we swim?' she asked him. Then, without waiting for a reply, she dived into the pool. Jon had never known a woman with so much energy — he tended to conserve what he had for sex, but Dana seemed to have boundless reserves of it.

Following her somewhat less gracefully into the pool he leant back against the tiled edge and waited for her to return. When she arrived back at his side she paused long enough to run her hand over his cock, then set off down the pool again. Knowing she was unlikely to stop until she'd done at least twenty lengths, Jon decided to go and wait in the jacuzzi.

The room was empty when he arrived and the steaming, bubbling water felt great as he lowered himself into it and closed his eyes.

He'd been up at the crack of dawn, staking out the jilted fiancée's house in Holland Park, but to no avail. If she was in there she wasn't answering the door or phone, or showing herself at the windows. Being cooped up in a car with Ernie all morning wasn't Jon's idea of a good time and by lunchtime he'd been thoroughly fed up.

He half drifted off to sleep, then woke up with a start to feel something tugging at his swimming trunks. Dana emerged from the bubbling water a few seconds later holding his trunks aloft like a trophy, then tossed them to the far side of the room.

'Dana, for fuck's sake,' he said. 'What on earth are you playing at? Anyone could come in.'

'Mmm,' she murmured, standing on the edge of the jacuzzi and pulling her own costume down to the waist, 'so they could.'

Jon gulped at the sight of her magnificent breasts. He'd seen them often enough before but never failed to be moved by the spectacle. They were very large, very firm and appeared to defy the laws of gravity. She had wide shoulders which tapered down to a narrow waist and the longest legs he'd ever seen.

She was beautiful, good-humoured and highly sexed – a fairly winning combination in Jon's book – but she had one character flaw as far as he was concerned.

Dana liked living dangerously.

INDECENT

It was bad enough that she kept trying to drag him along hang-gliding, rock climbing — or on whatever other lethal activity she had lined up — but recently she'd developed an alarming predilection for having sex in public places.

Jon found this a problem. It wasn't that he was averse to the idea in principle, it was just that he didn't relish making the front page of the tabloids — the *Daily News* included — having been charged with indecent exposure.

He was sure that Dana would get off somehow and he'd be left carrying the can.

As she stood above him on the edge of the jacuzzi, slowly and seductively she peeled her wet, clinging swimming costume down her thighs. He groaned and said weakly, 'Please Dana, not here.'

She was completely naked, her dark red hair and wispy red bush both dripping moisture. Slowly she parted her legs and looking upwards he could see the pink tip of her clit protruding from between her outer lips. She caressed her own breasts for a few moments and he watched mesmerised, wishing desperately and fervently that they were safely back in his flat.

When she stepped into the water and wrapped her legs around his waist he knew there was no point in fighting it. He might be well aware that this wasn't the smartest of moves, but unfortunately his dick had other ideas. It was already pushing purposefully up against the entrance to her pussy, trying to gain entry while the force from the jets of water buffeted them this way and that.

Grabbing her by the hips he managed to

manoeuvre himself fully into her and began to thrust forcefully – the quicker he could finish this the better.

The knowledge that anyone might walk in on them at any moment half terrified, half excited him. What if it was the blonde in the pink bikini? She might be so turned on by the sight that she'd slip out of her bikini and join them.

Fuelled by this fantasy and the risky nature of the situation, Jon came much faster than he usually did. Holding on to the rounded cheeks of her delectable backside he strained against her, groaning as he climaxed.

The force of it made him lose his precarious balance on the edge of the tiled ledge which ran about two feet below the surface of the water, and with barely a splash he went under. He pulled Dana with him and for a couple of seconds they sank towards the bottom, then Dana kicked strongly for the surface and his cock was wrenched out of her like a cork from a bottle.

Gasping and spluttering he rose to the surface himself, to find Dana already pulling her black swimming costume back on before rejoining him.

When at last he'd coughed up a couple of pints of jacuzzi water he spluttered, 'Fetch me my trunks. Please, Dana, before anyone comes in.'

'Oops, too late,' Dana said cheerfully, as Anne, one of her fellow instructors, entered the room.

'Hi, guys,' Anne greeted them, dropping her towel and climbing lithely into the water. 'Are you alright, Jon? You look a bit red in the face.'

'I'm fine thanks,' he muttered, trying to keep his

INDECENT

bum on the ledge and not let the force of the water push him to the surface, where he was sure his genitals would float as unappealingly among the bubbles as a dead rodent surrounded by water lilies.

He sat there despairingly as his skin turned pink and crinkly and the two girls chatted endlessly about their fellow staff members. Anne didn't appear to have noticed that he was naked below the surface of the churning water, but he couldn't be sure that Dana wouldn't find it amusing to draw her attention to the fact.

He was dreading anyone else coming in.

After what seemed like hours Anne stepped out and said she was going for a swim. As soon as she'd left the room Jon leapt out, retrieved his trunks and dragged them on, while Dana shrieked with laughter.

'I'm going to get dressed, go home and set about a bottle of whisky,' he told her. 'And if you choose to come with me I should warn you that you're going to spend the rest of the evening trying to make up for this.'

Her only reply was another shriek of laughter.

Ellen had had a dull evening.

She'd been to look at a flat in Islington – the only one of seven she'd phoned to enquire about which hadn't already gone. Did people ring in answer to ads in the evening paper and take the flat over the phone? she wondered. Because she'd started phoning as soon as she'd bought a copy of the paper from a nearby vendor and there was only this one left.

It was ghastly.

Described as a basement flat it was actually in a cellar, with only a dim light from one small high window in the sitting room and no windows at all in the bedroom, bathroom and kitchen. It was horribly depressing and there was a strong smell of damp. The landlady lived on the premises and treated Ellen to the story of her own life and that of her other tenants, while Ellen shifted her weight from foot to foot and tried not to yawn.

Returning to Kate's small but cosy flat was a great relief. Sitting in front of the TV with a dish of chocolate ice cream and a glass of Cointreau, she wished this was her own flat so she didn't have to go to all the trouble of finding one.

Prior to moving in with Simon she'd lived in a depressing bedsit and she was unwilling to return to that way of life. Perhaps she should think about buying, but she had no savings and she wouldn't be able to afford anything in any of the areas she could contemplate living in.

Kate arrived home at that moment, bringing with her a Chinese takeaway.

'Hi, have you eaten?' she asked, putting her head around the door. 'I've got enough for two if you're interested.'

Ellen had in fact had a frozen pizza earlier and had only just finished a dish of ice cream, but suddenly she felt hungry again.

'Well, if you're sure,' she said, 'I bought a bottle of Cointreau — would you like a glass?'

Kate shuddered at the idea. She didn't share

Ellen's sweet tooth, or her ability to eat and drink anything at any time.

'Er, no thanks — I think I'll have a beer with mine,' she said hastily, remembering the occasion she'd seen Ellen working late at her desk, absent-mindedly eating a beefburger and a packet of chocolate eclairs at the same time, washing them down with sweet sherry.

'How did the flat hunting go?' she asked a few minutes later as they ate their lukewarm and rather glutinous meal.

'Oh, the one I went to see was ghastly. It stank of damp and decades of cooking — and the landlady lived on the premises and obviously spends all her time watching the comings and goings of her tenants. A bit of a disadvantage when I'm about to enter a period of rampant promiscuity,' she ended dolefully.

'How is the promiscuity coming along?' asked Kate, 'I half expected to arrive home and hear the headboard thudding rhythmically against the wall.'

'No such luck,' replied Ellen gloomily, scraping the last morsels of sweet and sour chicken from the bottom of the foil tray.

'Well, there are always our male colleagues — they're a pretty libidinous bunch. How about Jon "never been known to say no" Wright? Or Ernie "fancy a shag?" Holdgate? Or if you really want to aim high, our esteemed editor Vernon Rees — a man I've never actually managed to make eye contact with, he's always so busy looking at my boobs or legs.'

'I'm not starting anything with anyone from

work,' said Ellen determinedly. 'I don't exactly relish every intimate detail of my sex life being known to all and sundry. I might as well just video the proceedings and hand out copies, or hop up onto a desk in the office with someone and get on with it in front of everyone. Anyway, I've hit on a good idea for meeting lots of new men.'

She told Kate about her planned series on lonely hearts columns.

'Breathtaking in its simplicity,' said Kate admiringly, shoving the empty food trays into the carrier bag. 'Can I look through the replies with you? And will you tell me all the details which are too salacious to put in your articles?'

'You'll be the first to know,' Ellen assured her. 'The number of sexual encounters I plan to have over the coming weeks will be positively indecent. I don't suppose there's any fried rice left?'

CHAPTER THREE

Kate dressed with great care for her lunch-time meeting with James. Her dark grey linen suit, black silk shirt and pale grey stockings would not have been out of place on a solicitor or an accountant.

The scarlet basque she wore underneath would have been more appropriate on a prostitute.

Tight-fitting and underwired, it pushed her breasts so far upwards they threatened to spill out completely. Red ribbon suspenders attached to the bottom held up her stockings and she wore a matching pair of scarlet satin panties.

She was shown into James's office by his secretary. Rising to greet her, he removed his glasses and shook her hand.

'Kate, this is a pleasure indeed.'

'And for me too,' she replied demurely, sinking gracefully into the chair he held out for her.

Opening her briefcase she took out her pen and a pad and they made polite conversation while his secretary carried in plates of sandwiches, a bowl of fruit, mineral water and orange juice.

'Will there be anything else, Minister?' she enquired.

'No thank you, Stella, you can take your own lunch now. I won't be needing you again until two – and no calls please while Miss Owen is interviewing me.'

Stella left the room and for a few minutes, while they could still hear her in the outer office, Kate went through the motions of conducting an interview.

Replying to a question on education, James went over to the door and silently locked it, before taking a bottle of Chablis out of a small fridge and opening it.

After pouring her a glass, he took the pen and notebook out of her hand, and, pulling her into his arms, kissed her, his tongue exploring her mouth while his hands roamed over her body.

He slipped her jacket down her arms and tossed it onto the sofa before unbuttoning her shirt and whistling softly when he saw the creamy orbs of her breasts overflowing from the tight basque.

'Uum,' he said appreciatively. 'I like it.' He removed her shirt and skirt like a child unwrapping a birthday present, then walked around her while she stood in a provocative pose with her hands on her hips.

Going over to his briefcase he produced four short silk cords and pointed to the chair in front of his desk.

'Sit down,' he ordered her.

Obediently Kate sat down. He tied each of her wrists to the arms of the chair and then parted her thighs, tying each ankle to a chair leg. Leaning against his desk in front of her he began to feed her small pieces of smoked salmon sandwich and sips of Chablis.

In between mouthfuls he caressed her, running his hands over her constrained breasts and her stocking-clad thighs, bending down to nibble the soft skin between her stocking tops and her panties.

Kate's breath began to come in little gasps and she strained against her bonds as he pulled the basque downwards, freeing her breasts and fastening his mouth onto one of her nipples. He sucked hard, then teased it with the tip of his tongue until she moaned and thrust forward against him. Pausing to take a mouthful of Chablis, he closed his mouth around her breast again and she inhaled in shock as she felt the icy liquid against her warm skin.

He fed her another sandwich and more wine, then moved so he was standing behind her, fondling her breasts and pressing her head back against his groin. She could feel how hard he was and rubbed her head against his erection, while he kissed and softly bit her neck.

She heard the sound of his trousers being unzipped and when he moved in front of her his cock was standing rigidly to attention. Shifting her behind forward on the leather seat of the chair she leant across and took him in her mouth. Sucking hard she took him even further in while he groaned and buried his hands in her dark blonde hair.

At last removing her mouth she murmured, 'More wine,' and he held the glass to her lips while she drank deeply.

James turned his attention to her satin-covered pussy, running his hand over the damp patch in the centre which immediately became even damper. Sliding his fingers backwards and forwards over the slippery material he soon had Kate wriggling on the seat, wanting more than he was giving her.

Hooking one finger into the scarlet satin he jerked hard, ripping her panties off and exposing her swollen pink honeypot.

Her head dropped backwards as he slipped a couple of fingers inside her and stroked her clit with his thumb. Her legs held wide apart by her bonds, she moved her bare bottom backwards and forwards over the worn leather of the seat in a sympathetic rhythm.

When she came she moaned loudly and strained against the cords, her whole body convulsing with pleasure.

Swiftly undoing the silken ropes which held her captive in the chair he pulled her to her feet and sat down himself, dragging her onto his knee.

Holding the arms of the chair Kate raised her backside then lowered herself eagerly onto his waiting erection.

Ellen was interviewing a woman who claimed to be a psychic. Madame Enid maintained that she was in touch with Elvis Presley and had various tapes of supposed conversations with him, in which he sent messages to the living.

It was unlikely that the interview would ever be used, but it could be kept on file as a potential filler for when the silly season started.

Ellen wondered why it was always Elvis Presley psychics seemed to be in contact with. If they really were, the poor man would be in such constant communication with the world he'd left behind he wouldn't have a moment's peace. It would be worse than the telephone continually ringing because he

INDECENT

wouldn't even have the option of unplugging it.

It was hot and smelly in the cramped little sitting room and Ellen kept shifting around on the uncomfortable sofa, trying unobtrusively to deter Madame Enid's various cats from taking up residence on her knee. It wasn't that she disliked cats, it was just that as she'd stroked one of them early on in the interview she'd definitely seen a couple of fleas jumping around on the matted fur.

She had the feeling that it might be stretching Kate's hospitality too far to introduce uninvited guests into the flat in the form of cat fleas.

Madame Enid stopped the tape recorder at the end of a conversation in which Elvis – speaking through the medium of Madam Enid – exhorted the president of the USA to avoid travelling by plane, as he had inside information that the president was scheduled to die in a plane crash.

The psychic had sent a copy of this tape to the White House, but to date had received no reply. Shaking back her long, tangled hair she fixed Ellen with a penetrating stare and said, 'I've a message for you from a deceased loved one. Are you ready to receive it?'

Ellen had a pragmatic approach to life and she wasn't easily rattled, but Madame Enid gave her the creeps. She wasn't sure if this was because the woman obviously hadn't bathed in weeks and didn't smell too good, or because she was clearly barking mad.

She wished someone else had been saddled with this particular interview. She knew that as a good investigative reporter she should now invite

Madame Enid to pass on her message, but she was desperate to get out of the stuffy room and into the fresh air. There seemed to be an inordinate number of plates of decomposing cat food in the room and she was starting to feel queasy.

Getting a grip on herself she said, 'I'm ready, go ahead.'

Her eyes closed, her hands stretched in front of her, Madame Enid began the low keening noise which prefaced all her communications with the spirit world. Having gone through her 'is anyone there?' routine her eyes flew open and she said, 'This is a message from your grandmother.'

Ellen kept her face blank and waited. Both her grandmothers were alive and well, one in Tunbridge Wells and one in Eastbourne, but there was no point at this stage in telling Madame Enid that.

Evidently not having received the reaction she was hoping for Madame Enid hedged her bets by saying, 'Or your great-grandmother.'

Terrific, thought Ellen. Aloud she asked politely, 'Which one?'

Madame Enid ignored her and her voice changed in timbre as she spoke — supposedly in the persona of Ellen's deceased relative.

'Ellen darling, watch out for an untrustworthy man.'

Ellen couldn't quite believe she was hearing this. As far as she was concerned about ninety-eight percent of the male population were untrustworthy, so the advice from the spirit world was pretty much a case of stating the obvious. Perhaps she could narrow it down a bit.

INDECENT

'What's his name?' she enquired.

The spirit wasn't to be drawn.

'He will cause you great pain,' Madame Enid quavered.

'If I don't know his name how can I watch out for him?' asked Ellen, reasonably.

'He will want you to give yourself to him without marriage. Resist him.'

Ellen thought that this wasn't really going to help her identify the unknown untrustworthy one, as every man she'd ever been out with had wanted her to give herself to them without marriage. Anyway, resisting men wasn't exactly high on her agenda at the moment – neither was marriage.

Putting her notebook away she said politely, 'I'll bear it in mind Madame Enid. Now I really must go. Thank you for your time.' Unable to stand the foetid atmosphere any longer, she fled from the house.

Once in the fresh air she took several deep breaths and began to walk briskly in the direction of the main road, wishing that someone else had been given that particular assignment.

Back at the *Daily News* building she paused on the steps then decided to go into the Vine for a quick drink. She owed herself a breather before returning to the office.

Jon and Ernie were propping up the bar and indulging in innuendo-laden badinage with the barmaid.

'It's lovely Lolita,' Jon greeted her. 'What are you having then?'

'Sweet Martini and lemonade,' she decided after a moment's consideration. 'With two cherries.'

She propped herself up against the bar next to Jon. Ernie immediately sidled round to stand on the other side of her, pressing his leg against hers and staring openly down the front of her baggy, off the shoulder top. White, with pink polka dots, the top skimmed over her breasts, leaving most of her shoulders exposed. She was wearing it with a short pink skirt which stopped just above her bare, tanned knees.

'Do you know what I like best about you, Lolita?' he asked, breathing beer fumes all over her.

'My sparkling personality? My razor-sharp brain?' she enquired innocently.

Ernie shook his head.

'No, your tits.'

Jon looked pained and said mockingly, 'Master of the delicate compliment aren't you, Ernie?'

Ellen smiled sweetly up at the photographer and widened her round blue eyes. Delicately she sucked the second cherry off her cocktail stick and ran the tip of her small pink tongue over her sugar-sweetened lips.

'You've got a fine pair there yourself Ernie,' she told him, eyeing the flabby rolls of fat on his chest. 'Jon, do you think if I inserted this cocktail stick into Ernie's navel he'd explode?' They both looked down to where Ernie's paunch strained unappetizingly against the buttons of his shirt.

Jon grimaced. 'It doesn't bear thinking about. Can you imagine what the contents of Ernie's stomach must be like? Stop being such a prick Ernie and get a round in. Ellen wants another fix of cocktail cherries.'

INDECENT

Somehow Ellen's quick drink became four as she joined Jon in sending-up Ernie. However desperate she became she couldn't imagine ever succumbing to Ernie's unsubtle overtures.

Jon was a different matter.

Shooting covert glances at him from under her lashes she knew she could be easily tempted – if only he wasn't her colleague. Although, if office gossip was anything to go by, she'd be lucky to catch him between other women – or as Ernie delicately put it, Jon's cock spent more time inside pussy than it did inside his trousers. The photographer continually complained that he spent half his waking life waiting in the car while Jon got his leg over whichever female he happened to be interviewing.

Jon was tall, slim and had an easy, boyish charm which Ellen couldn't help but respond to. In fact she'd never met a woman who didn't. Suppressing a tingle of lust in her groin as she caught a whiff of his cologne, she told herself firmly that in a few days when the replies to her ads came in, every night would be party night and her days of frustration would be over.

Liz's new secretary put her head around the door and said nervously, 'It's Ledd Lomas, he wants to speak to you. Will you take it?' She'd only been working for Liz for two days and already her nerves were in shreds.

'Yes, put him through. And Gina, fetch me some low-fat cheese dip and a plate of crudités. And pick up my ivory suit from the dry cleaners.'

'Which dry cleaners? And where do I get cheese dip from?' Gina asked desperately.

Ignoring her, Liz picked up the phone. The column featuring her interview with Ledd Lomas had appeared in that morning's paper. It was a particularly good hatchet job, even for her. In it she took swipes at heavy metal, teenagers, and rock stars in general; before specifically carving up Ledd himself.

She'd been half expecting his call.

Leaning back in her chair she said into the phone, 'Hello, Liz Peters.'

'It's Ledd. I thought we had a good time together that afternoon. Why did you write all that stuff about me?' His tone was injured in the extreme. 'And why did you tell me you worked for one of the fanzines?'

'I didn't,' answered Liz crisply. 'You just assumed I did. It isn't my fault if your publicist doesn't keep you informed.'

'Didn't you enjoy yourself?'

'What does that have to do with it?'

'I thought you liked me. You certainly seemed to like me when I was giving you one,' he replied aggrievedly.

Liz laughed, 'It was fine — as far as it went.'

'What's that supposed to mean?'

'It means it was okay for a quickie.'

'A quickie?' he repeated in a strangled voice, 'we were at it for over three hours.'

'Like I said — a quickie.'

There was a silence at the other end of the phone. Liz recalled the energy and enthusiasm with which he'd screwed her. He'd been unsubtle and not particularly inventive, but even so he'd had a raw sexual appetite which appealed to her. Mentally she reviewed their encounter and felt herself becoming wet. She had nothing better lined up at the moment, she might as well see him again.

'Don't take it personally,' she said at last. 'I was just doing my job and I did say you were sexy. How about getting together again tonight?'

'"Ledd Lomas has the strutting, self-conscious, macho sexiness of the young Brando,"' he read aloud from the paper. '"He's also smug, self-satisfied and stupid." What do you mean stupid? I've got four GCSEs.'

'Look, Ledd, I've got to go. Do you want to get together again tonight or don't you?'

'Alright,' he said grudgingly, 'but you'd better be prepared for me to fuck your brains out. Do you want to come here?'

'I'll meet you in the bar of La Maison at eight.'

She hung up before he could reply.

Now where was that incompetent girl with her cheese dip and crudités?

Vernon Rees was having a very uncomfortable early dinner with Ross Talbot, the owner of the *Daily News*.

Short, red-haired and pugnacious, Ross Talbot was in Vernon's opinion a complete philistine and virtually illiterate — which probably made him the ideal owner of a tabloid newspaper.

'You've really got to throw some fireworks under your staff,' said Ross belligerently, his nasal South

African accent grating unpleasantly on Vernon's nerves. 'They need a good kick up the arse. I've never seen such a weak set of stories in my life. What the fuck do you think you're editing – a women's magazine? Where's the scandal? Where's the sleaze?'

He paused to nod at the waiter who was displaying a bottle of burgundy for his approval. 'Your staff seem to spend more time running up bloody expense accounts than actually doing any reporting. Doesn't the term "investigative journalism" mean anything to you?'

Mercifully, the waiter brought their first course before Ross could really get up a head of steam. Vernon looked unenthusiastically at his plate of seafood. He didn't feel hungry anymore, he could feel the onset of indigestion before he'd even eaten anything and having to listen to Ross slurping his soup didn't help.

His respite was short-lived. Ross polished off the soup in record time and continued, 'Get them out on the streets really working for their living for once. They spend too much time pouring coffee and booze down their necks. Everyone has some skeleton in their cupboard and it's time your lot found a few.'

'Kate exposed that civil service kissogram scandal last month,' Vernon pointed out defensively. 'And Jon got the "Royal nights of lust" story from that sacked chambermaid the month before that.'

'Exactly!' exclaimed Ross triumphantly. 'Last month and the month before that. I want great stories breaking in my paper every week. This is journalism. No one gets to rest on their laurels.' He

INDECENT

glugged down a glass of burgundy and began to tuck into his steak pie, while Vernon tried to ignore the increasing discomfort in his abdomen and eat some of his own meal.

As far as he was concerned Ross was being unrealistically demanding. Sometimes it took months of digging to unearth a particular scandal and although the paper would then milk it for as long as possible, the story still had a finite shelf life.

It was hard to fill a daily paper without resorting to hard news, which the *Daily News*'s readership wasn't interested in, or trivia, which Ross objected to. Every so often there would be some really major scandal which had newspaper editors everywhere giving heartfelt thanks, but regrettably there just weren't enough of them. Digging dirt was expensive and time consuming, facts which Ross just didn't seem to accept.

'And another thing,' said Ross with his mouth full, waving his knife threateningly at Vernon, 'you're not keeping a tight enough control over the expense accounts. If Liz Peters ever pays for anything out of her own pocket it's news to me. Tell her to conduct her interviews over coffee rather than five course meals at the paper's expense in future.'

Vernon quailed from the idea of telling Liz anything of the sort. He could just envisage her reaction and quite frankly it scared the shit out of him.

'Uum . . . Liz has her own style of . . .' he began falteringly, then stopped as Ross gulped down the last of the burgundy and threw down his napkin.

'Just get me stories Vernon — that's what you're paid for. Get me dirt. Get me sleaze. Get me scandal — or heads will roll!'

Pushing back his chair abruptly, he strode off across the restaurant leaving Vernon mopping his forehead and staring with distaste at his plate of uneaten food.

When Liz swept into the bar of La Maison twenty minutes late, she found Ledd scowling into his glass of Budweiser. Arranging herself gracefully on the bar stool next to him, she ignored him until the barman had taken her order for a Mimosa.

'You're late,' he told her sullenly, nevertheless eyeing the plunging neckline of her black silk dress with interest.

'I was held up,' she returned offhandedly, lighting up a cigarette. 'Jean, may we have menus please?'

She recrossed her legs and Ledd stared openly at her thighs — was she wearing stockings and a suspender belt again? He'd jerked off earlier that evening picturing her in them and imagining what he'd get her to do to make up for that column she'd written on him.

He was buggered if he knew what they were doing here in this poncey restaurant when they could be in his suite screwing. After she'd hung up on him earlier he'd tried to speak to her again to tell her he didn't want to sit making polite conversation over dinner — if she was hungry he'd order something from room service between bouts of fucking.

But he hadn't been able to get through and her secretary had told him she couldn't be contacted.

INDECENT

He'd seriously thought of not turning up, but somehow the thought of how he'd make her pay for the things she'd said had drawn him here.

Now she was studying the menu — she'd barely glanced at him since she'd arrived. He couldn't be bothered to look at his own menu and when the waiter came to take their order he merely said indifferently, 'I'll have what she's having,' and swivelled round on his bar stool to face her.

'I hope you're a quick eater,' he told her. 'I've got plans for later this evening.' His eyes ranging lewdly over her body left her in no doubt as to what those plans were.

'So have I,' she said, 'so don't drink too much beer.'

'Frightened I'll get brewer's droop?' he leered. 'Don't worry it's never been known to happen to me.'

'No,' she returned acidly, shaking back her glossy chestnut hair, 'I just don't want you belching, breaking wind and excusing yourself every five minutes to empty your bladder — switch to wine.'

Gesturing imperiously to the barman she ordered a bottle of wine and pushed his half finished beer to one side.

'Bossy bitch,' muttered Ledd under his breath, thinking savagely he'd have her on her knees later for this. Glancing quickly around him in the dimly lit restaurant he pushed his hand up her skirt and immediately made contact with her stocking top and a few inches of smooth, warm thigh.

He expected her to recoil in shock and push his hand away. Instead she parted her legs so he could feel a few stray wisps of her bush and the damp warmth between her thighs. His dick immediately leapt to attention making him wish he wasn't wearing his leather trousers. Catching a glimpse of movement out of the corner of his eye he tried to withdraw his hand, but her thighs clamped together holding him trapped.

Over her shoulder he saw the maître d'hôtel bearing down on them and said urgently, 'The waiter's coming – do you want us to get thrown out?'

Releasing him, she smiled at the man as he said, 'Your table's ready, Miss Peters, if you'd like to come this way.'

Ledd was piqued.

It was bad enough that they hadn't appeared to recognise him when he'd arrived – in fact the maître d'hôtel had been outright offhand – but to be making a fuss of Liz as if *she* was the important one was enough to make him livid.

He wished he'd brought his entourage and taken over half the restaurant – they'd have livened up this stuffy joint alright. As it was he was going to have to eat a lot of food which had been mucked about with, just so he could get into this uppity bint's drawers again. Was it worth it when there were thousands of girls out there just waiting for the chance to drop their knickers for him?

Following Liz across the restaurant and watching the 'fuck me' roll of her shapely backside he thought perhaps it was.

Once seated at their table he drank a couple of glasses of wine and brightened up a bit – the meal couldn't last all night after all. He was taken aback when she said, 'So tell me, Ledd Lomas, what's on your sexual agenda this evening?'

'Eh?' he asked, confused.

'Well, as you're patently thinking about what you're going to do to me once you get me back to your hotel and as you're obviously not the world's most accomplished conversationalist, why don't you tell me about it? Or shall we just sit here in silence?'

'Er . . . well I thought we'd fuck.'

'I'd gathered that. Would you care to be more specific?'

Ledd didn't.

It was one thing doing it, or even thinking about it, but talking about it wasn't really on. How could he say, 'I want you on your knees sucking my cock,' in a crowded restaurant — anyone might overhear, there were Frog waiters dashing around all over the place.

After waiting a few moments Liz bit the end off a celery stick in a way which made him shiver, before saying, 'I'll tell you what I have in mind then.'

By the end of the meal Ledd's head was spinning and his dick was throbbing so much it felt like it was going to explode. He'd never known a woman talk so dirty. Following her out of the restaurant he found he was almost hobbling, his leather trousers felt so tight.

His limo was parked just across the street and he climbed in, telling his driver to take them back to the hotel, before closing the partition between them.

Unzipping his trousers, Liz ran her hands over his cock before kneeling sideways on the car's wide leather seat and going down on all fours. Hoisting her dress up over her waist she presented him with her backside.

She was wearing pewter-grey lace briefs which barely covered the cleft between her buttocks and he tore them down to her knees before jamming his cock into her welcoming pussy.

He caught a quick glimpse of her well-rounded bum framed by a lacy grey suspender belt before he entered her and his groin slammed into her buttocks. She felt molten inside as he banged her, holding onto her waist as he plunged feverishly in and out.

He came very quickly and sagged against her just as the car drew up outside his hotel. Pulling herself free Liz drew her briefs back up over her hips and straightened her dress, leaving him to zip himself up.

He stumbled out of the car after her and followed her towards the lifts. A trickle of moisture appeared on her inner thigh and he watched, fascinated, as it ran slowly down her stocking towards her silver ankle chain.

Once alone in the lift he pushed his hand up her skirt and felt inside her panties, wriggling a couple of fingers inside her as she leant back, legs splayed, against the mirrored wall and watched their reflection. He was amazed to feel himself becoming hard again and resisted the temptation to give her one there and then.

Better give himself a breather.

Instead he rubbed her clit until she shuddered and came, pushing down hard against his dripping fingers just as the lift came to a halt. He withdrew

INDECENT

his hand and she stood upright again as the doors slid open to admit an elderly couple who stared at them with distaste.

Ledd was well aware that the lift reeked of sex and that it must have been obvious that something was going on, but he was past caring.

Letting them into his suite a couple of minutes later he led her into his bedroom and quickly peeled off her dress. She wasn't wearing a bra and he reached out to fondle her breasts, but she eluded him.

'Open a bottle of champagne, will you?' she said coolly, walking into the bathroom, her high heels clicking on the tiled floor. Through the open door he saw her strip off her sopping panties and wipe herself between the legs with one of the hotel's fluffy white towels, before emerging again.

Taking the icy bottle from him she put her thumb over the top and shook it before directing the spray upwards at her pussy.

'Beats a bidet any day,' she remarked as the foaming liquid ran over the chestnut curls of her bush and cascaded down her legs. She was so shamelessly hedonistic standing there in her stockings, suspender belt and spike heeled shoes that Ledd grabbed the bottle from her and sprayed her breasts as well.

She gasped and her nipples hardened instantly, crinkling and thrusting pertly outwards. He began to lap at the champagne, starting with her breasts and working his way down to her honeypot while she grasped his cock and rolled it around between the palms of her hands.

'Take your time,' she murmured, running her thumb over the tip of his dick. 'We've got all night.'

CHAPTER FOUR

The only light in the luxuriously furnished room came from a dozen candles which threw strange shadows on the wall as they flickered in their silver holders. It was warm in the room but it wasn't the temperature which had the naked man perspiring freely — it was fear.

Tonight was his initiation into a society he'd heard whispers about for years and which at last he'd been given the opportunity to join.

He was blindfolded and his arms were tied behind him with a leather strap. He knew he wasn't alone because he could hear the sound of other people moving around the room, but he didn't know who they were or how many there were of them.

He jumped, startled as the sharp sound of a whip cracking whistled past his ear. Then he jumped again as he felt something hard and cool being drawn over his chest and then lightly over his buttocks.

'Kneel,' he was ordered — the voice a woman's, husky and with a foreign accent. He hesitated, then grunted in shock as something struck him across the buttocks. The blow wasn't hard enough to hurt but it was disorienting not to know what was coming next. Hastily he sank to his knees on the soft carpet and clenched his teeth as three more light blows landed in quick succession across his back.

He knew that total obedience was necessary if he was to be initiated into the society, but he wished he had a better idea of what he was letting himself in for.

An unseen leather-clad hand began to caress his back, running lightly over the faint tingling where the cane had struck him. He flinched as the hand probed between his legs from behind and took hold of his balls, handling them with careless ease.

The woman spoke again. 'Now you will drink from the temple of Venus.'

His head was seized from behind and thrust forwards until his face made contact with what was indisputably a woman's private parts. He smelt her musky, faintly scented odour as his nose was pushed into her damp, wiry bush.

'Drink!' urged the voice again as the leather-clad hand grasped his cock and began to squeeze it. With his tongue he searched for the entrance to her secret cavern and, finding it, began to lap at the portals. He felt the tiny nub of her clitoris and circled it before thrusting his tongue deep within her.

It was disconcerting.

It was disturbing.

It was unbelievably erotic.

His erection, at first tentative, grew harder as the leather-gloved hand expertly manipulated his cock. His senses were reeling as he gave himself up to it, forgetting the unseen audience and his own humiliating position, aware only of his increasing excitement.

* * *

INDECENT

'Just look what the postman's brought you,' said Kate, handing Ellen a large, brown envelope. 'Could this be the first batch of billets-doux from your potential bedmates?'

It was Saturday morning and the two women were having breakfast in Kate's sunny kitchen when the postman arrived. Dropping her spoon into her dish of sugar puffs, Ellen tore the envelope open eagerly.

'I wonder which lot this is? Oh, it's the arty magazine.'

'Great timing,' observed Kate. 'You shall go to the ball instead of watching Saturday night TV – one of them must be free this evening.'

Kate sipped her coffee as Ellen read the first letter, then let out a wail.

'Oh no! Just listen to this Kate. "My name's Christopher. I'm seventy-three. I like going to the theatre and spanking young girls." '

'Not at the same time I trust,' said Kate dryly. 'Still, at least he's upfront about it. Now, what will you wear? Do you have any white ankle socks?'

'Shut up, Kate,' said Ellen, tossing the letter to one side and ripping open another. 'I've no objection to older men but seventy-three is pushing it a bit. I'd be petrified he was going to have a stroke – I was rather hoping for someone reasonably athletic.'

She perused the second letter, frowning slightly.

'Well?' enquired Kate.

'This one throws pots in a converted warehouse in Wandsworth. He lives there with his "lady" Janette and assures me he has a lot to teach me, to help me find myself and lose my inhibitions. Whatever makes him think I've got any? He says Janette will come round to the idea of a *ménage à trois* in time, but for now I may find her a bit hostile. He suggests I go round there for supper and can I please bring some wine and a takeaway.'

'Just what did you put in your advertisement?' asked Kate, laughing.

'Petite, curvaceous brunette wants to meet attractive male to help expand her cultural horizons,' Ellen informed her, dropping the letter on the table. She opened the next one on the pile, taking five closely written pages out of the envelope. 'Maybe this one will be more promising.'

'Looks like the story of his life,' commented Kate. 'More coffee?'

'Mmm, yes please.'

Ellen read in silence for a few minutes then groaned.

'Do tell,' Kate encouraged her, placing a fresh pot of coffee on the table.

'The story of his life is just about it. He's detailed every one of his relationships and exactly why they went wrong. According to him, all women are selfish bitches who want to bleed a man dry and don't consider his needs at all. For example, "Naomi never listened to me, even though I'm a man of considerable experience and obviously knew better than her. She always insisted on going her own way without considering me at all. I tried to advise her but did she listen? She did not!!!" The exclamation marks are in green ink by the way. "She needed correcting but questioned my right to do it. She told lies to the police and I hope the miserable bitch rots in hell."'

INDECENT

Ellen grimaced and sipped her coffee.

'He goes on like that for five pages and through seven relationships. Oh, listen to this, "I know that you'll be different. I feel already that you'll understand me and what I need from a woman and that you won't be like the rest of the stupid cunts who haven't appreciated me and what I have to offer. I look forward to our life together, Ken." He's used four different colours of ink for emphasis.'

'Well, your Saturday night is obviously going to be more exciting than mine,' said Kate. 'So which is it to be? A visit to the ballet with the geriatric spanker? A cosy supper with the pot thrower and his hostile lady in Wandsworth — let's hope she doesn't decide to throw any pots in your direction — or an evening considering the emotional and physical needs of the psychotic Ken?'

Ellen shuddered.

'As potential interviewees they're all great, but as dates they're absolutely useless.'

'Try another,' encouraged Kate.

'I'm not sure I can face it.'

'Go on, try this one.' Kate handed her another envelope.

Ellen unfolded a single sheet of thick white paper.

'Oh, this one's more promising. He actually suggests taking me to dinner which endears me to him already. Are there any of those chocolate biscuits left by the way?' Kate reached for the biscuit tin and pushed it across the table. 'He's called Gordon. He's thirty-two and he's a marketing consultant. He's recently moved down to London from Edinburgh and he likes the theatre, cinema and eating out. He's the man for me.'

Rolling over in bed Jon put his arm around Dana and ran his hand sleepily over the curve of her hip, before covering one full breast with the palm of his hand. He found sleeping women particularly erotic — he liked the innocently abandoned postures they assumed as they lay there cocooned in their soft, relaxed warmth. Dana was lying on her side with her knees drawn up and her bottom thrust in his direction and, as he'd woken up with a hard-on as usual, it seemed like too good an opportunity to miss.

Stealthily, so as not to wake her, Jon began to explore her fantastic body. It was a game he liked to play, seeing how far he could get before she woke up. He grazed over her nipple in a circular movement, feeling it harden beneath his palm, then began tracing the rounded contours of her backside, just delicately brushing the surface of her smooth skin.

She stirred in her sleep and shifted position slightly as Jon eased his hand between her thighs and began to stroke her with a pressure so light he barely made contact. Her wispy bush was warm and damp and, as he increased the pressure, she moaned faintly and moved one leg further up, rendering more of her private parts accessible to his exploring hand.

He could feel her clitoris swelling as he stroked it, becoming slippery with her natural juices. Holding his breath he slowly pushed a finger inside her, checking to ensure she was wet and ready.

She was.

His dick had been nudging hopefully between her thighs and he guided it into position, then inserted it an inch at a time, continuing his gentle massaging of her clit. She moaned again and drew her knees even farther up, so her gorgeous bum was nestled against his stomach. With his cock in position he rubbed her clit faster, knowing her responses well enough to tell she was on the brink of orgasm. As she came, moaning and pushing back against him, he began to slip smoothly in and out of her, moving his hand from her clit to her breasts and teasing her nipples the way she liked best.

She was awake now and began to move drowsily with him, wriggling against his groin in a way which drove him wild.

As he climaxed she squeezed him with her internal muscles, adding to the pleasure of the release but causing him to cry out.

There was a sudden vigorous banging on the wall from Dana's next-door neighbour and Jon collapsed against her as they both tried to stifle their laughter.

Gordon had one of those soft Scottish accents which made Ellen go weak at the knees. He seemed delighted by her call and readily agreed to meet her that evening.

Putting the phone down she suddenly felt nervous. She'd only been to bed with three men in her entire life and felt that her sexual experience was very limited. She certainly hadn't planned it that way. It was just that the men she had been out with always seemed set on a long-term relationship after just one date and she was too nice to say no.

Not any more — now it was time to play the field.

Returning from an early evening drink with a political contact, Kate found her in the tiny second bedroom surrounded by every garment she possessed.

'I don't know what to wear,' she wailed. 'Nothing's clean and he's taking me to a really posh Italian restaurant.'

She was wearing a tight, black lace bra which looked at least two sizes too small for her generous breasts and a matching pair of black lace briefs. Her suspender belt, however, was pink and one of the suspenders was missing and had been replaced by a safety pin.

'I don't know where my black suspender belt's got to,' she said when she saw Kate looking at it. 'I think I must have left it in Simon's flat. Do you think the pink's okay with black?'

Kate privately thought that the colour of Ellen's suspender belt would be the last thing on the mind of her date. The younger woman's dark hair was tumbling over her shoulders in glossy curls and she was looking exceptionally alluring with a lot of dark eye make-up and a bright pink lipstick.

'I've a black one you can borrow if you like,' she offered. 'I'll go and get it.'

Returning with the wisp of black lace she found her lodger looking indecisively at two outfits.

'Which one do you think?' asked Ellen. The choice was between a flamboyant flowered cotton dress with a tight bodice or a shocking-pink lycra mini-dress. Kate personally wouldn't have been caught

INDECENT

dead in either of them, but she said kindly, 'Well, the pink would suit your lipstick.'

Wriggling herself into it Ellen looked doubtfully at her reflection in the mirror. It was very low cut and as the tight bra had pushed her breasts upwards, they were exposed almost down to the nipples. It was also so short that whenever she moved, anyone watching would be treated to tantalising glimpses of suspenders and stocking tops.

Let's hope you fancy him,' said Kate at last, 'because you re going to be beating him off with a stick.'

'Do you think I look tarty?' Simon's accusation still rankled.

'You look very nice,' Kate told her soothingly. 'Do you want me to ring for a minicab for you? You're going to be late.'

Gordon looked like he couldn't believe his luck when he saw Ellen.

They met in a quiet bar near Shaftsbury Avenue and she identified him easily. He was as he'd promised, sitting at a table by the wall with a copy of the magazine featuring her advertisement on the table in front of him.

He took in her provocatively innocent face, curvaceous figure and long legs, then said disbelievingly, 'Ellen?'

'Yes. Hello, Gordon,' she greeted him, seating herself at the table with a flash of stocking top.

'I thought you were probably going to ask me for change for the cigarette machine, or the way to the ladies,' he told her. 'I didn't expect you to be so sex . . . pretty,' he amended hastily.

He wasn't bad himself, thought Ellen, appraising him. Of medium height, he had a pleasant if unremarkable face, light brown hair and grey eyes.

'What would you like to drink?' he asked her. Ellen pounced gleefully on the cocktail list and chose one at random, after ascertaining that its constituents included several types of liqueur. He was drinking red wine and looked doubtfully at the cocktail as he placed it in front of her. Served in a glass with a sugared rim, it was a vicious, bright green in colour and decorated with a tiny paper parasol and a curly-wurly red-and-white-striped straw.

She sipped it ecstatically while he made an obvious effort not to stare at her breasts, although she noticed him mopping beads of sweat off his forehead a couple of times.

'I've booked the table for nine o'clock,' he said, 'but I can change it if that's not okay.'

'No, that'll be fine,' she assured him. 'I'm starving — I love Italian food.'

She had another cocktail before they walked down the road to the restaurant, where after one look at Ellen the waiters vied with one another to serve their table.

When Ellen was living with Simon they rarely ate out. He thought it was a waste of money and as Ellen couldn't cook and Simon would only do so for dinner parties intended to further his career, they lived on packet food and takeaways.

Ellen liked eating and she enthusiastically

INDECENT

worked her way through a pasta dish, a steak and two helpings of chocolate trifle before settling back to enjoy a glass of Grand Marnier.

She didn't say much throughout the meal – she was too busy relishing the food – but it didn't take her long to realise that Gordon, although very pleasant, was deathly boring.

He told her about his job and the promotion which had led to him being transferred to London, in stultifying detail. He also seemed to take it for granted that they would be seeing a lot of each other in the future. Suddenly remembering that she was supposed to be working, she steered the conversation in various directions trying to cover as much ground as possible.

When the bill arrived she offered to pay her share but he wouldn't hear of it. She accepted his invitation to go back to his flat for coffee with alacrity. He might be dull but he was quite attractive and his voice, if she didn't actually listen to what he was saying, was very sexy.

He lived in Ealing and his flat, which covered the top floor of a three-storey Victorian semi, was pleasant if featureless.

Over coffee she confided her flat hunting difficulties. She'd been to see two more that afternoon, neither of which was remotely suitable.

'I'd love somewhere like this,' she said, looking enviously around the recently decorated sitting room, 'but it'll be years before I manage to save enough for a deposit.'

She'd told him that she was a secretary in a large insurance company, knowing that he wasn't likely to ask her much about a job which sounded so dull.

'Move in,' he said suddenly. 'I was half thinking of taking a lodger, just for the company. Move in here — I won't charge you any rent if you'll just make a contribution towards the bills.'

Ellen stared at him in amazement.

'But you don't know me,' she said at last.

'No, but we can easily rectify that,' he pointed out, moving to sit next to her on the sofa and pulling her into his arms.

Jon's idea of a pleasant Sunday was to sit around the flat reading the Sunday papers, then later do something undemanding like seeing a film, meeting a few friends for drinks, or eating out. As Dana's ideal Sunday was one spent in pursuit of some life-threatening activity, invariably involving a lot of strenuous effort, they usually went their separate ways.

Today she was going hot-air ballooning and Jon had offered to drop her off on his way to meet some friends for lunch at a pub on the Thames near Marlow.

It was a beautiful day, sunny and warm, and Jon enjoyed the drive out of London in his open top MX5 — it had been a hard week and the prospect of a day in the country was very appealing.

When they arrived at the field where the balloons were waiting to take off, he succumbed to Dana's request to come and take a photo of her as she prepared for the ascent.

Clad in a bright blue tracksuit she leapt athletically out of the car without bothering to open the door and led the way across the field to where a red-and-white balloon floated gracefully above its frail-looking basket. She was greeted with enthusiasm by various men, all of whom looked as if they'd leap at the chance to get into her tracksuit bottoms.

Climbing nimbly into the basket she struck several provocative poses while Jon fumbled with the viewfinder. When he'd taken several snaps she called to one of the other balloonists. 'George! George! Will you come and take a couple of photos of Jon and me together?'

George obligingly came over and took the camera while Jon, who didn't particularly like having his photo taken, moved reluctantly to stand by the basket. Dana leaned out and wound her arms around his neck while George snapped away.

'Just climb in for a minute, Jon,' Dana urged him. 'It'll make a great photo.'

'Come on, Dana,' he protested, glancing up to where the six-foot-high flame roared intermittently upwards into the flimsy looking balloon. 'It makes me feel nervous just looking at one of these damn things — let alone getting in one.'

'Please, Jon, just for a minute,' she persisted, smiling at him winsomely. George scowled at Jon as if he was behaving like an oaf and, sighing to himself, Jon reluctantly got in.

He stood next to Dana feeling like a complete pillock as George captured the moment on film. Dana insisted in scrambling about adjusting the gas pressure and messing with the ropes in a way which made him distinctly nervous. Suddenly she exclaimed, 'Damn! Oh, Jon, I've dropped my earring. I think it went over there.'

Getting on his hands and knees Jon searched for the missing piece of jewellery, then let out a cry of alarm when there was a sudden loud roar as the flame leapt upwards and the basket lurched sickeningly.

'Dana! What the fu . . .!'

He dragged himself upright holding onto the side of the basket, just in time to see it rise several feet in the air. He thought about jumping, but already the balloon was quite a distance from the ground and ascending fast.

'Dana!' he yelled. 'Get this thing back on terra firma!'

Leaning back against the side of the basket Dana was convulsed with laughter.

'Dana please! You know I can't even go up an escalator without getting vertigo. Please Dana, take it back down again.'

The figures on the ground were getting smaller. In the grip of a scrotum-shrivelling terror Jon sank to the floor, his knees buckling.

'Just relax and enjoy yourself,' said Dana as he slumped against the side of the basket, his eyes closed.

'You planned this,' he accused her weakly. 'I'll never forgive you if you don't land it immediately.'

'It's a lovely day for a flight,' she told him. 'I thought you'd enjoy some time alone with me in the fresh air.'

Jon kept his eyes tightly closed and tried to ignore the uneasy feeling in his stomach. He heard a sudden loud pop and jumped about a foot in the air. His eyes flew open just in time to see Dana pouring champagne into two glasses.

'An old ballooning tradition,' she said soothingly, handing him a glass. 'Champagne on a first flight.'

Jon forced his shaking hand to close around the glass and gulped the contents down in one, then held it out for a refill.

'Dana, please tell me you're going to land this thing soon,' he pleaded, trying to get a grip on himself. By way of a reply Dana sat next to him in the bottom of the basket and removed her shoes, followed by her tracksuit bottoms and then her blue cotton knickers.

'Oh no,' moaned Jon. 'Dana don't even think about it. I can't, really I can't. My dick only functions at ground level.'

Taking no notice Dana knelt by his side and unzipped his trousers, taking out his limp cock and grasping it firmly. Jon gulped down another glass of champagne and closed his eyes, saying weakly, 'You're wasting your time.'

He felt her mouth close delicately over the tip and she began to suck, gently at first then more persuasively. Jon willed his cock to stay soft, certain that any undue movement on their part would send the balloon plummeting from the sky like a stone.

Dana's mouth felt like warm velvet in contrast to the outside air, which was growing noticeably cooler the higher they ascended. Feeling the first hint of impending rigidity as his treacherous cock succumbed to the moist blandishments of her tongue, Jon forced himself to think about the least sexy thing possible. Unfortunately he couldn't concentrate; the altitude, or possibly the champagne, was making him light-headed.

As his cock grew in her mouth and the basket rocked in the breeze, he made one last effort to stop her. Sitting up he grabbed her weakly by the shoulders and tried to pull her away from his private parts. Her teeth nipped warningly at his shaft and he slumped back against the side of the basket again, defeated.

Now he could only pray that she'd bring the whole thing to a conclusion with her mouth, so that nothing would be required of him in the way of movement or effort. But the business-like way in which she'd stripped off her lower garments made him sure that this was a faint hope.

Sure enough, when she'd coaxed his cock into sitting up and taking notice, she dropped a last couple of butterfly kisses on the tip and removed her mouth. Lithely straddling his recumbent form she murmured, 'Do try to be a little more enthusiastic, sweetheart – it's not everybody gets an opportunity like this.'

She lowered herself expertly onto his dick – the only part of him which wasn't limp with terror – and wriggled pleasurably.

The basket swayed alarmingly as she moved her hips up and down, until suddenly an unexpected jolt of electrifying randiness seized him. It was like being on a roller coaster – sickeningly terrifying but with great crests of excitement.

As this might well be his last ever fuck he thought he should at least make it a good one.

INDECENT

Reaching forward, he wrenched down the zip of her tracksuit top, under which she was wearing a plain, pale blue cotton sports bra. Dragging it up above her voluptuous breasts he saw her nipples stiffen immediately in the cool air and tiny goose pimples form on her smooth skin.

Rolling over so she was underneath him, he fastened his mouth over one breast and began to screw her vigorously. The basket swung wildly with each thrust until the bottle of champagne fell over and he felt the cold liquid splash over his ankles.

Dana wrapped her legs round his waist and moaned as he shafted her to a swift, erotic tempo. The balloon climbed further up into the air and they were thrown frantically from side to side by the erratic swinging of the frail basket.

Jon forgot that they were several hundred feet above ground and likely to drop from the sky and hurtle downwards at any moment. The only thing he was aware of was Dana's body moving wantonly beneath him and his fast-approaching climax.

He came in a great hot gush, pumping into Dana with a long drawn out cry, before rolling off her and lying on his back with his eyes closed.

He wasn't sure whether he fell asleep, or just passed out from a combination of the excitement and the altitude, but when he came round he felt as if he'd been out for quite a while. He opened his eyes and lay squinting up at the sky wondering where the hell he was.

As the flame above his head roared suddenly upwards he jumped nervously. He didn't understand why it didn't set fire to the balloon and turn the whole thing into a terrifying conflagration.

Like a best-forgotten nightmare it all came back to him in a horrible rush of clarity. He scrambled to his knees as Dana, fully dressed again, brushed past him intent on adjusting the gas pressure and carrying out other necessary manoeuvres, which to Jon seemed extremely complicated.

Reluctantly he peered over the side. A field seemed to be rushing upwards at a frightening rate as Dana called, 'Hold on, we're about to land!'

A few seconds later the basket hit the ground, then bumped gently along a few times before finally coming to rest. Jon wasted no time in climbing clumsily out, staggered a few yards, then collapsed gratefully onto the grass.

'Thank you, thank you,' he repeated hysterically several times, clutching at two clumps of bulrushes as if they were a lifeline.

'Good, eh?' said Dana cheerfully, flinging herself down beside him on the grass while the balloon deflated silently behind them.

'Don't speak to me,' he growled. 'Don't ever speak to me again in fact. That was the worst thing anyone has ever done to me — ever!'

'Come on, Jon,' she said, unperturbed. 'Admit that you enjoyed it really. It's not everyone who gets the opportunity to have it away among the clouds.'

'As far as I'm concerned fucking among the clouds is strictly for the birds. Do you realise we could easily have been killed?'

'What a way to go though,' she returned sunnily.

Turning his head to glare at her Jon became aware that over on the other side of the field, across the road was what was undoubtedly a pub.

Rising to his feet he looked sternly down at her.

'If my legs will carry me I'm going into that pub, downing several drinks then ringing for a taxi to take me to meet my friends. How you get yourself and that hideous contraption back to base is of no interest to me. I'll pick the car up later.'

He stood up and began to stumble weakly towards the pub.

'Jon.'

'What?'

'You'd better zip yourself up if you're hoping to get served. Your flies are still undone.'

CHAPTER FIVE

When Ellen tottered weakly into the flat late on Sunday afternoon she found Kate giving herself a manicure while watching a current affairs programme.

Zapping the TV, Kate looked enquiringly at her lodger.

'I trust that your dishevelled appearance means that you've had a wonderful time and not that you've been mugged.'

Sinking into a chair Ellen said dazedly, 'That pretty much sums it up.'

Her hair was tousled and her mascara had smudged beneath her eyes giving her an endearing panda-like appearance.

'Well?' prompted Kate. 'How did it go?'

'Great. Just great. I've done nothing but eat, drink and have sex since last you saw me. We dined at a really good Italian restaurant then went back to his flat and spent most of the night screwing each other's brains out. Then this morning we had another prolonged bout until I got hungry and he took me to a lovely old pub where we had steak and chips and lots to drink. Then we went back to his flat and screwed again.'

She sighed dreamily.

'Gordon hadn't had sex since he split up with his last girlfriend six months ago, so he was as keen as I was. He wants me to move in with him.'

'And are you going to?'

'No.'

Ellen's pleasure in her date had only been slightly marred by Gordon's determination that they were going to see a lot of each other in the future. He'd wanted to drive her home so she could pick up some clothes, then take her straight back to Ealing.

He'd taken her refusal to give him either her phone number or address quite badly. In the end she'd promised faithfully to phone him within the next few days but she could tell he hadn't believed her and that he was bitterly disappointed.

Stretching, Ellen murmured, 'I think I'll go take a shower.'

Soaping herself lethargically under the hot water, Ellen's hand slid gently over her swollen private parts. She was sore now but it had been worth it. Gordon had made love to her with a gratifyingly single-minded concentration — very different from Simon's cursory caresses. Although he obviously tried to hold back, he came quickly the first time. She didn't mind because within a few minutes he started to kiss and stroke her again, giving her pleasure with his hands and mouth until he became hard.

Emerging from the shower, Ellen dried her hair and curled up on her bed. She must have dozed off because when she looked at the clock it was approaching eight o'clock and she was hungry.

She found Kate in the kitchen peering vaguely into the fridge.

'There doesn't seem to be anything to eat,' she

greeted Ellen. 'I'm sure I went shopping one day last week.'

Ellen lowered her eyes guiltily.

'Sorry, Kate — I probably ate it. I'll call at the shops on the way home tomorrow, I promise. Do you fancy a curry? I'll take you to the Indian round the corner if you like.'

'Sounds good to me.'

The two women set off half an hour later, Ellen walking gingerly and rather stiffly after her prolonged session with Gordon.

Once ensconced in a booth they drank Kingfisher beer and Kate asked which of the men Ellen was planning to see next.

'I'm not sure,' she replied thoughtfully. 'No one for at least a couple of days — I can hardly walk as it is.'

She'd read the rest of the letters on Saturday afternoon and some of them seemed quite promising.

'The trouble is,' she said, spooning mango chutney onto a poppadom then taking a large bite, 'that because it was an ad in that arty magazine most of the replies suggest that we go to the opera or theatre together — and I'm a complete philistine. If I have to sit through some three hour performance without even a packet of crisps to keep me going, I know I'll just go to sleep.'

'How about a film?'

'Same problem really. The only films I enjoy are strictly mainstream. The art movie circuit bores me rigid. One of my boyfriends at university was always dragging me along to see subtitled Polish films with names like *The Inconsolable Tears of the Disabled War Widow*, or *The Last Goods Train to Kiev*. Then he'd want to have an informed discussion about it afterwards and go on and on about camera angles.'

Ellen signalled to the waiter to bring them two more beers before continuing, 'Anyway, if I agree to go to the opera or something we'll be watching instead of talking, so I won't be finding out about him. How am I going to write an amusing piece if the evening consists of sitting watching fat people singing too loudly in a foreign language?'

'You've got me there,' returned Kate. 'Why not just say that you want to spend the evening getting to know him, so can you go for a drink or a meal?'

'Yes, I think I'm going to have to — oh good, here comes the waiter with our starters.'

Vernon had called a meeting for ten-thirty Monday morning to relay Ross Talbot's sentiments regarding his staff's general inadequacy as investigative reporters.

He did this with some trepidation. Journalists were a bolshie lot in general and didn't take too kindly to criticism.

He ended, '. . . so later this week I'm going to see each one of you individually and I want to hear your ideas for getting more stories. Think big, think dirty, think *investigative*.'

Without waiting for any response he hastily left the room and returned to his office, unlocking the drinks cupboard and pouring himself a stiff whisky. He hadn't dare glance at Liz while he was giving his pep talk, this sort of thing tended to make her angry — and that was without any reference to expense accounts. He'd decided to mention that particular issue some other time.

There was an imperative rapping at his door and Vernon hunched further down in his chair and hoped that whoever it was would go away.

It was a vain hope.

The door was thrown open and Liz strode in, her brows drawn together and her eyes flashing dangerously.

'I hope none of that was aimed at me Vernon,' she said angrily.

'No, no of course not,' he hastened to assure her. 'I just thought that as a senior member of the team you should be there.'

Liz threw herself into a chair and looked meaningfully at his drink.

Crossing hastily to the cupboard he asked placatingly, 'Drink, Liz?'

'Bloody Mary.'

Liz had a hangover and wasn't in a very good mood. Searching for some non-contentious topic of conversation, Vernon asked, 'Did you have a good weekend?'

'My weekend was crap,' she returned. She was obviously still fuming. 'My secretary didn't come in today — the agency called to say she was off on indefinite sick leave. I need another one, I need someone good and I need them within the hour. Get onto it will you!'

Downing her drink in one, Liz left the room.

Returning to her office she began to pace the floor in her high-heeled shoes. Liz's problem was simple.

Sexual frustration.

She hadn't had sex since her night with Ledd after

their dinner at La Maison. He'd been out of London that weekend playing a pre-tour gig in Newcastle. She'd gone out on Saturday night and cruised a few bars but she hadn't picked up anyone who appealed to her.

Sunday had been spent alone in her flat hoping Ledd might ring on his return from Newcastle, but the phone had been annoyingly silent.

She knew that there were at least a dozen men who would be more than happy to see her but, for some reason she couldn't quite fathom, she wanted Ledd.

Their second time together had been pretty cataclysmic. She'd begun by calling the shots but had ended by letting him do what he wanted with her.

And he'd wanted to do a lot.

He was leaving next week on a world tour and it galled her to think of him wasting his not inconsiderable sexual energy on erotically unsophisticated groupies.

Lighting a cigarette, Liz sat down at her desk and picked up the phone – time to get a grip on herself and phone one of her many casual lovers.

A lunch-time rendezvous was definitely in order.

Sitting casually on the edge of Ellen's desk, Jon commented, 'You're looking pleased with yourself this morning, Lolita. Could it be that you've spent the weekend enjoying the love of a good man?'

Ellen giggled. 'Could be. How about you – did you have a pleasant weekend?'

'Pleasant doesn't enter into it. If I told you how I'd

spent my Sunday morning you wouldn't believe me.'

'Try me.'

Jon shook his head. 'You'd think it was the lurid imaginings of a diseased brain. You're looking very fetching today — I presume they didn't have that tee-shirt in your size.'

He was referring to the fact that Ellen's tight yellow tee-shirt was stretched to capacity in a desperate struggle to contain her breasts. Tugging it down Ellen muttered, 'I can't decide whether it shrank in the wash or if I've put weight on.'

Jon ogled her shamelessly.

'Well, if you have, don't worry — it's in all the right places.' Changing the subject he asked her, 'So what's going to be your first move in digging megadirt by the shovelful for our esteemed owner?'

'Haven't a clue,' she told him cheerfully. 'How about you?'

'I think I'll go and befriend some of the better connected ladies at the health club,' he said. 'See what I can come up with.'

'I suppose I'll have to give it some thought,' conceded Ellen. 'In fact I think I'll sit here for a while and contemplate my strategies.'

'I'm sure your strategies are absolutely delightful,' teased Jon, 'but that won't be enough for Vernon. He's got Ross the Toss breathing down his neck and he's shit-scared of him. But then — who isn't?'

'I haven't met him yet.'

'Think yourself lucky — he's nobody's idea of a charmer. When Ross shouts we all jump. He'd fire the lot of us without a second thought. Anyone who crosses him is out, as many have found to their cost.'

'I can't wait. Does he honour us with his presence very often?'

'Thankfully, no. His usual custom is to summon Vernon and tear him off a strip, then send him back here to relay his latest orders. You can always tell when Vernon's been with him — he comes back looking like he's been given two months to live. Oh well, time to hit the street and look for the action. See you, Lolita.' Uncoiling his tall body from Ellen's desk, Jon left the office.

The corridor leading to the toilets was deserted. As Jon strolled along it Liz suddenly appeared from the Ladies and blocked his path.

'Fuck me,' she invited him without preamble, and with the economy of words which had led her to being the leading columnist on the *Daily News* for the last five years.

It wasn't that Jon was in any way reluctant — like the rest of the male staff he'd often fantasised about screwing Liz — it was just that he wasn't too thrilled at having the time and place dictated to him. He also had a desperate need to empty his bladder.

'Er, why don't we discuss this over a drink,' he suggested.

'Now,' she said firmly.

Turning down women had never been part of Jon's repertoire.

'I just need to . . .' He gestured towards the Gents.

Liz folded her arms and leant back against the wall.

'Hurry up. I'm waiting — and I don't like waiting.'

Jon relieved himself, washed his hands and

INDECENT

glanced hastily at his reflection in the mirror before returning to the corridor. Liz was still in the same position but as he approached her she shot out an arm and grabbed him by the hand, leading him quickly into the Ladies.

'Not in here!' he protested. 'How about your office?'

Ignoring him Liz dragged him into one of the cubicles and bolted the door.

Not for the first time that week, Jon found himself wondering what it was about him that made women drag him into potentially dangerous and embarrassing situations.

There was barely room for the two of them and Jon could feel the rim of the toilet seat pressing painfully against his leg. With a deftness borne of long practice Liz unzipped his trousers and slipped her hand inside. He caught his breath as she extricated his fast-hardening member and began to manipulate it skilfully.

Undoing the three buttons on the front of her mustard-coloured jacket he was delighted to discover that the only thing she had on underneath was a cream lace camisole.

It was the work of a moment to flip the shoulder straps down and expose her perfect breasts. Small and high, they had disproportionately large nipples the same pale brown as milk chocolate. Already sharply extended, they pressed determinedly into the palms of his hand as he caressed them.

Liz was a woman with a mission and after a few seconds she reached beneath her skirt and slipped her cream lace panties down to her ankles, stepping carelessly out of them and leaving them on the toilet floor.

Opening her legs invitingly she leant back against the cubicle wall, her back arched and her breasts and hips thrust forwards. Jon pushed a hand between her thighs and his fingers were immediately engulfed in the sort of hot sticky wetness he loved to find waiting for him.

He'd always suspected she was hot – she was certainly rumoured to be – but this was surpassing his wildest speculations.

'Fuck me!' she ordered him again, gasping as he explored her dripping pussy. 'Fuck me now!'

Slipping easily inside her, he responded to the hard grinding of her hips by grasping her backside with both hands and forcing her to let him dictate the rhythm.

She was like a woman possessed – her legs spread, her head thrown back as she welcomed each forceful thrust.

The smell of disinfectant mingled with her heady perfume and the side of his shin kept chafing painfully against the edge of the toilet seat as he moved against her.

Jon was just on the brink of his climax when he heard the door to the Ladies open. Unable to help himself he let out a strangled groan and came, then felt Liz shudder as she did the same.

Leaning against Liz, he heard as if from a great distance the sound of someone using the adjoining cubicle. He tried not to breathe too loudly but it seemed like an eternity before whoever it was finished and left the toilets.

INDECENT

Extricating himself from Liz, he grabbed a handful of toilet tissue and passed it to her, before wiping himself and dropping the paper in the toilet.

'That was close,' he breathed, as she pulled her panties back up her stocking-clad legs. 'I wonder who it was?'

'Who cares?' she returned impatiently, buttoning up her jacket. Opening the cubicle door she checked her appearance in the mirror.

'Will you go and make sure there's no one outside?' he asked her. Without replying she walked over to the door and opened it, then vanished into the corridor. Peering nervously out he was relieved to see that the coast was clear. He was about to go into the Gents when he realised she was standing waiting for him.

'Well, thanks – it was really great,' he told her, feeling something was expected of him.

'Was?' she queried, raising one eyebrow. 'I think you mean it will be. Come into my office.'

Not being able to fix a lunch-time rendezvous with one of her lovers at such short notice hadn't phased Liz.

Ellen only managed to contemplate her strategies for a few minutes before she was despatched on a story.

Paul Fenton had started with one shop selling good quality ladies underwear at reasonable prices and was now the head of a multi-million pound conglomerate with shops on every high street.

He designed a lot of the lingerie himself and made

a point of visiting each shop in his empire every few months — usually without warning. His success was attributed to the tight personal control he kept on all aspects of the business, and now he was rumoured to be about to sell to an American company.

His secretary told Ellen that he was in a meeting and couldn't be disturbed, but allowed her to take a seat in reception. Her stomach rumbling, Ellen watched hungrily as the woman ate a yoghourt and an apple. It wasn't exactly her idea of a sustaining lunch but she was starving.

Forty minutes later a door opened and several people came into the reception area. She recognised Paul Fenton at once — he was the only man not wearing a suit. In his early thirties, he had prematurely grey hair and wore his jeans and polo shirt with an air of authority.

'Paul,' his secretary said after he'd shaken hands with his departing business associates, 'there's a young lady to see you — a reporter.'

'Not right now,' he began, then caught sight of Ellen and changed his mind. 'On second thoughts I'm sure I can spare a few minutes. Would you like to come this way?'

'Hello,' said Ellen standing up and holding out her hand, 'I'm Ellen Marshall from the *Daily News*.'

'Delighted to meet you, Ellen.' His hand was warm and dry and his grasp pleasantly firm. In fact, thought Ellen, he was really a very attractive man — tall, lean and blue-eyed.

He led her into an untidy, cluttered office and invited her to take a seat, sweeping several samples of flimsy material from the chair onto the floor to enable her to do so.

'So what can I do for you, Ellen?' he asked pleasantly, his eyes appraising her warmly.

Ellen smiled sunnily.

'Just give me a few minutes of your time to tell me about your future plans for the company.'

'Oh, I think that'll take more than a few minutes.' He glanced at his watch. 'Why don't I tell you about it over lunch?'

Ellen's sunny smile became positively beatific.

'Lunch would be lovely.'

He took her to an old-fashioned French restaurant serving large portions of delicious garlicky food. He watched with amusement as she tucked in with gusto, and didn't even raise an eyebrow when she asked for some ginger ale to add to the bone dry wine he'd chosen to accompany the meal. The head waiter looked to be on the verge of apoplexy as he added the sweet fizzy drink to half a glass of wine.

'I think I've offended him.' she commented, gesturing at the waiter's departing back with her knife.

'I'll certainly never be able to eat here again,' he said, laughing when he saw Ellen's look of consternation. 'It's alright, I'm sure your youth and beauty will stop him from taking it too much to heart. He probably thinks you're my schoolgirl niece. Smile at him a couple of times and he'll forgive you. Anyway, aren't you supposed to be interviewing me?'

Ellen looked abashed.

'Sorry, I find it difficult to concentrate on anything else when I'm eating. Are you about to sell your company?'

He talked obligingly about his future plans while Ellen continued to relish her food, but it soon became obvious he wasn't really giving anything away. She studied him as he talked. He certainly was her type. Sexy in an understated sort of way and a very amusing conversationalist.

They didn't finish lunch until after three. By the time the meal was over Ellen was replete and, after drinking three glasses of Tia Maria on top of the wine, fairly drunk.

When he'd finished being charmingly evasive about the future of the company Paul started to talk about underwear. It was a subject he was obviously passionate about.

'What a woman is wearing under her clothes is fundamental to the way she feels about herself. If she's off to meet her lover she needs to feel that her underwear renders her desirable. If she's on her way to work she wants something practical which still makes her feel feminine.'

Finishing his cup of coffee, he continued, 'Did you know that the majority of women in this country wear the wrong size bra?'

'I think I did read that somewhere,' admitted Ellen.

'It's because they just walk into a chain store and grab whatever they think looks pretty. When they get it home and discover it doesn't fit properly they can't be bothered to change it. Every one of the staff in my shops is properly trained to ensure that customers buy bras which are actually right for them.'

He suddenly looked hard at Ellen's breasts.

'Please forgive me for being personal but you, for example, are patently wearing a bra too small for you. It can't be very comfortable and it's not giving you the support you need.'

'That's true,' agreed Ellen, glancing down at her generous bosom. 'I do have difficulty buying underwear. Or even if it seems okay when I buy it, somehow it never stays that way.'

Scribbling his signature on the credit card slip Paul said, 'I think I can help you — let's go.'

Back at his office he led her to a large storeroom and began pulling bras out of boxes. Handing her about a dozen he indicated a curtained changing area.

'Try these.'

Pulling her tee-shirt over her head Ellen unclipped her own rather faded black bra and began to try the others on.

'This one seems okay,' she said walking back into the room wearing the third she'd tried. He looked at it critically.

'No, it's not quite right. Try the others.'

She was aware of his gaze on the smooth swelling of her breasts where they emerged from their lacy cradle and a sudden rush of heat swept over her. Trying to suppress it she went back into the changing cubicle and tried another. It was pale pink and made of such fine material that it fitted like a second skin. Going back into the room she stood in front of him with her hands on her hips.

'What about this one?'

Reaching forward he adjusted the shoulder straps, then stepped backwards to look at her.

'Maybe this wasn't such a good idea,' he said suddenly. 'I think I'd better go and leave you to it. I'll send Janis in to help you.'

'Why, what's the matter?' she asked puzzled.

'The matter is, that even though I see women wearing my underwear on a daily basis I'm not usually alone with them. And what's more I don't usually get an almost overpowering urge to ravish them — which is what I think I'm about to do to you if I don't get out of here right now.'

He backed away from her but Ellen followed him, winding her arms around his neck.

'And what if I'd like you to ravish me?' she said huskily.

Burying his face in her hair he pulled her close to him, tracing the contours of her back with his warm hands.

'Well that would be a different matter — would you?'

In reply she pulled his head down and kissed him hungrily — she felt as if she were on fire she wanted him so badly. With a deft movement he undid her bra and it slipped to the floor leaving her breasts free.

'You've done that before,' she accused him softly as his hand brushed over one hard, puckered nipple.

Picking her up he carried her over to a couch against the wall, reaching behind her to unzip her skirt and pull it down over her hips. To her embarrassment she remembered belatedly that she was wearing a rather tatty pair of cotton panties with red hearts on them. Damn, how she wished she was wearing something lacy and seductive. They didn't even match the bra she'd been wearing.

'Those are truly horrible,' he remarked, easing them down her bare legs to reveal the dark fuzz of her bush, 'and you're never to wear them again.'

Bending his head he kissed and licked his way over her breasts and down the smooth skin of her stomach. She wriggled slightly as his tongue touched a ticklish bit, then moaned as he dropped several light kisses on her mound.

His tongue probed delicately at the entrance to her honeypot, circling the bud of her clit and sending shivers of pure pleasure through her body. Naked except for her stiletto-heeled shoes, Ellen stretched languorously out on the sofa and opened her legs. She was squirming and panting with lust by the time he surfaced from between her legs and stripped off his jeans and polo shirt.

She almost flinched when she saw the size of his erect member. Rising massively from a dense mass of dark hair it looked very red, very hard and more than ready for action.

Awed, she reached out and touched it with the tip of her forefinger, spreading a droplet of moisture over the end.

'Goodness, it's big,' she breathed, hoping she'd be able to take him inside her without discomfort.

Paul placed a cushion under her hips and gently parted her legs even further.

'Relax,' he murmured, pushing three fingers inside her and stroking the velvet folds of her pussy in a way which soon had her squirming and groaning again. When he was sure she was ready, he positioned himself above her and slid partially inside.

Ellen felt herself being stretched internally to accommodate him and held her breath as he began to move slowly backwards and forwards within her, gaining a little more ground every time he pulled back, then forging ahead again. Soon he was completely inside her, filling her with sensations she'd never experienced before.

She began to move with him, her hips rotating erotically on the rough cotton cover of cushion beneath her. Gasping, she felt herself on the brink of orgasm far sooner than usual. Then, with a cry, she toppled over the edge as he continued to plunge into her.

She sustained two more panting, choking climaxes as they screwed – her body convulsing and her back arching as they moved frenziedly together on the sofa. When he finally emptied himself into her it was almost a relief – Ellen didn't think her body could take any more pleasure without a break.

The storeroom felt airless and a drop of sweat ran down her cleavage as he slipped out of her. Glancing down she saw that even flaccid, his cock still looked enormous. They lay in silence for a while until his gaze fell on her discarded heart-covered panties.

Leaning over he reached out and picked them up, then suddenly ripped them in half and threw them into a wastepaper bin.

'No one as beautiful as you should wear panties

like these,' he told her sternly. 'You should only wear gorgeous silk lingerie.'

Ellen spent the rest of the afternoon happily trying on every conceivable sort of underwear, parading around the storeroom in front of him feeling gloriously decadent.

'You've got such a luscious body,' he panted later as he screwed her again – this time over a large trestle table among rolls of sensuous fabrics. He paused to hook one of her legs more firmly over his back. 'It's a crime not set it off to advantage.'

'Mmm,' moaned Ellen, feeling like she was about to soar off the edge of a cliff, so great was the feeling of intense, mounting pleasure.

She was wearing a tight-fitting bodice in pale blue satin, with a pair of matching camiknickers – the first she'd ever worn. She'd been surprised when he'd insisted she keep them on while he screwed her. None of her past lovers had ever suggested such a thing and she had to admit it added a frisson to the situation. The sensation of his groin moving over hers but separated from it by a fine layer of silk, was erotic in the extreme.

Hours later when she returned to the flat carrying several carrier bags crammed with underwear, she found Kate busy doing some background research. Her colleague raised her eyebrows when, after greeting her airily, Ellen began to unpack the bags.

'I suppose it would be inquisitive to ask why you appear to have been buying up half the stock of a Paul Fenton shop rather than interviewing him?' Kate enquired, putting down her pen. 'Incidentally, did you get your copy in? Vernon was doing his fruit when I left, saying you should have been back hours ago.'

'Yes, I stopped by the office on my way home. Look at all this. Isn't it gorgeous?'

By now the whole of the sitting room was swathed in frilly lingerie.

'Would it be indelicate if I wondered aloud whether you actually bought these fripperies or whether Paul Fenton was so besotted by you he just pressed them into your unresisting hands?' queried Kate, picking up a lace-edged slip.

Ellen giggled. 'He didn't think I was wearing underwear which did justice to my exquisite form, so he gave me these. Would you like a couple of sets? Pick anything you want,' she urged generously.

'I'm glad to see that after an initial slow start the promiscuity now seems to be off and running. I admire your stamina. Last night you were tired, tender and walking with difficulty. Today you're right back in there.'

'Actually,' admitted Ellen ruefully, 'I didn't notice at the time but it was probably a bit soon to get intimate with anyone again – I'm already aching all over. Still, nothing that a hot bath and a good night's sleep won't cure.'

CHAPTER SIX

There were a dozen men in the room.

Naked, except for their masks, they stood in a line one behind the other, their hands clasped obediently behind their backs.

Lying on a couch set on a raised platform at the far end of the room lay a woman, her voluptuous body encased in a tight bodice of supple black leather. Strips of leather around her thighs held it in position but left the secret place between her legs open and exposed. Long black leather gloves hid her slender white arms to just above the elbow and a pair of thigh-high boots with spike heels adorned her shapely legs.

She had dark auburn hair and looked to be in her early thirties, but as she too was masked it was difficult to tell. Her eyes glittered as she surveyed the waiting line of men, an air of expectation hanging heavily over the candlelit room.

Patrolling the line of men were three other young women also leather-clad, but these three carried whips.

The woman on the couch began to caress herself, one hand running languidly over the jutting curves of her breasts and the other moving between her legs.

One of the men in the line grasped his cock and began to stroke it, his eyes glazed with lust as he watched her. There was a sharp cracking noise and the lash of a whip flew through the air and landed squarely across his back.

'That is forbidden,' hissed the Amazonian blonde wielding the whip. She struck him three more times, hard enough to sting but not enough to break the skin. 'On your knees,' she ordered, towering fiercely over him.

He obeyed, clasping his hands behind his back and bowing his head. 'Kiss my boots,' she continued, grabbing him by the hair and forcing his face downwards. Abjectly he dropped kisses on the highly polished surface of her boots until she ordered him to cease, then despatched him to the end of the line.

At last it was time.

At a nod from one of the women the first man in line strode forwards and joined the woman on the couch. He entered her immediately and began to plunge in and out, his performance closely observed by the watching men. Most of them had erections and all of them were gripped by the proceedings on the couch.

After only a few seconds he came and immediately rolled off the couch, kneeling briefly to say, 'Thank you mistress.' His place was taken by the second man while the three guards continued walking up and down the length of the line, handing out random punishments to anyone not obeying the stringent rules.

One man reached out and pushed his hand between the legs of the statuesque brunette guard as she strode past him and the others were torn between watching his punishment and continuing to observe the action on the couch.

He was ordered out of the line then spread-eagled over a desk while two of the women took it in turns to strike him with the handles of their whips until he begged for mercy. When they let him up his previously diffident erection was standing stiffly to attention and one of the women gave it a contemptuous flick with her whip before ordering him to the end of the line.

The initiates continued to take their turn in servicing the auburn-haired woman, her moans of pleasure becoming greater and greater with each man as she writhed frenziedly beneath them.

One of the men was unable to raise an erection so the blonde guard sank to her knees before him and took him in her mouth. When it was his turn he was ready, but came as soon as the tip of his member pushed against the auburn bush guarding the entrance to the secret lair.

The last man laboured over the glorious leather-clad body for a long time but couldn't obtain the release he sought. One of the guards mounted the platform and began to whip his plump white buttocks as he moved up and down, until at last he pumped his juices ecstatically into the woman moving so wildly beneath him.

'Hi, it's Ledd.'

'Yes?' Liz's tone wasn't very encouraging.

'Aren't you going to ask me how the gig in Newcastle went?' Tucking the phone under her chin Liz studied her long red fingernails.

'I get the feeling you're going to tell me whether I want to know or not.'

'We went down a storm. There was nearly a riot afterwards — you should have been there.'

Liz was actually pleased to hear from him but she wasn't going to let *him* know that. It was Wednesday afternoon — why the hell hadn't he called her before this? But as he talked, describing the gig in detail, she felt the familiar demanding heat uncurling in her groin.

Her session in the toilet with Jon a couple of days earlier had taken the edge off her frustration and the follow up in her office had been even better. It was actually very useful to know that there was at least one man in the *Daily News* offices she could call on if her need became unbearably urgent. Now here was Ledd again.

'How about coming over?' he mumbled at last. 'I've been thinking about you a lot.'

'Really? And what have you been thinking?'

'That you're the best fuck I've ever had — and I've had plenty.'

'Anything else?'

'Yeah. I love those suspender belts and stuff you wear. Are you wearing one now?'

'Yes.'

'What colour is it?'

'Beige.'

There was a silence at the end of the phone then Ledd repeated, 'How about coming over? I'll send the car for you if you like.'

'I'm busy at the moment — get it to pick me up here about six.'

INDECENT

Liz put the phone down and her scarlet lips curved in a smile. She'd punish him for taking so long to ring her.

Kate was sitting in the front row of a press conference being held by James. He was speaking with his usual conviction about the need to increase exports, his deep voice ringing authoritatively around the room.

Kate studied him as he spoke – he was a very impressive speaker. He wore his impeccable dark suit well and his greying temples and horn-rimmed glasses hit just the right note. She knew James would ask her opinion of his performance later so she tried to concentrate on his delivery. She wondered if anyone else knew he practiced his speeches and the accompanying gestures in front of the mirror.

His eyes met hers occasionally while he was speaking but she knew he was also making eye contact with everyone else in the room at least once during his speech.

Glancing at her watch, Kate guessed he was about to begin his summing up.

Time for her surprise.

Unobtrusively hitching up her skirt, she waited until he next glanced her way. When he did so she slowly uncrossed then crossed her legs, taking her time over it so he could see she wasn't wearing any panties.

He faltered over his sentence then looked away, still continuing to talk but putting less emphasis on the key words than he usually did. Kate carried on taking notes, knowing he was exerting superhuman control not to glance her way again. She waited until his eyes were turned in her general direction then uncrossed her legs in a leisurely fashion, pausing as if to straighten her skirt while her thighs were parted. She saw his Adam's apple bob as he swallowed, then he finished his speech somewhat abruptly.

He invited questions, answering the ones he wanted to and fielding the others with practiced ease. Kate knew it was killing him not to look at her and raised her hand.

He shot her a dark look from beneath his brows before saying, 'Yes? It's Miss Owen isn't it?' She nodded and began to ask him about export grants.

Both her voice and expression were serious but they both knew that she was about to expose herself again. She waited until she'd finished her question, then as she sat back in her seat she briefly flashed herself at him. There was a pulse going in his temple but only she knew what had put it there.

Half an hour later as the Minister talked to the journalists informally over coffee, Kate couldn't help but admire the way he worked the room. He had something to say to everyone and she knew his memory for names and faces was phenomenal. As she expected he eventually worked his way to her side.

'Ah, Miss Owen. That was an interesting question you posed.' He took her arm and drew her into a corner as he continued to talk about the question she'd asked. As soon as he judged they were out of earshot he lowered his voice but his professional smile remained firmly in place.

'I nearly came in my underpants — what were you thinking of?' he demanded.

'Just of brightening your otherwise joyless day,' said Kate, smiling demurely.

'You certainly did that — and that of all your fellow journalists if anyone had spotted you. You ruined my summing up — I left out at least half the points I meant to make. My mind went a complete blank when I realised I was gazing straight up your skirt at your fanny.'

A couple of people walked by and he raised his voice slightly to ask, 'Another cup of coffee?'

'That would be very nice, Minister.'

He led the way to the high, cloth-covered trestle table at the end of the room, manoeuvering her behind it as he poured them both more coffee.

'Would you?' he asked, indicating the milk and sugar. As Kate leant forward to reach for them he slipped his hand up her skirt from behind and pushed it between her legs.

'You're soaking wet,' he muttered. 'I take it you found it as exciting as I did. I want to fuck you so much, I wish we were alone.'

Kate gritted her teeth and tried not to give way to the excitement which threatened to overwhelm her. She concentrated on slowly putting milk, then sugar into both their cups, though neither of them took sugar. James's hand was sliding seductively backwards and forwards between her legs and she felt a trickle of moisture edging its way down her inner thigh and dampening her stocking top.

He removed his hand just as one of his staff moved

around the table to join them.

'Minister, you have a meeting scheduled for six o'clock.'

Glancing at his watch James said smoothly, 'I'm on my way. Miss Owen, if you'd care to walk me to my office I'm sure my secretary can find you the information you asked for.'

She followed him out of the room, almost running to keep up with him as he hurried through the warren of corridors. His secretary was sitting at her desk leafing through a sheaf of papers.

'Stella, could you possibly go along to William's office and pick up that file on the revised EEC export procedures he promised me?'

Stella left the room and James ushered Kate into his office, locking the door behind him with one hand and unzipping his trousers with the other. Pushing her down onto his desk he plunged into her, his hands finding her breasts as he thrust away, desperate for release.

For two wonderful, hot, shuddering minutes they banged away on the desk, the urgency of their mutual need blotting out everything else. Neither of them tried to prolong it — there just wasn't time. Kate's legs were clasped around his waist and she gasped at each strong thrust, until in a great rush of heat they both came.

Within seconds James was on his feet, zipping himself up and offering Kate a spotless white handkerchief to wipe herself on. Hastily tidying her hair, she took a couple of deep breaths and nodded as he stood poised to unlock the door.

Two of his staff were hovering in the outer office

waiting for the meeting to start. His Permanent Secretary greeted Kate by name and she smiled sweetly at him and asked him how he was before leaving the room on distinctly wobbly legs.

Walking back along the corridors she hoped no one suspected anything. It had really been a foolish risk to take, particularly so soon after he'd had her to lunch in his office.

They'd better be careful not to be seen together anywhere for a while.

To Liz's annoyance Ledd's suite was crammed with people. He was talking to a couple of men in grey suits who looked like accountants and he merely waved a casual greeting. She recognised his publicist, his manager and a couple of other people from his entourage but the rest were strangers.

Malcolm ambled over and asked her what she'd like to drink.

'Nothing,' she retorted, her aquamarine eyes glacial, 'I'm not staying.' Turning sharply on her heel she walked out of the room. Ledd caught up with her at the lifts.

'Where are you going?' he demanded. 'You've only just got here.'

'And now I'm leaving.' Liz's foot tapped an impatient tattoo on the floor as she waited for the lift to arrive.

'Why? What's up?'

'What's up is that I don't feel particularly inclined to sit around waiting for you to finish your business – you knew what time I was coming.'

'Give me a break, Liz,' he said sullenly. 'We're off

on a world tour next week – there's a lot to get sorted out.'

'Then I suggest you get back in there and continue sorting it out.'

The lift arrived at that moment and Liz stepped into it and pressed the button for the ground floor. Cursing, Ledd stepped in too.

'Come on, doll, I'll only be another five minutes or so.'

Wheeling round to face him Liz hissed, 'That's five minutes too long as far as I'm concerned – and *don't* call me doll!'

He grinned suddenly and pulled her roughly into his arms.

'I love it when you get all hoity-toity – it gives me a hard-on.'

It certainly had, Liz could feel it pressing into her stomach as he pushed her back against the mirrored lift wall and kissed her, his hands fondling her backside. She couldn't help but respond, sliding her tongue into his mouth and feeling her stomach lurch with lust.

The lift stopped at the ground floor and, disengaging herself from his embrace, Liz stepped out into the foyer with Ledd following her.

'Don't go,' he pleaded, grabbing her hand. 'What will I do with this?' He gestured downwards to where his erection stood out from his leather trousers like something carved in bas-relief. He leered at her lustfully and she hesitated.

'Look, why don't we go into the bar and have a drink and I'll phone Malcolm and tell him to clear everyone out – then we'll go back up,' he urged her.

INDECENT

Liz allowed herself to be led into the bar. After all, how could she punish him properly if she left now?

At around midnight she began to collect her scattered garments from around the bedroom while Ledd watched her.

'I've got a great idea,' he said suddenly, sitting up in bed, the sheet falling from his pale, hairless chest.

'What's that?'

'Why don't you come on tour with us? It'd be a gas.'

Liz winced — she did wish he wouldn't keep using expressions like that. Still it was an interesting idea.

'On tour? With Sledgehammer? Why?'

'So we could screw all the time. All that travelling gets boring — if you were with me it'd be great.'

Liz sat on the edge of the bed thoughtfully pulling her slip down over her head. Noticing that both her stockings were badly laddered she discarded them, slipping her shoes back onto her bare feet.

The idea had distinct possibilities.

She had to admit she'd been feeling restless recently — there was really no reason why she shouldn't take a couple of weeks off and go with Ledd. On second thoughts, perhaps she could tie the trip in with work in some way and claim substantial expenses, while in reality Ledd could pick up the tab.

The more she thought about it the more she liked it.

'Convince me,' she said.

Ledd lay back on the bed his hands behind his head. Taking Liz along would be much better than availing himself of the services of a different groupie every night. She was a more imaginative fuck and it would be good for his reputation to have such a classy-looking lady in tow. He was well aware that men always stared hungrily after Liz − she looked so hot, even though at the same time she had that disdainful 'don't fuck with me' air.

It had been galling him for a while that other singers had girlfriends who were top models or gorgeous actresses − he deserved better than the sort of girls he had been pulling.

'You'll enjoy it,' he told her. 'Luxury travel, limos, hotel suites − the lot. And endless opportunities for screwing each other's brains out.'

Combing her chestnut hair in front of the mirror Liz asked, 'Where are you opening?'

'The Hollywood Bowl.' Ledd smirked at her complacently as if expecting her to be impressed.

'Then where?'

'San Francisco.'

That clinched it. Liz liked America. If they'd been opening in Sweden nothing would have prevailed on her to go along − but California was a different matter.

Preparing to depart she picked up her bag.

'Alright,' she said casually, 'but I want my own suite at each hotel, I'm not sharing yours with assorted hangers on.'

'You got it, girl.'

Leaving the room Liz snapped over her shoulder, 'And *don't* call me girl!'

The phone rang just as Ellen was on her way to bed.

'Hello darling,' said a deep resonant voice which she couldn't place but which sounded vaguely familiar.

INDECENT

'Hello,' she replied, trying to think who it might be.

'This afternoon was wonderful,' he continued. As Ellen had spent the afternoon in the office on the telephone following up potential leads, she found this puzzling.

'Was it?' she asked blankly.

'Who is this?' the caller demanded suddenly. 'I wanted to speak to Kate Owen.'

'It's Ellen Marshall — hold on I'll just get Kate.'

'Damn!' James greeted Kate when she picked up the phone. 'I'd forgotten you had a temporary lodger. I'd better not ring you at home until she's moved out.'

'Why, what did you say to her?' asked Kate amused.

'It doesn't matter, I didn't tell her my name. How are you this evening, darling?'

'Tired. How about you?'

'Busy ploughing through some paperwork. I was wondering, how would you like a few days in Barcelona?'

'I'd like it a lot. Why, what's happening?'

'I've been invited to speak at a conference being held there and I thought if you could get some time off you could join me. I'll be the only English delegate so it should be fairly safe.'

'Mmm, I'll see if I can get away. I've never been to Barcelona.'

They chatted for a while then Kate said goodbye and headed for her bedroom. Ellen was hovering just outside the bathroom door.

'So you spent a wonderful afternoon, did you?' she teased. 'And I thought you were covering a press briefing at Westminster. Who was that by the way? I thought I recognised his voice.'

'Goodnight, Ellen.'

With a smile Kate vanished into her bedroom.

Liz waited until late afternoon before going to speak to Vernon.

He knew immediately that she wanted something by the expression on her face and he suppressed a shiver of longing. Whatever it was, he hoped she wanted it badly.

Very badly.

'Do you have a few minutes Vernon?' she asked him sweetly.

'Certainly, Liz. Sit down my dear. Would you like a drink?'

'Vodka and tonic, please.'

She sat on the chair opposite his desk, crossing her legs and hitching up her skirt.

'I've been giving some thought to your little talk the other day and I've found a great story. You said you wanted sleaze and scandal — well, I think I know where I can get you bucket loads of it.'

Vernon could just see a glimpse of stocking top and was finding it hard to concentrate on what she was saying.

'Where?' he managed to say.

Taking her time, Liz slowly removed her jacket, underneath which she was wearing a round necked ivory silk top. She was braless and her small pointed breasts with their upturned nipples were plainly visible.

Vernon gulped and knocked back a generous

mouthful of whisky, unable to tear his eyes from the delectable sight.

'I thought I'd go on tour with Sledgehammer for a couple of weeks. Orgies, drugs, smashing up hotel rooms – you name it, they're bound to be doing it.'

Making a huge effort, Vernon managed to say, 'Well, it's a good idea Liz but it's fairly standard stuff. After all, no one expects a rock group to behave in any other way – an evangelical preacher behaving like that on tour would be another thing altogether.'

Keeping a smile on her face nearly killed Liz but she managed it.

'You know the way I approach things, Vernon, I'd bring a whole new slant to the situation.' She brushed her fingers casually over her left breast as she spoke.

'I'm sure you would, Liz, and I like the idea in principle, but I really don't think there's enough mileage in it for us.'

Liz's eyes glittered angrily and she opened her mouth to say something and then thought better of it. Pausing to sip her drink she leant back in her chair, her breasts jutting forwards, straining against the thin material of her top.

She waited until Vernon had had time to appreciate the sight then said, 'The tour starts in Los Angeles. I thought that while I was there I could do a few celebrity interviews for my column.'

Glassy-eyed, Vernon fortified himself with another swig of whisky.

'That ... that sounds interesting. Who did you have in mind?'

Liz reeled off a few names then rose sinuously to her feet.

'Tell Hannah you're not to be disturbed,' she ordered him softly, running the tip of her tongue over her red lips.

Without taking his eyes off her Vernon slowly lifted the phone and spoke to his secretary. While he did so Liz unzipped her skirt and stepped out of it with her back to him, revealing her naked backside. The alluring globes of her buttocks were bisected by the two back suspenders of a black suspender belt. She was also wearing black seamed stockings — but no panties.

Turning round she slowly removed the silk top and idly ran her hands down over her nipples.

Dry mouthed, Vernon watched as she moved her chair nearer and, using it as a step, climbed onto his desk. Towering above him she opened her legs — a sight that was the closest thing to heaven Vernon had ever experienced.

'I want to go on tour with Sledgehammer for a couple of weeks,' she murmured, her hands on her hips. 'I can go, can't I, Vernon?'

Several pairs of male eyes followed Ellen across the room as, deep in thought, she walked over to one of the battered filing cabinets. She was wearing a pair of black leggings, which looked like tights, tucked into spike-heeled boots. Her short red jacket only came down to her waist, with the result that her curvaceous bottom was very much on display.

She looked like the principal boy in a pantomime and there had been some speculation as to whether she was wearing panties — no one could actually see the outline of them beneath the close fitting material.

Bending over to pull a file out of the bottom drawer Ellen was only aware of Ernie's approach when she felt his hands on her backside. She knew it was Ernie because only Ernie smelt like that.

She deduced correctly that he'd been drinking as his hands kneaded and squeezed the fleshy mounds of her buttocks. A strong whiff of stale beer assailed her nostrils as he said, 'I'm mad about your bum, Lolita. Fancy a shag? There's no one in the storeroom.'

Straightening up she stamped down hard on his instep with her high heel. Ernie swore and reeled backwards, hopping around in agony.

'What did you do that for?' he demanded. 'I was only being friendly.'

'Sorry, Ernie,' Ellen apologised sweetly. 'A sudden spasm — being manhandled has that effect on me.'

'You're a lezzo, that's what you are,' he complained. 'That or frigid.'

Ignoring him, Ellen returned to her desk and began to read through the file, unwrapping a milk chocolate flake as she did so. She'd just inserted the end of the chocolate bar into her mouth and was circling it with the tip of her pink tongue, when there was an anguished cry from the injured photographer.

'Now she's going to eat a flake,' he moaned. 'It's more than a red-blooded man can stand.' Looking straight at him Ellen opened her mouth wide, showing her small white teeth, then bit down hard. Ernie let out a howl and blundered backwards, unfortunately for him bumping into Liz.

The usually noisy office fell silent as Ernie wilted under the onslaught of a vicious tongue lashing from Liz. Everyone kept their heads down and avoided looking in their direction — no one wanted to be next on Liz's shit list.

Placidly munching her flake, Ellen read through the file on her desk.

She had an appointment to interview an ageing actress who'd recently published her autobiography. Ellen had just finished it and it made wonderful reading — was there anyone in movies at the time that Donna Hamilton hadn't been to bed with? And surely that story about David Niven couldn't be true? — it just wasn't anatomically feasible.

Donna Hamilton lived in a flat near King's Cross and had invited Ellen for cocktails. The once-gracious house was in an area much gone to seed, but the interior was warm and comfortably furnished, if rather cluttered with Donna's memorabilia.

Ellen enjoyed the interview even if she did have difficulty choking down the very dry Martinis that Donna kept mixing. She longed for some lemonade to add to them but it didn't seem polite to ask.

She left at around eight and headed for the tube station in the balmy evening air. Her high-heeled boots clicked on the pavement as she walked along trying to decide whether to return to the office or go back to the flat.

She suddenly became aware that a sleek black car which had overtaken her a short time ago had turned round and was now keeping pace with her.

INDECENT

She looked enquiringly at the driver who pressed a button to lower the window.

'Can I help you?' she asked, thinking he was lost. He was foreign looking, possibly an Arab.

His liquid dark eyes appraised her carefully then in slightly accented English he said, 'Hello, beautiful – how much?'

'How much for what?' asked Ellen puzzled. Then, rather belatedly, the light dawned.

He thought she was a streetwalker.

She mentally castigated herself for being so slow on the uptake – she was in King's Cross after all and she'd passed several women loitering on street corners.

Maybe there was a story in this somewhere.

'What was it you wanted?' she enquired, smiling at him.

'Your company for the evening.'

Glancing around Ellen remembered there was a hotel on the next corner which had a bar. She certainly wasn't about to get in the car, but she wanted to talk to him.

'Why don't we go for a drink and discuss it?' she suggested brightly. At that moment a car pulled away from the kerb a few yards ahead of them, vacating a parking space. He nodded and pulled into the space, then joined her on the pavement. It was only then that she noticed the car had diplomatic plates.

Even better.

She appraised him carefully as they walked towards the hotel. He looked to be in his late thirties and was of medium height with thick dark hair. In the rather seedy cocktail lounge of the hotel they took their drinks over to a corner table.

'What's your name?' she asked him.

'Ali. What's yours?'

'Ell... Ellie,' she amended hastily. 'So what exactly are you looking for, Ali?'

'A few drinks – maybe a meal. Then I'll pay you well to do what I want.'

'And what do you want?'

Lowering his voice he told her. A slow flush crept over Ellen's cheeks as he spoke. Goodness, this was a long way from Simon's unimaginative approach to sex. She'd heard Arabs had different tastes but this was something else.

His hot dark eyes lingered on her breasts as he spoke, making her wriggle slightly on her seat.

'Do you do this a lot?' she asked.

'I've only been in England for two months but this is about the fourth or fifth time. I like the company of ladies very much and where I work there are mostly men.'

Deciding it wouldn't be a good idea to ask which Embassy he was attached to, and anyway she'd memorized the number on the licence plate so she could easily find out, Ellen considered giving Ernie a ring to come and get a photo. But no, maybe on balance it would be better just as a story.

Her head was starting to spin slightly after Donna Hamilton's Martinis and now a gin and tonic. Better get something to eat or she'd be on her back. The idea made her giggle and he laughed with her, softly stroking some stray dark curls back from her face.

He had very full red lips and they were now close

to hers. She couldn't help but lean forward and he kissed her, gently at first then more passionately. Feeling the familiar tingling between her legs, Ellen allowed him to deepen the kiss. His hand on her thigh was sending sparks of desire shooting up into her groin.

They were interrupted by the barmaid, an elderly woman with dyed red hair. Emptying the ashtray on the table next to theirs she said, 'You know better than that, dear. Not in here.'

Ellen blushed hotly. Now the barmaid thought she was a streetwalker too.

'Come,' said Ali, 'let's eat.'

He took her to a small but plush Armenian restaurant which Ellen liked a lot, except for the horrible wailing piped music. They drank a rough red wine with the meal and, although she kept trying not to drink much, somehow her glass was always full. Ali told her about his home and how he missed his family, while under the cover of the tablecloth he stroked her thigh.

Over liqueurs and tiny cups of dark bitter coffee he moved closer to her on the banquette. She was aware that he was gently massaging her lower back but it was a surprise when he pushed his hand down the back of her leggings and slipped his fingers into the cleft between her buttocks.

Her male colleagues had been right, she wasn't wearing any panties.

His tanned fingers massaged seductively away and, as if of its own volition, her backside raised itself briefly from the seat, enabling him to slip his hand beneath her.

Felice Ash

Ellen couldn't believe she was doing this.

She was sitting in full view in a restaurant while a man she'd just met slowly eased his fingers into her honeypot – surely someone would notice. But the restaurant was dimly lit and their table was in a secluded corner. She sucked in her breath as the tip of one finger made contact with her clit and began to tickle it. She could feel her juices trickling downwards, making her slick and molten where he was touching her.

In the grip of an uncontrollable sexual excitement she opened her legs beneath the table so he could get a couple of fingers up inside her.

'Aaaah!'

The long drawn out moan escaped from her unbidden as an intense climax took her by surprise. A couple of other diners looked in their direction, but luckily the music was the type which sounded like a lot of wails and groans set to music anyway.

She closed her eyes for a few seconds while Ali withdrew his hand and wiped it fastidiously on his napkin. How had he brought her to orgasm so quickly? It usually took her much longer than that.

'Shall I call for the bill? Or would you like more coffee or another liqueur?' he asked courteously.

Ellen shook her head, too dazed to speak.

CHAPTER SEVEN

Ellen hadn't actually intended to have sex with Ali but somehow events ran away with her.

After leaving the restaurant he helped her into his car, caressing her breasts briefly as she sank back into the luxurious leather seat. He drove competently through the darkening streets with his hand on the sopping crotch of her leggings, keeping her in a state of intense sexual arousal.

He lived in a modern service flat in an expensive block in Knightsbridge with its own underground garage. Walking towards the lift Ellen was uncomfortably aware of the way the leggings had worked their way into the cleft between her legs, half chafing, half stimulating her.

His flat bore all the hallmarks of an expensive interior designer. There was a lot of black, grey and white with ultra-modern furniture and leather sofas.

Once in the sitting room he led her across to the floor-to-ceiling windows which looked out over Hyde Park. Turning her so that she had her back to the room he gripped the waistband of her leggings and tore them down the back. She protested but he ignored her, ripping them from her shapely legs so she was standing in her red jacket and boots, naked from the waist down.

Holding her by the hips he pushed her groin forwards until it made contact with the cool surface of the glass. There were several lamps lit in the room and Ellen was uncomfortably aware that anyone in the park looking up would be able to see her. She could only hope fervently that no one down there had a pair of binoculars with them.

Ali fell to his knees behind her and in sudden contrast to the cold glass she felt the heat of his mouth as he began to lick his way over her private parts, invading her secret places with his lips and tongue.

His fingers feathered their way down from her waist, smoothing and stroking her bush as if it were a kitten while his mouth continued its welcome exploration.

His lips closed over her clit and sucked hard, causing an immediate explosion of pleasure as she came for the second time that evening. Rising to his feet Ali stripped off her jacket, tee-shirt and bra, fondling and squeezing her breasts, rolling her hard nipples gently between his fingers while she thrust her naked derrière back into his groin.

Suddenly she felt herself pushed up against the window again, her breasts flattening against the glass as he unzipped his trousers and impaled her smoothly from behind. Lost in an erotic haze Ellen hoped again that there wasn't a voyeur out there having a field day. She must look very odd as her breasts, stomach and groin pressed rhythmically into the glass with each forceful thrust.

She also hoped that it was very strong glass.

The rest of the night was almost like an intense

erotic dream. There seemed no break to the flow of their movements, no definite moment where one type of screwing became another. He explored every inch of Ellen's body, leaving nothing untouched.

There didn't seem to be anywhere in the flat that he didn't fuck her.

Bent backwards over the sofa, her legs around his waist.

On her hands and knees on the thick carpet, her rump in the air.

Over the dining room table, her hips raised by a couple of cushions.

In one of the squashy leather armchairs.

On the king-sized bed, riding him deliriously while he thrust away beneath her.

She lost count of the number of orgasms she sustained.

It was a warm night and by the early hours they were both slick with sweat and each other's juices. Opening his eyes to smile at her as she lay there panting next to him, he licked a droplet of perspiration from one perfect breast.

Standing up, he swung her into his arms while Ellen wondered weakly if she could carry on much longer. He lowered her into the bath, positioning her so she was reclining with her legs wide apart and her feet up on the tiled surround.

She shrieked when the icy blast of the shower spray caught her squarely between the legs, cooling her hot and swollen private parts and dousing them with chilly water.

She struggled to sit up but he leapt into the bath with her, holding her down while he soaped her thoroughly, then rinsed her off.

She did the same for him then they screwed one last time, sliding soapily around in the bottom of the bath while the shower spray continued to drench them.

It was six o'clock when Ellen left Ali's flat and stumbled along towards the park looking for a taxi. The combination of a hangover and lack of sleep made her feel like death. Her hair hung in a tangled mass over her shoulders from sleeping on it while it was still wet and her face was pale and puffy.

She'd rummaged through Ali's wardrobe for something to wear instead of her torn leggings. The best she could find was a pair of black silk shorts which made her look even more like the tart that Ali thought she was. There hadn't been any stage of the proceedings when she felt she could tell him that she was in fact a journalist. She wondered what he would think when he woke up and found she'd left without asking for money.

She flagged down a taxi and directed the driver to Kate's flat.

'Busy night was it, love?' he asked, when his eyes met hers in the rear-view mirror. She sighed. Today she'd better go into the office in something demure – she wasn't keen on being taken for a prostitute. Her reply when he suggested she needn't actually pay the fare, just let him get in the back with her for a while, was pithy in the extreme.

Barcelona was hot.

That was fine with Kate – she liked it hot. James

INDECENT

had flown out the day before and would be tied up at the conference until early evening. When she'd checked into her room at a hotel just off La Rambla, Barcelona's main street, she decided to go for a stroll in the late afternoon sunshine.

A busy road with a central paved area, La Rambla ran upwards from the sea for about a mile to the Placa de Catalunya. Pavement cafés, flower stalls and stands selling tourist paraphernalia filled the centre and Kate wandered around for a while before taking a seat in one of the cafés.

A waiter took her order then darted confidently into the heavy traffic to bring her drink from the other side of the busy road. Sipping her glass of San Miguel, Kate watched the passing crowds from behind her dark glasses. She was struck by the casual grace of the young Spaniards, most of whom had dressed with a degree of style not found in their English counterparts.

An attractive man in his early twenties approached her table and smiled down at her. She found herself smiling back, liking the look of him. He had a strong face with an aquiline nose and a body which looked lean and fit. He spoke to her in Spanish then, when he realised she didn't understand, in English, asking if he could buy her a drink.

Regretfully she shook her head. Had she been in Barcelona alone it might have been a different matter, but she was meeting James soon.

When she'd finished her drink she explored the gothic quarter of the city for a couple of hours then returned to the hotel. James was waiting for her in the bar, looking every inch the Englishman abroad as he drank a gin and tonic. Ten minutes later they were in his room, making love while the curtains stirred in the warm breeze from the open window.

When they'd finally finished Kate propped herself lazily up on one elbow and looked down at her lover.

'So, what's on the agenda tonight?' she asked.

'Dinner, a few drinks and a stroll along La Rambla, I think,' he returned. 'Talking of which, I'm quite hungry now I come to think of it. Do you want the first shower?'

Kate was in the bathroom with the shower going when she noticed there was no shampoo. Opening the door she was just about to call James to ask if he had any, when she heard the phone ring. Padding barefoot down the short corridor linking the bathroom to the bedroom she stopped short when she heard the words, 'National security'.

Without really thinking about it she stayed where she was, out of sight but within earshot. Most of James's side of the conversation was monosyllabic, but when she heard him say, 'It could cause a national scandal – even bring the government down if the information got in the wrong hands,' she knew she'd inadvertently stumbled onto something.

When she heard him replace the receiver she returned silently to the bathroom and stepped under the shower, absent-mindedly washing her hair with shower gel. What was this all about?

She didn't know but she certainly intended to find out.

Liz took an instant dislike to Ledd's tour manager, Bruce.

INDECENT

They met at the lead guitarist's birthday party which was being held at his manor house in Surrey. She and Ledd had been driven down in Ledd's limo and were having a drink in the stone-flagged hallway when Bruce joined them.

Ledd introduced him and Bruce's eyes swept over her dismissively as he nodded an offhand greeting.

'Beat it for a bit will you, love?' he said, 'I need to talk to Ledd.'

Without waiting for a reply he continued, 'There's a problem over the dates for the Chicago gig . . .'

He didn't get any further.

'Just a minute,' interjected Liz coldly. 'Firstly, my name is Ms Peters as far as you're concerned. Secondly, *I* was talking to Ledd, so *you* can beat it until I've finished. Thirdly, since you are here you can go and get us another couple of drinks.'

The tour manager's face became mottled with rage as he turned to stare at Liz for a moment before demanding of Ledd, 'Who does this bitch think she is?'

'I'm Liz Peters from the *Daily News*, and I'll be covering the tour,' she retorted coldly, 'and as you're the tour manager I expect you to make sure that I get what I want when I want it — and right now that means another drink.'

'You fu—' he began, then let out a strangled gasp as Liz casually threw the contents of her glass of champagne at his groin.

'You heard the lady,' said Ledd, putting his arm around her. 'Piss off and do what she says.'

As soon as Bruce had walked off swearing under his breath and mopping at his damp groin with a handkerchief, Ledd took hold of Liz's hand and led her towards the stairs.

'Where are we going?' she asked, struggling to keep up with him on her spike-heeled shoes.

'To find somewhere we can fuck – it turns me on when you're like that. You're really something, you know. I don't know how you manage it.'

He flung open several doors on the first floor, briefly inspecting the rooms until he found what he was looking for.

'Here we are then,' he told her. 'Have you ever done it on a billiard table before?'

Liz hadn't.

Kate and James ate on the bougainvillaea-covered terrace of an old-established family restaurant in the centre of Barcelona. After the meal they walked slowly back to the hotel, stopping to have brandies at a couple of pavement cafés on the way.

It was quite late by then but the traffic was still heavy as they crossed a busy square. In the centre of the square was a large traffic island grassed over and planted with flowers, bushes and shrubs. They decided to walk across it rather than around it, pushing their way with some difficulty through the bushes planted on the perimeter. They had almost reached the far side when James stopped and pulled Kate against him, bending down to kiss her to the sound of the cicadas and the late-night traffic in the background.

Kate responded eagerly, sliding her tongue into his mouth and pressing her full breasts against his chest. He slipped a hand inside the front of her dress and fondled one hard crinkled nipple, his other hand caressing the swell of her buttocks.

She was surprised when he suddenly lifted her and laid her on her back on the coarse grass.

'James, we can't!' she gasped, as he knelt beside her unzipping his trousers. He ignored her, reaching up beneath her dress to slip her panties off. 'James!' she exclaimed again, then inhaled sharply as his fingers found the slippery nub of her clit. He rubbed it gently with a sensual circular movement and she forgot that she'd been about to remonstrate with him, instead lying silently gazing up at the stars as he skilfully manipulated her towards orgasm.

When he entered her she was more than ready for him, her legs clasping his thighs as he slid deep inside her. They moved together silently under the dark velvety sky, oblivious to the sound of a group of people passing a few yards away on the other side of the bushes.

A few seconds after James erupted into orgasm, he was startled to feel that his back was becoming wet. Raising his head reluctantly he saw that it was beginning to rain quite hard. At least he thought it was rain until he realised it was a sprinkler a couple of yards away giving the grass a thorough night-time watering.

Getting hurriedly to his feet he reached down to help Kate up, but not before she'd been drenched too. She shrieked as the water soaked into her thin beige dress. Half laughing, half annoyed they fled through the bushes back onto the pavement running around the traffic island, then turned to look at each other.

'Oh no!' cried Kate in dismay, looking down at her dress. The water had rendered it virtually transparent. It clung to her curves like a second skin, making it obvious she wore nothing underneath.

'Where are my panties?' she asked him frantically, as a group of passing men slowed down to gaze admiringly at her. Dragging her hastily back into the bushes to the accompaniment of appreciative cat calls from the men, James put his damp jacket around her shoulders.

'Stay there, I'll get them.' Diving back into the spray he found them in a wet crumpled heap on the ground. Kate pulled them back on but they'd been rendered transparent too and did little to help to conceal her charms.

'How can we go back to the hotel looking like this?' she demanded, torn between amusement and distress.

'Mmm, I see what you mean,' he said looking at her closely. 'Pity the jacket isn't a couple of inches longer – I can see your bush quite clearly.'

In the end Kate hovered in the shrubs while James flagged down a taxi to take them back to their hotel. Once there he went up to his room and brought down a lightweight mac for her to don before emerging from the car, much to the amusement of the taxi driver.

Back in her room Kate removed his mac and jacket then began to strip off her dress saying, 'What on earth possessed you to take such a risk? If we'd been arrested for public indecency your political career could have been on the line.'

'Politicians take much bigger risks than that,' he murmured, watching her undress with interest. 'On a scale of one to ten what we just did scores about three.'

'What sort of risks?' enquired Kate suddenly alert, her journalist's antennae quivering.

'You name it politicians do it – vice girls, cottaging, indecent exposure ... talking of which, I've a sudden overpowering desire to stand under a hot shower and cover you in soap suds.'

'How does that rate on a scale of one to ten?' asked Kate demurely, dropping the towel she'd been rubbing her hair with.

'It depends where you do it.'

Ellen's article on being mistaken for a streetwalker went down very well with Vernon. She had naturally not revealed all the details of her encounter with Ali, just enough to make a good piece.

'Good work, my dear,' he praised her. 'Just the sort of thing our readers love. Now, how's the first article on your blind dates coming along?'

'Well, I've been on two blind dates now and I have another lined up tonight so it should be ready tomorrow – or the day after,' she added hopefully.

'Tomorrow,' he said, making a note. 'Another nice meaty piece I trust?' He smiled wolfishly at her and she nodded as she gathered up her papers and left the room.

Ellen's first article was to be about the men she met through the arts magazine. Gordon had been the first, followed a few days later by Nigel.

Nigel had been a low-ranking civil servant of such mind-numbing pretentiousness that she'd seriously considered leaving after only fifteen minutes.

They'd met in a bar in Convent Garden. He had greasy hair, ill-fitting grubby clothes and a supercilious manner. He poured scorn on her choice of drink — sweet sherry and lemonade — and proceeded to lecture her on the subject for forty-five minutes.

The rest of the evening was no better. He talked about himself at great length, giving her his opinions on recent films, books and concerts without once asking her what she thought. He was patronising, ill-mannered and deathly boring. Eventually at around ten o'clock he glanced at his watch.

'We'd better get going,' he told her. Greatly relieved Ellen rose to her feet, brushing a shower of crisp fragments from her skirt. She'd been so bored that she'd got through three packets and as a result now had a raging thirst. Once outside Ellen flagged down a cab. To her surprise he waved it on again.

'I'm not made of money,' he told her. 'Come on, we'll get the tube. Incidentally you'll have to leave before midnight, my landlady doesn't allow guests after that time.'

Ellen stared at him in astonishment. Had she missed part of his monologue? She didn't recollect accepting an invitation back to his flat.

'What on earth makes you think I'm coming home with you?' she asked.

'Well that's what this is about isn't it?' he demanded. 'We've explored each other's psyches, now it's time to take that to its logical conclusion and see if our bodies are in tune. I hope you're not going to play hard to get,' he added peevishly. 'That's just so typical of the irrational female mentality it makes me livid. You've been leading me on all evening – you're not even my type but I'm prepared to make allowances.'

Completely taken aback Ellen wished she could think of something pithy to say. Unfortunately she couldn't so she settled on, 'Well, it's been nice meeting you, but I really must get back,' before turning away and flagging down another taxi.

'It's your loss,' he shouted after her as she climbed into the cab. 'I'm brilliant in bed, women beg me for it, I'm...'

Thankfully the end of his sentence was lost as the taxi drove away.

Her third blind date was with a salesman for a Birmingham manufacturing company which made plumbing sundries. In his mid-forties George was pleasant, plump and balding. They met in a pub in Soho and after he'd got her a drink his first words were, 'Now, what's a gorgeous young girl like you doing putting adverts in magazines? You can't find it hard to meet men surely?' He looked longingly at her stocking-clad legs as he spoke.

Ellen stirred her Babycham with her cocktail cherry.

'I like to meet different people,' she said evasively.

'I don't think you were bargaining for someone like me,' he told her bluntly. 'I suppose I'd better come clean. What I know about the arts and culture wouldn't cover a bottle top. Someone had left that artsy-fartsy magazine in my hotel room last time I was down here. I just answered your ad on an impulse because I'm in London a couple of days a week and I get tired of my own company in the evenings. And I'm much too old for you anyway,' he ended lugubriously.

Ellen giggled, he was really quite endearing. He reminded her of a dog she used to have when she was a little girl.

'Shall I tell you something?' she murmured, sucking the cherry slowly off her cocktail stick.

'Tell me anything you like,' he invited her good-humouredly.

'I don't know anything about the arts either — except that they bore me rigid,' she admitted.

'Then why the ad?'

'My mother wanted me to meet a nicer class of man,' she replied mendaciously. He burst out laughing.

'She sounds just like my ex-wife, she's obsessed by our daughter marrying into the professional classes.'

'Are you divorced?'

'Yes, just last year, but we'd been separated for years and hadn't got round to doing anything about it until Elaine met a new bloke.

'Did you mind?'

'No, I was relieved really, I still felt responsible for her. Whenever the boiler wouldn't light or her car broke down she still phoned me, even though she ran off with a civil engineer from Loughborough seven years ago — but that didn't last long. Now she's marrying an accountant. Seems like a nice enough bloke.'

INDECENT

He drained his glass and stood up. 'Same again or would like something different?'

'The same please.'

When he returned he asked, 'So what do you like doing if you don't like the arts?'

'Eating and drinking,' replied Ellen promptly. He bellowed with laughter again, slapping his plump thigh.

'Me too. Well what do you say we have a couple more drinks then go and have a good meal somewhere?'

Ellen beamed at him.

'That sounds great to me.'

She really enjoyed the evening. After amiably discussing where to eat, they settled on a restaurant renowned for its old-fashioned English cooking — particularly the roast beef.

George was endlessly solicitous, asking if the table they were shown to was alright, urging her to order whatever she wanted from the menu and deferring to her taste in wine.

They both had a lot to drink and she was often reduced to helpless laughter by his droll, downbeat sense of humour. Despite the fact that he wasn't really her type Ellen started to find him attractive — anyone who could make her laugh so much was okay in her book.

And all the alcohol she'd consumed had put her in a sexy mood.

At the end of the evening as they stood outside the restaurant he took her hand in both his and kissed it fervently.

'Thank you for a great evening,' he said. 'Now I

suppose I'd better put you in a taxi home before I forget I'm an overweight middle-aged man who's old enough to be your father.'

Ellen looked flirtatiously up at him from beneath her long lashes.

'You mean you're not going to ask me back to your room for a nightcap?'

'I don't think I'd better – I'm only human after all.'

'What if I said I'd like you to invite me back?'

'Would you?'

In reply she hailed a taxi and taking his hand pulled him into it behind her, directing the driver to his hotel. She snuggled up beside him smiling winsomely.

'Are you sure?' he asked her hesitantly.

'I'm sure,' she replied, pulling his head down and kissing him.

Jon was feeling fairly pleased with himself when he entered the steam room at the health club. Vernon had tried to send him up to Leicester with Ernie to interview the wife of a well-known jockey who'd just announced he was gay and was leaving his wife for his male lover.

Jon took one look at her photograph and decided that even to get a good story he couldn't contemplate using his usual technique.

Added to which Ernie had patently eaten curry the night before and kept belching and farting while they were in Vernon's office. The idea of being cooped up with him in a car for most of the day was more than Jon could stand.

INDECENT

He'd told Vernon he was following up a lead which looked as if it was going to result in a big story and Vernon had reluctantly agreed to send someone else.

Jon had hurriedly left the building before Vernon could change his mind. He decided to take refuge in the health club — he didn't actually have any leads at all at present, but there was always the possibility something would turn up.

The steam room was empty and so thick with vapour that he had to grope his way across to the slatted wooden benches by touch. He climbed up to the top bench and stretched out on his stomach, closing his eyes and looking forward to relaxing for a while.

He must have drifted off to sleep in the soporific heat because the next thing he heard was the sound of a woman saying in a low throaty voice, 'Mmm, that's nice.'

Opening his eyes, he turned his head and saw two women on the bottom bench on the other side of the room. One of them, a petite brunette in her twenties, was lying on her back completely naked, displaying small but very pert breasts, slender hips and long legs.

The other woman sitting beside her was older, perhaps in her late thirties. She had a towel loosely wrapped around her waist, exposing a pair of firm ripe breasts. Shoulder-length streaky-blonde hair hid her face for a few moments as she sat looking down at her companion, but then she threw back her head to laugh and Jon saw she had a lovely sensual face.

Leaning forward, she kissed one of the brunette's

upturned nipples then began to massage her breast, her slender hand moving languidly around and over it.

Thinking he must be asleep and having an erotic dream, Jon closed his eyes and counted to three before opening them again. In addition to caressing the brunette's delectable breast, the blonde was now running her hand over her stomach, grazing her long nails over the smooth skin in a way which made the blood pump through Jon's veins at what felt like twice its normal rate.

It was obvious they had no idea he was there, the steam was particularly thick around the bench he was lying on, only a few feet below the ceiling. Moving slightly nearer the edge to get a better view he thought that really he should make his presence known. That's what a gentleman would do after all.

But then, he wasn't a gentleman.

And anyway his first responsibility was to the paper and he scented a story, particularly as he thought he recognised the blonde woman. For a few moments he tried to remember who she was then gulped and lost interest in placing her — at least for the moment — when she slipped her hand between the dark girl's legs.

He could feel his hard-on digging painfully into one of the wooden slats and shifted position. A wreath of vapour hid the pair from his sight for a few moments and when it had drifted past he saw that the brunette had parted her legs and her hips were moving dreamily in response to the gentle pressure from the other woman's fingers.

He just about suppressed a moan of pleasure at the

sight, particularly when blonde parted her companion's legs even further giving Jon a bird's-eye view of her glistening cleft, the pink tip of her clit peeping shyly out from between the soft folds of her labia.

With the tip of her finger the blonde woman began to stroke the protruding clitoris, gently encouraging it to swell and emerge even further from its hiding place. When she bent her head and began to lap at it with her tongue, silky blonde hair spilling over smooth slender thighs, Jon thought he would die of pleasure.

The steam hid them from sight again, then he heard the unmistakable sound of a woman in the throes of orgasm. When the vapour cleared a little he saw the brunette lying with her eyes closed, her chest rising and falling while her friend stroked her breasts.

A few moments later the dark girl sat up and the two women kissed deeply before the blonde lay on her stomach, her gorgeous rounded backside fully exposed.

Sitting astride her companion's legs, the younger girl began to massage her back, expertly working her way downwards until she was kneading her buttocks with firm, smooth strokes. The blonde woman's head was turned sideways so Jon could see the pleasure on her face as she submitted to her friend's expert ministrations.

Both women were gleaming with perspiration – Jon felt pretty sweaty himself, a combination of the heat and the raging excitement at what he was seeing.

The brunette's fingers eventually glided between her friend's parted thighs, teasing the soft petals of flesh apart and then pushing inside so deeply that her small hand vanished almost up to the wrist. The blonde woman began to moan and push her hips against the bench, her rounded buttocks making erotic circles in the air.

It was the most arousing scenario Jon had ever witnessed, the constantly swirling steam imbuing it with a languid, dream-like quality.

Shifting position, the brunette pushed one of her knees between the other's legs, parting them even further and kneeling astride her left thigh. She began to rub herself backwards and forwards along it, stimulating her own clit as she massaged the blonde's with her fingers. Jon thought he was going to burst a blood vessel as he watched, gripping hold of the bench and trying not to give into the urge to go and join them — they seemed to be managing quite well without him after all.

A few seconds later the blonde let out a cry and arched her back, her eyes closed and her body shaking with ecstasy as she came. The brunette continued to rub herself faster and faster up and down the thigh clutched between her legs until she too let out a shriek of pleasure and convulsed into orgasm.

Jon felt weak and spent — as if he'd just run a marathon or done five hundred press-ups. He closed his eyes and when he eventually opened them the blonde was sitting up leaning back against the wall her towel around her waist, while the brunette secured her own towel so it covered most of her slender frame.

Bending to kiss her friend goodbye, she vanished into the steam and Jon heard the sound of the door opening then closing.

A satisfied smile on her face, the blonde woman stretched contentedly then looked upwards, just as the steam billowed across the room in the draught from the door, leaving Jon suddenly fully exposed to her gaze.

For a long moment they stared at each other, their eyes locking. Then she said, 'My my, what have we here – a Peeping Tom?'

Whatever reaction Jon had expected it wasn't this. He thought she might cry out and run from the room, or clutch her towel to her luscious bosom and scream. Instead she just watched him lazily as he wrapped his own towel firmly over his burgeoning erection and climbed down. She made no attempt to cover her charms, leaning back with her arms behind her head, her full pink lips curved in a smile.

Suddenly he recognised her.

'Hello, Mrs York.'

Her smile didn't falter.

He sat down beside her on the bench thinking how different she looked. The wife of the party chairman, she usually wore her streaky-blonde hair pulled back off her face and elegant understated clothes which only hinted at the superb figure they concealed.

'And who are you?' she asked casually.

'Jon Wright.'

At this stage he usually added 'from the *Daily*

Felice Ash

News' and presented his credentials. But in his current state of undress his only credentials were covered by a towel and he wasn't sure whether presenting them to the ravishing Amelia York would go down well.

'Do you often play the voyeur?' she asked him, her tone mildly accusing.

'Oh, come on,' he protested, 'I was already in here when you arrived — and I was half asleep. By the time I'd realised what was going on, you were well into it and I doubt whether you'd have welcomed an interruption.'

His eye was caught by a bead of sweat rolling down one full breast. It paused for a moment on her swollen nipple and he had to suppress a strong desire to lean across and lick it off before it fell onto her stomach.

She saw him looking.

'Did it turn you on?' Her eyes rested for a moment on his towel-covered erection.

'What do you think?'

She smiled knowingly, dabbing at her damp brow with a corner of her towel.

'Incidentally, how come you recognised me? I keep a fairly low profile.'

'Beautiful women tend to stick in my mind. And anyway it's my business to recognise people.'

'What business is that?'

'I'm a reporter for the *Daily News*.'

A fleeting look of consternation passed over her face then her expression became thoughtful.

'So what will it be? "Party Chairman's Wife in Steamy Lesbian Sex Romp"? That should sell a few copies. What a pity you didn't get any photos.'

'How can you be sure I didn't?'

She looked at his groin again.

'Is that a camera under your towel or were you just glad to see us?' she quipped. '*Did* you take any photos?'

'No, but you've got to admit it's still quite a story. Our readers will love it.'

She was silent for a few moments then she smiled at him, leaning closer and fluttering her eyelashes seductively.

'Is there any way I can persuade you not to write about this?'

Under its terrycloth covering Jon's dick telegraphed a very decided 'yes'.

CHAPTER EIGHT

Two braziers burning in the corners of the stone-flagged room kept the temperature well into the seventies. It wasn't a particularly chilly evening but all the men present were in various stages of undress so the heat was welcome.

Seated on benches at rough trestle tables they were enjoying both the food and the free flowing wine which they drank from silver goblets.

They were served by girls in simple long white dresses. The girls seemed demurely attired until they walked in front of one of the ornate candelabra and against the light it became plain they were naked beneath the gauzy gowns.

As the meal progressed the men became more boisterous, fondling the girls' buttocks and breasts as they passed the food round and poured more wine.

One of the men, wearing only his shirt and socks, pulled a plump redhead onto his knee and plunged his hand down the front of her dress. Giggling, she wriggled around on his knee and tried to remove it. Fastening his mouth onto her neck he became even more amorous and thrust a hand between her legs, feeling at her cleft through the thin material.

Another man lifted a curvaceous flaxen-haired girl onto the table facing him and slowly began to lift her dress up her calves. When he reached her knees she made a token protest and tried unsuccessfully to pull the flimsy material from his grasp. In the ensuing struggle her dress ripped up to the waist revealing a neat triangle of fluffy flaxen pubic hair. Pushing her knees apart the man paused to stare gloatingly at the moist, deep red entrance to her honeypot, then moving forward onto the edge of his chair licked his lips in anticipation and buried his head between her pale thighs.

A voluptuous beauty with hair the colour of polished ebony was lying across the table on her back, while a man naked except for his tie stood between her legs and serviced her enthusiastically, his hands gripping her buttocks. Her head was tipped backwards to accommodate the cock of a man standing on the other side of the table who was also fondling her stupendous breasts.

By the end of the meal the room was in an uproar as both men and women pleasured each other uninhibitedly. Most of the girls were naked by now, or their dresses had been carelessly bunched up around their waists.

Such was the abandoned gaiety that when the door opened and six leather-clad women strode in, it was a few moments before anyone noticed. Gradually a silence fell over the room as the revellers hastily separated and tried to cover their nakedness, the girls melting unobtrusively into the background.

A titian-haired woman with a magnificent figure tightly corseted in a black leather bodice stepped forward. Tapping a riding crop against her thigh she slowly surveyed the scene of depravity which met her eyes.

INDECENT

Eventually she spoke, her words sending shivers of dread down the spines of everyone present.

'You men have defiled the vestal maidens, taking them for your own pleasure against all the rules of the society.'

She paused for a moment for maximum effect before continuing.

'Your punishment will be most severe.'

Lying back on the sofa in his living room, Jon drank deeply from a can of lager and reviewed the events of the day while absently channel-hopping on the TV with the remote control.

Amelia York and her female lover.

What a great story it would have made.

But now it looked like he was onto an even better one.

When the luscious Mrs York had invited him for a drink to discuss the situation he'd accepted with alacrity. After hastily showering and dressing he'd met her in the club's reception area.

Wearing a tailored cream suit, her silky hair pulled back in a thick coil, she looked so cool and poised he found it hard to believe that only an hour before she'd been naked and perspiring as another woman masturbated her to orgasm.

They'd walked to the marbled luxury of the Hyde Park Hotel and in the bar she repeated her question.

'Is there any way I can persuade you not to write about this?'

Jon was on the horns of a dilemma. On one hand he knew that he'd inadvertently stumbled on a real scoop and one which would win him considerable

Brownie points with Vernon.

The hard-headed journalist in him urged him to write the story ... but on the other hand Amelia York was an extremely attractive woman and the look she gave him promised a world of sensual delights which his dick was urging him to take her up on.

Sensing his indecision, Amelia crossed and uncrossed her stocking-clad legs giving him a tantalising glimpse of a lace edged slip. Clearing his throat Jon asked, 'Er, what do you have in mind?'

'What would you like?'

'You,' he told her frankly. Then, 'Do you mind if I ask you something?'

'Ask away.'

'Do you prefer women?'

She laughed throatily, 'I take my pleasure where I can find it, but I'm very discreet.'

The look Jon flashed her was frankly sceptical.

'I'm not sure that a scene with another woman in the steam room of a health club counts as discreet — anyone could have walked in.'

She pouted prettily.

'Actually we hung an "Out of Order" sign on the door. The club had only just opened for the day and there isn't usually anyone around at that time. We hadn't bargained for someone being there before us and certainly not someone tucked away out of sight. I'll be more careful in future.' She smoothed a strand of still slightly damp hair back off her face as she spoke.

'Aren't you worried about the potential scandal? It could cost you your marriage.'

INDECENT

'It's worth the risk. You'd think so too if you were married to my husband.'

Jon raised an interrogative eyebrow.

'Why is that?'

She laughed again, rather wryly this time.

'He isn't interested in me. His ... interests lie in other directions.'

Jon took a sip of his drink, trying not to look anything other than mildly surprised. Career and pleasure suddenly became pleasantly intermingled. He'd screw the delicious Mrs York and at the same time — well not exactly at the same time — he'd pump her for information about her husband's proclivities.

Still, no point letting her know she was off the hook just yet.

'Persuade me,' he said, sitting back in his chair.

Several hours later, as they lay back in a tangle of creased sheets in a room in the hotel, Jon asked her casually, 'So, where do your husband's interests lie?'

Flushed and sated as she was, she nevertheless took his hand and guided it back between her legs. As he obligingly slid his fingers in and out of her dripping pussy she gasped, 'He's a member of this weird club ... harder ... yes that's it ...'

'What sort of weird?' he asked, continuing to stimulate her.

'It's like a secret society ... you have to be invited to join ... it's very exclusive ... half the prominent men in the country are members ... mmm, yes do it like that ...'

'And what sort of things do they get up to?' With

his other hand he caressed her breasts.

'I'm not sure . . . S & M I think . . .'

'Where do they meet?' murmured Jon, now concentrating his efforts on her engorged clit.

'A private members club in Mayfair,' she panted, her breasts rising and falling as, with a cry and a long-drawn-out groan, she achieved her fifth orgasm that day.

That was all he'd been able to find out and later he could tell that she regretted having let so much slip, refusing to discuss it any further.

It had been quite a day.

Opening another can of lager, Jon idly wondered how Ernie had gone on in Leicester.

The plane flew west in the late afternoon sunshine. Or was it the early evening sunshine? Liz wasn't sure. The flight from London to Los Angeles passed through so many time zones that she'd lost track. Better to set her watch to LA time now and forget about it.

Glancing sideways, she saw that Ledd was still asleep in the seat next to her, his hand resting on her thigh. She'd discovered today that Ledd didn't like flying. He'd been pale and withdrawn in the limo on the way to the airport and at first she'd put it down to a hangover. Once in the VIP lounge he'd waved away the champagne, washing down several pills with a glass of mineral water instead.

'Valium,' he'd muttered by way of explanation. Shortly after that he'd fallen into a virtual coma and had to be helped onto the plane by a couple of his entourage.

Liz had been looking forward to a certain amount of covert sexual activity while in the air and to have Ledd slumped comatose beside her had put her in an even worse mood than usual. She kept the cabin staff dancing attendance on her, but there was a limit even for her as to how many drinks and snacks she could consume.

Anyway, Liz knew better than to drink too much on such a long flight. When they arrived on the West Coast it would be the middle of the night as far as her body clock was concerned, but only mid-afternoon LA time.

She was so damn bored.

After lighting another cigarette she took a folder out of her bag and began to read a profile of the country singer she was scheduled to interview in a couple of days. Her latest secretary had supplied her with a lot of background information on the man and she supposed that now was as good a time as any to read it.

Rhett Renton. Liz snorted derisively at the name before turning to the first page. According to this particular profile he was a good ol' boy from Arkansas turned born-again Christian. Which probably meant that he was from Massachusetts and had a law degree, thought Liz.

Still, studying a photo of him leaning negligently against a fence she had to admit that he was sexy as hell. The hat was ridiculous of course, but wearing them seemed *de rigueur* with country artists and he did look good in the skintight jeans.

Liz had three interviews lined up in Los Angeles – the country singer, an actor and a senator. They were all male, sexy and rich and if Liz had her way she'd never interview anyone who didn't fall into those categories.

Rhett Renton's biographical details were pretty standard stuff. One of a large number of children from a poor family, he had a couple of minor convictions in his late teens for stealing cars. In his mid-twenties he had a lucky break while singing in a local club and was now fast approaching mega-stardom.

Having finished reading, Liz yawned then irritably elbowed Ledd in the ribs.

'Wassa matter?' he mumbled groggily.

'If you don't wake up and entertain me I'm going to go and find someone who will,' she threatened him.

'Later, doll,' he muttered blearily, then sank back into unconsciousness.

Ellen had never used any sex aids. In fact the whole subject was a bit of a closed book to her. When Vernon called her into his office and asked what she knew about them she looked blank. He was delighted.

'Virgin territory,' he exclaimed rubbing his hands together. 'Here, take a look at this.'

Flicking through the pages of a glossy sex-aids catalogue Ellen's eyes widened. It was obvious what some of them were for, but the purpose of quite a few things featured was more obscure.

'I thought an article on the sex-aids industry would be a good idea,' he told her, his eyes resting on her breasts. "Depraved Artefacts Or Valuable

Social Service?" – that sort of approach. You could interview people who make them, sell them and use them. Perhaps try a few yourself.' He bared his teeth at her. 'And you know I'm always here if you need any help or want to discuss anything. Good work on the first blind date article by the way. Which magazine ad are the next batch from?'

'*Time Out.*'

'Good, good. Did you have many replies?'

'About a dozen.'

'Good, good. Well, mull over the sex-aids article and let me have your ideas sometime tomorrow.' He smiled benignly at her breasts as he dismissed her. Clutching the magazine, Ellen went back to her desk.

She was looking forward to her next lot of blind dates. The most difficult thing was that they usually wanted to see her again, and after Simon she wasn't in any hurry to start a new relationship, however much she liked someone. She'd seen Gordon the Scottish marketing consultant one more time after the first date.

It hadn't been a successful evening.

He spent the whole time trying to persuade her to move in with him and failing in that had attempted to find out her phone number and address so he could contact her again. In the end she'd refused an invitation to go back to his flat because the situation was becoming increasingly fraught. It was enough to make her determined to keep to one date in future.

George, too, had wanted to see her again but

accepted it philosophically when she prevaricated.

Reading through the catalogue made Ellen feel that there was a whole world out there she knew nothing of. She was just staring at a photograph of several vibrators in different designs, sizes and colours when Ernie loomed up behind her.

'Oh ho, what's this?' he demanded, leaning over her shoulder. 'Lolita, you don't have to go to these lengths for sex when you can call on Ernie Holdgate – satisfaction guaranteed – whenever you get hot knickers.'

Jon sauntered up to Ellen's desk and glanced at the photo.

'Lengths just about sums it up. Is yours twelve inches long, Ernie? Or black for that matter? Does it come with detachable heads? Let's face it, without that sort of versatility your appeal is limited. And that's before we get onto your other myriad deficiencies.'

Taking the catalogue from Ellen, he turned to the section on inflatable dolls.

'This is what you want Ernie. You need never spend a night alone again. How about Gilda? She's battery-operated in two vital areas and comes with a choice of hair colour.'

Ernie turned a livid shade of magenta, swore at Jon and slunk off down the office.

'I see that you got landed with the sex-aids article, Ellen. Vernon tried to interest me in it but I thought I'd pass. Do feel free to call on me if you need any help though. My expertise is at your disposal.'

'That's what Vernon said.' Ellen was staring in a puzzled way at a particular photograph.

'Jon . . . what do you think this is used for?' she asked.

Jon left work early to meet Dana. It was her birthday and she'd requested a silk nightdress as her present.

Jon was delighted. He would have given her whatever she asked for, but a silk nightdress would be something he could enjoy too — unlike the tennis racket she'd chosen for Christmas.

Dana spent a long time going through the selection in the lingerie section of the department store before eventually narrowing the choice down to three.

'Can I try these please?' she asked the saleswoman.

She turned to Jon, 'Are you coming to watch me try them on?'

The saleswoman looked outraged.

'We don't allow gentleman in the changing rooms,' she announced icily, looking at Jon as if he were a complete pervert. Dana pulled a rude face at the woman's back as she led the way.

'Hang around near the door and I'll come out instead,' she ordered him, 'and don't go talking to any strange women.'

Jon leant against the door by the entrance to the changing room speculating what the various women browsing through the lingerie would buy. He particularly fancied a sloe-eyed, dark-haired woman who was choosing a teddy, and spent several agreeable minutes imagining her wearing the different ones she held up.

Felice Ash

The disapproving saleswoman was behind the till attending to a customer when Dana put her head round the door. Seeing that the woman was occupied and had her back to them, Dana hissed, 'Quickly, before she comes back.' Grabbing his hand she pulled him into one of the changing cubicles.

'She'll call security and have me thrown out if she realises I'm in here,' protested Jon. 'That's if she doesn't have me arrested.' He sank reluctantly into the chair in the corner.

'Stop moaning and tell me what you think of this.'

Dana twirled around in front of the mirror. She was wearing an ankle-length nightdress in pale shimmering green which set off her red hair to advantage. It was such thin silk it was virtually transparent, and he could see the thrust of her breasts and backside quite clearly. There were angled mirrors on all four of the walls and he could see her reflected back at him from all directions.

'Very sexy,' he commented faintly, reaching out a hand and running it over her bum. She let him caress her for a few moments then twitched out of his reach, pulling the nightdress over her head and discarding it.

The next one she tried on was pale pink. Short and frilly it clung to her body, accentuating her breathtaking curves and emphasising the length of her legs. It suddenly felt hot in the changing room and Jon, already in his shirt sleeves, loosened his tie and undid his top button.

Dana preened in front of the mirror, running her hands over her silk-covered breasts.

'I don't think the silk's as soft as the green one,'

she decided. 'What do you think?' She undulated over to him and sank gracefully into his lap.

Jon stroked her full breasts, flattening the palm of his hand against her nipples and feeling them harden through the fine fabric. He could feel the heat of her body and smell her fresh scent as she wriggled her bottom experimentally into his groin.

'Well?' she demanded.

'I haven't decided yet.' He traced the curving line of her hip, detouring inwards to graze over her mound.

Dana rose sinuously to her feet and whisked the garment over her head.

'Or what about this?'

The third one was black lace. It plunged so far down between her magnificent breasts that the deep vee almost reached her navel. It had thin shoulder straps and made her pale skin appear an even more translucent shade of porcelain. As she turned this way and that in front of the mirror he realised he could see the dark circles of her nipples on a 'now you see them, now you don't' basis under the open weave of the lace.

It was a huge turn-on.

It was even more of a turn-on when she bent over him with her cleavage inches from his face and kissed him. He returned the kiss, feeling sweat breaking out on his brow as he slid his hands into the front of the nightdress and fondled her breasts.

He was just trying to estimate how long it would take them to get back to his flat, or whether in fact hers was nearer when she pulled away.

Jon mopped his brow with a handkerchief and stood up.

'I'd better go and wait outside. If I stay here I won't be able to stop myself screwing you up against the wall.'

When he saw the expression on her face he backed away towards the door in horror.

'Dana, no. We can't – not here.' With a sudden flash of perception he realised that she'd been planning this all along.

She wanted him to fuck her in one of the changing rooms of the exclusive department store.

He stood there trying to will himself to leave as Dana, hips swaying, walked over to the chair he'd just vacated and bent over it. He felt as if he'd been turned to stone – one part of his anatomy in particular – as she slowly pulled the seductive nightdress up her hips and over her waist, revealing her rounded backside and the ripe, succulent fruit of her sex.

He knew he should get out of there fast but unfortunately his dick was already expressing a decided and single-minded interest. It strained towards Dana's invitingly parted legs as if drawn by a powerful magnetic force. He could see her reflected from all sides, each image enticingly erotic. He knew he was lost when she reached between her legs and began to stroke herself.

Cursing briefly but fluently under his breath he unzipped his trousers muttering, 'This is absolutely the last time I let you do this to me.'

He plunged into her with no foreplay, pumping vigorously in and out of her wonderfully wet interior. He gripped her firmly around the waist determined she wasn't suddenly going to wriggle away from him and prolong this torture.

A tap at the cubicle door made them both freeze.

'Do you require any assistance, Madam?' They both recognised the haughty tones of the saleswoman. Dana managed to call, 'No thank you,' then thrust her rear hard into Jon's groin to encourage him to continue shafting her.

He obliged. He could see them both in the mirrors and the eroticism of their reflection helped him bring things to what he hoped was a speedy conclusion.

Dana had other ideas.

When he pulled out of her, wiped himself on his handkerchief and zipped up his trousers she turned her head to look at him beseechingly.

'I haven't come yet.' Jon came the closest he'd ever been to expressing a total lack of interest in his partner's satisfaction. He briefly considered begging her to wait until they'd got back to his flat and promising to spend the entire evening satisfying her over and over again, if only she'd get dressed so they could get the hell out of there.

But it went against the grain. Instead he reached between her legs and rubbed briskly away — this was no time for finesse.

She'd barely stopped gasping before he dragged the black lace nightie over her head and passed her her clothes. When she was dressed she handed him the three nightdresses saying, 'I'll have the black one, please. I need to go to the Ladies so I'll see you by the escalators.' Then she vanished.

Leaving the changing rooms with some trepidation, he wasn't particularly surprised to see the saleswoman bearing down on him with a furious expression on her face.

Tempted as he was to simply drop the garments and flee, Jon told himself that after years of foot-in-the-door journalism he should be able to cope with one irate saleswoman.

'What were you doing in there?' she demanded fiercely.

'My wife was taken ill and called for my assistance,' he returned smoothly. 'She's in the Ladies now. We'll take the black one – could you hurry please? I need to get her home.'

He might have carried it off if the black nightie hadn't had a large damp stain across the hem. The saleswoman dropped it into a bag and took his credit card with a face like thunder.

He half expected her to call, 'And don't come back!' after his departing form as he slunk off towards the escalators.

A heatwave had hit Barcelona.

Standing on her small balcony in the early evening, Kate leant forward against the ornate stone parapet in an attempt to catch some of the breeze which was ruffling the leaves of the trees. It felt like a blast from a hairdryer. She'd only just showered but already her thin silk dress was sticking to her.

A woman appeared on the balcony to her left, fanning herself with the room service menu. She looked across at Kate.

'Goodness, did you ever experience such heat? It's definitely too hot to eat but try telling my husband that.' She was weatherbeaten, in her fifties and uncompromisingly English.

'It certainly is,' agreed Kate. 'Maybe it'll cool down later, but for now I'll settle for a couple of long cold drinks.'

Kate gave a start as unseen hands lifted her dress at the back, and she felt the unexpected but unmistakable sensation of a tongue sliding between her thighs. It said a lot for her self-control that she didn't cry out, particularly since the tongue was icy cold — James had obviously just been sucking an ice cube.

She pushed her thighs together while making a frantic flapping motion with her hand, gesturing for him to go away. She thought it was unlikely that the woman could see anything but she couldn't be certain.

'Forgive me, but don't I know you?' asked the woman.

'Er ... I'm not sure.' Kate felt her thighs being firmly parted by two strong hands then the tongue, slightly warmer now, plunged determinedly into her vulva.

'I'm positive I do,' said the woman briskly. 'I'm Vanessa Rushton.'

Kate felt James pause mid-probe, then she could have sworn his body shook for a few moments with silent laughter before he continued to flick his tongue over her labia.

Damn James. How could she pay attention to what the woman was saying while he was doing that?

Feeling positive something was expected of her but not sure what, she smiled vaguely.

'And you are?' the woman prompted her.

'Kate Owen.'

Vanessa Rushton peered at her as closely as she could from a distance of several yards.

'I know — you're a journalist,' she announced triumphantly. 'You work for that dreadful rag.'

James was now delicately sucking at her clit, sending delicious sensations through her body.

'Er, yes I am, I'm afraid,' was the best she could manage.

'I knew it! Never forget a face. What are you doing in Barcelona, my dear? Business or pleasure?'

This was just too difficult. Kicking backwards at her tormentor she caught him squarely on the chest with her heel, but he merely caught her ankle with one hand and held her foot firmly down against the floor without breaking rhythm with his tongue.

'Business,' she managed to say. 'I . . . I'm covering a conference.'

'Dickie and I are on our way to our villa in Valencia — thought we'd have a night in Barcelona on the way. Well, you absolutely must join us for a drink later.'

Normally adept at shrugging off unwelcome invitations without giving offence, Kate could only say weakly, 'That would be nice.'

'Eight o'clock in the courtyard bar, then.' With a final wave of her menu the woman vanished back into her room.

Her departure was well timed. Holding onto the rough stone of the parapet with her lover's head up her skirt, Kate felt the first breathless shudders of her climax. It seemed to go on forever, leaving her spent, weak and wringing wet.

James withdrew from beneath her dress and pulled her backwards into the room.

'You beast,' exclaimed Kate as they fell onto the bed together. 'How could you put me through that? And now I'm committed to having a drink with that woman and her husband. She must think I'm really strange — all I could do was stand there with a vacuous, bemused smile on my face. And I still haven't a clue where I've met her before.'

Convulsed with laughter James tried to pull her into his arms. She punched him hard on the chest and they struggled for a few moments before he managed to pin her down on the bed.

'You don't know the best bit,' he told her.

'What's that?' she demanded suspiciously.

'Dickie Rushton, the well known "hang 'em, flog 'em and castrate 'em" backbencher is my cousin and the charming Vanessa is his wife. What's more, they grabbed me in the foyer and insisted I have dinner with them. I was just about to tell you when you stepped out onto the balcony.'

'What?' Kate stopped struggling and lay back on the bed, her dark blonde hair in a tangle beneath her.

'Sorry, darling. Vanessa is an unstoppable force. There's never any getting out of one of her invitations. The best I could hope for was to bolt down dinner in double quick time then say I had to come back to the hotel to do some work.'

'Oh no,' groaned Kate. 'It's our last night. Now I'll

have to sit in the bar with them and pretend I barely know you. Honestly James, that's not my idea of a good time. Besides,' she added, 'how come you've never mentioned that Dickie Rushton is your cousin?'

'It's not a connection I'm particularly keen on for obvious reasons,' he admitted.

Kate could see why. Dickie was the most often-quoted backbencher of the current parliament. He could always be relied upon to say something inflammatory, particularly on occasions when diplomacy and tact were called for. He was also a well-known lecher. The idea of spending the evening in his company didn't exactly thrill her.

'I must be careful not to let them see me leaving your room. We'll have to spend the night in mine,' he warned her as he went into the bathroom.

Kate reluctantly dressed for the evening. She discarded her damp silk dress for a more substantial linen one. When James saw her drawing a pair of clean silk panties up her long legs he protested.

'Leave them off, darling, it'll give me a big thrill to know you're not wearing any under that dress while randy old Dickie sits there giving you the eye.'

'Not a chance,' said Kate firmly. 'Tonight we're both going to be the epitome of respectability. And if you even think about trying to feel me up under the cover of the tablecloth I'll stick a fork in your hand so hard you'll need surgery to have it removed.'

The evening was even worse than Kate had anticipated. James went down to meet Dickie and Vanessa in the courtyard bar fifteen minutes before she put in an appearance herself. Shaded from the sun for most of the day the courtyard was relatively cool, though the temperature was still probably in the eighties.

The two men rose when she arrived at the table and Vanessa introduced them.

'I know Miss Owen,' mumbled Dickie, his brick-red face an even higher colour than usual. 'That was rather a mangling you gave me in your paper last week, Miss Owen – or may I call you Kate?'

'Certainly you may. I might have given you a mangling but at least you can't complain about the amount of column space we give you.' She smiled at him sweetly before turning towards James.

'Hello again, Minister. That was an excellent speech you gave this afternoon.'

'Thank you. Won't you sit down?' Kate had in fact been sightseeing that afternoon, but she'd heard James practising his speech earlier in the day so she knew what it was about.

It soon became clear that the Rushtons were heavy drinkers and within an hour they'd made significant inroads into the hotel's sherry stocks.

At around nine Kate stood up and tried to excuse herself. She'd planned to take a stroll along La Rambla and nibble a plate of tapas instead of having a full meal. To her dismay, the others wouldn't hear of it. She glared at James, trying to telegraph her desire to escape, but he was obviously determined to keep her with them.

Reluctantly she resigned herself to her fate and accompanied them to an opulent restaurant a few minutes walk away. The food wasn't particularly good but its big attraction was that it had air conditioning and accordingly was packed.

The service was slow and the evening dragged on with Dickie holding forth about the working classes, Vanessa talking over him and trying to draw Kate out about herself, and James pressing his thigh meaningfully against hers under the cover of the starched tablecloth.

Excusing herself after coffee, she went to the Ladies and lingered there, hoping they would be ready to leave by the time she got back to the table. Dickie was waiting for her outside the door when she emerged into the corridor.

'Always fancied you,' he told her, backing her up against the wall. 'How about lunch when we're back in Blighty?'

Luckily at that moment James appeared, ostensibly on his way to the toilets. Kate hurriedly went back upstairs and was relieved to see that the bill had been paid and their departure was imminent.

Back at the hotel she resisted an attempt to usher her out to the courtyard bar and fled up to her room. A few minutes later there was a tap on her door and James came in.

'What a ghastly evening,' he groaned, flinging himself down on the bed. 'Let's go up to my room quickly while they're still ensconced in the bar.'

'How could you insist I join you for dinner when you knew there was nothing I'd like less?' she accused him. 'I was looking forward to a quiet stroll and a plate of tapas. Instead I get the third degree about my love life from Vanessa and Dickie mentally undressing me over the silverware. Honestly, James, I think I'll let you spend the night on your own for that.'

'I'm sorry, darling, I just couldn't face it alone. I'll make it up to you I promise.'

'How?' she asked him suspiciously.

'I'll . . .'

They were interrupted by a tap on the door.

'Who the . . . ?'

'Get rid of them fast,' hissed James, bolting into the bathroom and closing the door.

It was Dickie.

He pushed his way into the room without waiting for an invitation and tried to grab her. Kate retreated hastily to the other side of the bed.

'For heaven's sake!' she exclaimed. 'Get out of here! What would your wife say?'

'Don't care,' he mumbled, 'Told her I was going to bed. She's talking to some people in the bar.' He made a bull-like rush at her and managed to grab her round the waist. Holding him off with outstretched arms she tried to stay calm — difficult when he was attempting to paw her breasts and drag her towards the bed.

'If you don't leave at once I'll call the porter,' she threatened.

'Lovely woman like you shouldn't be alone at night.' He managed to get her off balance and onto the bed, crushing her with his weight. Kate shrieked and tried to struggle from under him. Where the hell was James?

There was an imperative knocking on the door, then the sound of James's voice calling, 'Miss Owen, are you alright?' She knew he'd slipped out of the bathroom, then outside into the corridor while she struggled with his cousin.

'Help!' she called. A moment later Dickie's huge bulk was dragged off her while James, all dignified outrage, demanded to know what he thought he was doing.

Dickie stood with his head drooping guiltily while James upbraided him.

'I was just bringing Miss Owen some background notes on the conference I thought she might find useful. What a good job I chanced along. You've just made a complete ass of yourself, Dickie, and I for one wouldn't blame Miss Owen if she called the police. You're absolutely contemptible and I really don't know how I'm going to stop myself telling Vanessa. She obviously needs to keep a closer rein on you. Really, Dickie, you aren't fit to be around decent women.'

Dickie registered drunken consternation.

'Sorry. Didn't mean any harm, such a lovely woman.' His eyes glazed and he swayed groggily. 'Reminded me of Tracey at the club. Do you know Tracey? Oh no, I forgot, you aren't a member. Too strait-laced. Tracey likes to cane me . . .'

'Miss Owen, please, I beg you, forgive my cousin,' James interrupted hastily. 'Although I think you have every right to press charges I'd really appreciate it if you didn't.'

'Get him out of here, please. I'll decide what to do in the morning.'

James frogmarched an abject Dickie out of the room. When he returned a couple of minutes later he found the door locked.

'Let me in please, darling,' he begged her.

'I've had quite enough of you and your family for one evening. Goodnight, James.'

Kate went thoughtfully into the bathroom and began to clean her teeth.

Now, what club was that?

CHAPTER NINE

At Los Angeles airport Liz decided it would be hours before Ledd and his entourage made it through immigration and customs — particularly with Ledd still barely conscious.

Ordering a resentful Bruce to make sure her luggage got to the hotel as quickly as possible, she detached herself from the rest of the party and went through the formalities of entering the country with just her hand luggage, then took a taxi to the hotel.

Arriving at the hotel first also meant she could check over the suites allocated to their party and appropriate the best one for herself, knowing this would enrage Bruce.

The suite she chose overlooked the glittering turquoise pool set among tall exotic palm trees and brightly coloured flowers. Before landing, the plane had circled round over the city and thousands of similar patches of turquoise water had shimmered enticingly in the afternoon heat.

By the time she'd showered and changed into the set of clothes in her hand baggage she felt well ready for some action. Ledd was obviously going to be of no use to her until he'd recovered from the flight and she certainly wasn't going to spend her first night in Los Angeles tucked up in bed with a book.

Time to cruise a few bars.

Wearing a peach camisole with an ivory silk jacket and trousers she took the lift down to the ground floor. Tall and very striking with her chestnut hair and aquamarine eyes, she attracted a considerable amount of admiration as she strode through the foyer.

She was just getting into a cab as a limousine pulled up outside the hotel and Ledd was half helped, half lifted from the back. Hopefully he'd be on form again tomorrow.

The first bar she entered was full of jaded-looking businessmen recovering after a working day. She sat at the bar and ordered a Mimosa, emphasising her English accent, and then waited for someone to approach her.

She didn't have to wait long.

A succession of men attempted to pick her up but none of them was what she was searching for — jaded definitely wasn't what she had in mind. After one drink she moved on. Eventually in the third bar she tried she found him.

He was tall, blond and tanned — the archetypal California man. His body looked fit and hard without being over muscular and he moved with sexy animal grace. She would have been surprised if he were much older than twenty although he nonchalantly showed an ID to the barman when requested to do so.

He must have felt her smouldering gaze on him because he glanced up and appraised her casually as he waited for his drink, then strolled over to greet some friends at the end of the bar. She knew he'd be back and she was right.

INDECENT

'Hi, beautiful. Can I buy you a drink?'

She wheeled slowly round to face him, giving him the full benefit of her dark-lashed aquamarine eyes.

'Maybe,' she responded huskily.

'Hey, you're English!'

'I certainly am.'

'I'm Paul. What's your name?'

'Liz, Liz Peters.'

'What are you drinking?'

'Another of these.'

He signalled for the barman and ordered more drinks before turning back to her.

'So, what are you doing in Los Angeles, Liz? Are you on holiday or here on business?'

'Business primarily, but I'm hoping to fit in some relaxation too.' She slipped her jacket off as she spoke giving him the full benefit of her smooth, bare shoulders. Her peach camisole clung to her small high breasts, drawing attention to her pointed nipples. He changed colour slightly and his Adam's apple bobbed.

'Uh... do you know Los Angeles, Liz? I'd be happy to give you a tour.'

'I've been a couple of times before but I don't know it as well as I'd like to.'

'Say, why don't we drive down to the ocean and watch the sunset,' he suggested enthusiastically. Liz liked the idea.

She'd already noticed that his clothes, watch and wallet were extremely expensive even by Californian standards, which probably made him a rich kid. When they walked out to the parking lot and she saw his car, an open-topped red Thunderbird, she revised her opinion.

A *very* rich kid.

He drove fast down the steep winding road to the ocean, even though the traffic was still fairly heavy. The air smelt of petrol fumes, salt and a faint but heady herbal scent she couldn't quite identify. She sat relaxed with her head resting against the back of the seat enjoying the drive, her hair tousled and her nipples stiffened by the cool evening breeze.

He pulled up outside a bar overlooking the beach and they sat by the window watching the sun sink slowly through the glorious crimson-streaked sky. A strange and unaccustomed peace stole over Liz. It was such an unfamiliar feeling that she found it unsettling, but she put it down to the long flight and her bewildered body clock.

Back in the car he kissed her, his hands smoothing over her bare shoulders, skimming lightly down her sides, just missing her breasts.

He cleared his throat. 'I live just over there.' He gestured along the coast. 'Would you like to come back for a drink?'

'Sure.'

They drove in silence as a hazy twilight fell and Liz felt goosebumps appear on her arms – whether from the slight drop in temperature or from excitement it was hard to tell.

The house overlooked the ocean and had a wooden deck where terracotta pots of hibiscus and geranium were strategically positioned for best effect around the smart beach furniture. She wondered whether he'd pretend it was his own place, but as he let her in he told her casually that his parents were at their other house in Bel Air and only came out to the beach at weekends.

She asked for a tour and then, in what was obviously the master bedroom, turned and pulled him into her arms. He kissed her enthusiastically, caressing her shoulders again. Then, when she pressed even closer, he slipped the shoulder straps of her camisole down her arms.

When the camisole slithered around her waist he gulped and flushed slightly, bending down to take one milk-chocolate-coloured nipple into his mouth. His tongue felt red hot against her cool skin and Liz felt pleasantly if unaccustomedly languorous as she tipped her head back and enjoyed the sensation.

The ground seemed to be slipping away underneath her and it was a few seconds before she realised he'd picked her up and was carrying her over to the bed. Placing her on the blue satin bedspread he undressed her, kissing each bit of her skin as he uncovered it. By this time Liz was usually impatient for the real action to begin and would be unzipping his trousers or thrusting his head between her thighs.

For once she was content for events to take their course and submitted with cat-like enjoyment to his caresses.

She must have dozed off because she came to with a start as he climaxed, opening her eyes just in time to see his face contort with pleasure. She thought distantly and incoherently that she mustn't go back to sleep before she'd had her own climax. Then her eyes closed again.

* * *

Liz awoke to a pale grey dawn and some very confused memories. There was a muffled pounding sound somewhere in the background and it took her a couple of minutes to remember where she was and to realise that the sound must be the ocean.

Turning her head, she saw that Paul was sleeping peacefully beside her, his tanned chest only half covered by a crumpled pale blue sheet, an arm thrown back over his head.

Closing her eyes, she dimly remembered several hazy scenes of sexual activity as his body had moved over hers in the night. Had they only made love the once? For some reason she got the impression it had been several times, but surely she'd fallen asleep halfway through the first time?

After stretching slightly her body gave off unmistakable signs of recent intense sexual activity and she definitely felt sore.

Puzzled, she slipped out of bed and went into the bathroom. There was tangible evidence of a great deal of sexual activity trickling from between her legs, and what appeared to be dried semen in her hair. Stepping into the shower she soaped and shampooed herself thoroughly, trying to clear her head and remember what had happened.

Wrapped in a towel, she padded barefoot to the kitchen and poured herself a glass of orange juice before stepping out onto the deck. The morning was cool and clear, the ocean and beach bleached out by the first rays of the early morning sun rising somewhere behind the house. A solitary jogger ran alongside the pounding waves as they crested, crashed onto the sand, then retreated in a swirling mass of foaming bubbles.

It all seemed a long way from Liz's service flat in London, where the only view from the windows was of a similar block of flats on the other side of the road.

She shivered as her wet hair dripped onto her bare shoulders and finishing her glass of orange juice she went back inside. Paul was still sleeping peacefully.

Well, she'd soon change that.

Yanking the covers from his recumbent form she sat on the edge of the bed. He opened his eyes and yawned, then smiled at her sleepily.

'Hi, what time is it?'

'I've no idea. Fill me in. What happened last night, did I pass out?'

He sat up and scratched his chest before crossing his arms behind his head.

'Yep. I can't tell you what it did for my ego to have a woman I was screwing pass out — it's never happened to me before.'

'You didn't feel the need to try to rouse me before continuing?'

He had the grace to look sheepish.

'Sorry, honey, I was too far gone to stop. Though I did try mouth to mouth resuscitation.' He grinned at her winningly.

'I see. May I ask just how many repeat performances there were?'

He shifted uneasily on the bed before replying.

'Four.'

'Does that include the one in my hair?'

He flushed and suddenly looked about sixteen. Lowering his eyes he mumbled, 'Sorry, I've always wanted to do that and none of my girlfriends would ever let me.'

Standing up, Liz towelled her hair vigorously while looking thoughtfully down at him. Dropping the towel on the floor she went over to where two dressing gowns hung from behind the bedroom door. Pulling the belts free she returned to the bed and taking his left hand lashed it swiftly to the bedpost while he watched her bemusedly.

'What's going on?' he asked uncertainly, while she did the same to his right hand. Without replying she glanced around the room, pulling his belt out of his trousers and using it to secure his left ankle. A silk scarf thrown over the back of the chair provided the fourth tie.

'You had your fun last night,' she pointed out coldly. 'Now it's my turn.'

Sitting astride his chest she moved upwards until she was poised above his face.

'Hey, I don't do that,' he objected. 'Women go down on me, I don't go down on them.'

'You do now,' she informed him, lowering herself and effectively silencing his protests.

Jon threw himself wholeheartedly into his investigation of the mysterious secret society.

He began by phoning all the women he knew who had contacts — however tenuous — in the government, which proved to be a considerable number. They included a large proportion of women he'd interviewed at a crisis time in their lives and with whom he'd enjoyed some sort of sexual encounter.

Most of them seemed keen to take up where they'd left off and he soon discovered that an invitation to a drink usually led to a lot more.

Jon had always considered himself to be a man who just couldn't say no where sex was concerned – it was an activity in which he invested a lot of enthusiasm, energy and stamina. But even he found he was beginning to flag after a week of non-stop rendezvous with the first names on his list.

He found himself extremely relieved that Dana was in Corfu with a couple of her female friends and wouldn't be calling on his services for a while.

After a particularly demanding day of intensive erotic activity he dragged himself into the office in the evening feeling as if he'd been turned inside out and back again. As soon as he'd put a few notes on disc he'd crawl home and allow himself the luxury of a full, uninterrupted night's sleep alone in his double bed.

Sitting shakily at his keyboard, he weakly tapped in all the information he'd been able to glean to date – which when he considered all the effort he'd expended didn't amount to very much.

He groaned when he saw Vernon at the other end of the office and bent his head hoping the editor hadn't spotted him. He knew he wasn't exactly flavour of the month because, despite his frequent absences and huge expenses claims, he hadn't actually produced anything useful and had made excuses not to cover the last three stories Vernon had assigned to him.

And as if that wasn't bad enough, Ernie had been unashamedly listening in to Jon's phone calls as he set up his various rendezvous and had been telling anyone who'd listen that Jon was off to 'pork another toffee-nosed bint'.

'Nice of you to drop by, laddie.'

Vernon wasn't actually Scottish but this was his preferred mode of address to his male staff. He loomed threateningly over the desk, holding a sheaf of expenses claims — with Jon's in pride of place on top.

'Congratulations, you win this week's prize for the most ludicrously inflated expenses claim. Of course, you've only achieved this sought-after accolade in Liz's absence but if you stay on form you may well usurp her long-held position.'

'Vernon I—'

The editor cut ruthlessly across him.

'So, what do you have for me, laddie? Some major scandal involving one of the members of our revered Royal Family complete with photos, signed statements from at least a dozen witnesses and a personal interview with the subject of the scandal in which they reveal all, sparing themselves nothing?'

'Well, not quite but . . .'

'Or could it be that you hold some irrefutable proof that key members of the government have been replaced by aliens from another galaxy?'

'That's an interesting idea but . . .'

'Or is it possible,' continued Vernon, warming to his theme, 'that under the pretext of following up leads which you claim may result in an earth-shattering story of hitherto unprecedented magnitude, you are in fact out wining and dining an astonishing number of ladies at the paper's expense?'

Jon sighed, mentally cursing Ernie and his big mouth, but he kept quiet because when Vernon was in this mood it was best just to let him talk himself out.

'Not content with spending your own time and not inconsiderable salary in pursuit of the pleasures of the flesh, you now seem hell-bent on expending the paper's time and money to the same sorry ends.'

Vernon paused to gaze dourly and rather enviously down at him, shaking his head as if in sorrow.

'Laddie, laddie, is it worth it? You'll soon be reduced to a husk of your former self. And for what? A few moments of fleeting pleasure here and there?'

'Hardly moments,' protested Jon nettled, but Vernon was still in full spate.

'So get it off your chest, laddie. What is this story which requires you to spend your waking hours humping half the female population of our great metropolis?'

He folded his arms and waited.

'Well,' began Jon cautiously, 'it involves a lot of very prominent men.' He paused and mentally assessed the situation. If he told Vernon everything he knew he'd risk the editor putting other journalists on the case too. Which would make it a bigger risk that the members might get wind of the investigation and the society could well be disbanded before he managed to unmask it.

On the other hand, if he refused to divulge what

information he had gleaned to date he risked facing Vernon's not inconsiderable wrath.

Trying for the middle ground he said carefully, 'I've got a whiff of a mega scandal with security implications. I have to tread very carefully at this stage or the whole thing could evaporate. You know as well as I do, Vernon, that women talk to me, so I'm trying to see as many contacts as I can – and it's expensive. But eventually it should pay dividends.'

Vernon was obviously not appeased.

'Would you care to be more specific? Perhaps indulge me by naming a few names?'

'I can't really at this stage, I'm afraid.'

Vernon looked at his watch. 'You've got ten seconds to persuade me you're really onto something.'

'It's not that simple. This is a very delicate situation which needs careful handling.'

'Nine . . . ten!' announced Vernon triumphantly. 'By tomorrow at six a.m. I want you outside the Faranx factory in Ellesmere Port covering the strike there. Take Ernie and some iron rations and don't come back without a good story – however long it takes. And if you need to stay overnight you can sleep in the car because I don't want any more expenses claims submitted until at least December.'

Vernon strode off down the office leaving Jon with his head in his hands. Ellesmere Port by six a.m. – they'd have to leave in about five hours. In the whole of the last week he'd only managed about four hours sleep and it didn't look as if tonight was going to be any better.

INDECENT

* * *

By the time Liz arrived back at the hotel she was in a much better mood.

She'd made Paul bring her to orgasm twice with his tongue before climbing off his face. Moving further down his body and sitting astride his groin she ignored his pleas to be released.

Grasping his cock firmly, she'd rubbed it tormentingly backwards and forwards over her clit then slipped it slowly inside her for a few seconds. He strained upwards, trying to penetrate deeper but Liz was still sore after last night and raised herself so it slipped out again.

She treated his cock as if it were simply an instrument for her pleasure, using it to bring herself to two more shuddering climaxes. When she eventually left the bed and headed for the shower he strained at his bonds and called after her desperately, 'Hey! Don't I get a turn?'

'You had your turn last night.'

After showering she returned to the bedroom to dress, helping herself to a liberal spray of perfume from a bottle on the dressing table and ignoring his demands that she release him.

By the time she shrugged elegantly into her jacket the sun was shining brightly outside. She wondered if Ledd had surfaced yet.

Time to return to the hotel and find out.

Picking up Paul's trousers she extracted his car keys and looked coldly down at him as he lay spread-eagled on the bed.

'I'm taking your car to drive back to my hotel. When I get there I'll send your keys to the bar we met at last night — you can pick them up from the barman.'

'You can't leave me here like this!' he raged, wrenching at his bonds. 'I won't be able to get free and my parents aren't due here for four days — I'll be dead by then. And I need a piss.'

She looked at him contemptuously — there was always a possibility he might not be enterprising enough to work out a way of getting free, and dehydration could be a problem.

Stepping forward she untied one of his wrists saying, 'Just in case you were thinking of calling the police and reporting your car stolen, remember that I'm a journalist with plenty of contacts here. I think I could guarantee a front-page spread in tomorrow's paper which would make you look very silly.'

Turning on her heel she left the room.

After a brief visit to her suite to change into a bikini, Liz found Ledd sprawled out on a sun bed by the pool under a large yellow-and-white-striped umbrella.

He was the only person in the pool area who was fully dressed — although for once he wasn't in the leather trousers — and all exposed areas of his skin were glistening with sun screen.

He greeted her sheepishly.

'Hi, doll, you slept nearly as long as I did.'

She didn't disillusion him, merely indicated to the Mexican cabana boy where she wanted her sun bed, appraising him from behind her dark glasses as he dragged it into position.

'Rub me with sun screen,' she ordered Ledd,

stretching herself out in the sun. 'Incidentally, why are you fully dressed?'

Ledd looked pained. 'Sledgehammer aren't a load of bleedin' suntanned puffs. We've got our image to think of — we're supposed to look like we haven't been out in daylight in years.'

He sat on the edge of her lounger and squirted a large dollop of cream on her back. 'You were sleeping like the dead this morning. I phoned your room when I woke up and sent Malcolm to bang on your door when you didn't answer, but you must have been out cold.'

'You didn't tell me you didn't like flying.'

'Naw... well... I'm not too thrilled about it myself. Tours are torture for me because we're on and off planes all the time. They always have to leave long enough between gigs for me to recover. How come you didn't spend the night in my bed?'

'Whatever for? You were completely comatose.'

'Yeah well, sorry about that.'

'Where are the rest of your ghastly entourage?' asked Liz enjoying the sensation of the warmed cream being massaged into her back.

'Round and about. The rest of the group have gone sightseeing, the roadies are sorting out the gear... dunno where everyone else is. Running up phone bills probably.'

He began to squeeze cream on the back of her thighs. She knew what he was going to say several seconds before he said it.

'Why don't we go up to your room and make up for lost time?'

'I've got a better idea. Why don't you order me a

croissant, some coffee and a Bloody Mary. I haven't had anything to eat since the last unbelievably disgusting meal on the plane.'

'A picnic?' echoed Ellen. 'What a lovely idea.'

She'd just called Dean, one of the men who'd answered her ad in *Time Out*, and he'd suggested that they go for a picnic in the country.

His letter had been the most amusing of the batch she'd received from this particular ad, and accordingly he'd been the first she'd replied to.

He was twenty-seven, a botanist and claimed to like the countryside, good food and good conversation.

Ellen was an urban creature who'd never spent much time in the country, but she was prepared to admit that it looked quite pretty from train windows. The temperature in London had soared that week so the idea of spending an afternoon somewhere cool and green really appealed.

Kate arrived back from Barcelona to find Ellen in a fetching black lacy bra and pants, rummaging through her drawers trying to decide what she should wear for a picnic.

Leaving her suitcases in the narrow hallway, Kate went to the fridge and poured herself a glass of mineral water.

'Did you have a good time?' asked Ellen, joining her in the kitchen.

'Great thanks, although it was very hot. It's pretty hot here come to that. Where are you off to?'

'On a picnic in a wood somewhere.' Ellen looked so childishly pleased with the idea that Kate thought she would easily have passed for about sixteen. 'What do people wear on picnics do you think?' she continued hopefully.

'Something long, white and Edwardian with a parasol?' suggested Kate.

Ellen pulled a face. 'Not my type of thing. I'd better hurry up and decide. I'll have to leave in a few minutes.'

Eventually she settled on a sleeveless black tee-shirt worn with a short cream cotton skirt and a pair of strappy sandals. As she was fastening the sandals over her bare feet she heard the unmistakable sound of a distant crack of thunder. Going over to the window and leaning out she stared upwards at the sky. There wasn't a cloud in sight but the air had that still and humid feel to it which sometimes preceded a storm.

Passing her lodger's bedroom a couple of minutes later, Kate stopped outside the door.

'Won't you be rather warm in that?' she asked faintly. 'What is it anyway?'

Ellen was wearing a belted mackintosh in clear, crackly PVC.

'It's a sort of pacamac,' she told Kate cheerfully. 'My grandmother gave it me for my birthday. I thought I could take it to sit on and then wear it if it rained. Why, what's the matter?'

'I'm not sure. It's just that there's something *bent* about it. It looks like the sort of thing fetishists fantasize about.'

'I'd forgotten I'd got it. I came across it when I went back to Simon's flat to get the rest of my things. Oh, look at the time – I'd better get moving.'

Ellen's contribution to the picnic was a bottle of sweet Sauterne, some sausage rolls, a box of chocolate eclairs and a bag of cherries. Thrusting them all into a plastic carrier bag she shouted, 'See you later,' to Kate and left the flat.

Dean picked her up at the station in his beat up VW. Tall and thin with untidy tow-coloured hair and murky green eyes, he had one of the widest smiles Ellen had ever seen.

After throwing her carrier bag into the boot they set off for the wood he knew. He didn't stop talking all the way there but Ellen soon realised this was nervousness. They parked the car by a weather-beaten five-barred gate then walked in among the trees.

'I know the perfect spot,' Dean assured her, leading the way and continuing to talk.

Ellen was soon panting as she struggled to keep up with him. Stumbling through piles of last year's autumn leaves, bracken and ferns she wished she'd worn more sensible footwear. It should have been cool in the shade of the trees but the air seemed almost steamy and beads of perspiration began to appear on her forehead.

'Is it much further?' she gasped at last. 'I feel as though I'm in a tropical rain forest, not somewhere thirty miles from London.' When they'd first entered the wood they'd seen a couple of other people walking dogs, but as they penetrated deeper and deeper they didn't come across anyone else.

Dean paused to turn and look at her.

'Am I going too fast? Here let me carry that.' He indicated Ellen's PVC mac and tried to take it from her arm. It stuck to her damp skin and she had to peel it slowly off. He was already carrying her bag of food as well as his own but it didn't seem to slow him down much.

Eventually they reached a secluded moss-strewn clearing where a patch of sunlight broke through the trees and fell on the bank of a small gurgling stream. Dean threw down a faded old tartan rug and began to unpack the bags while Ellen lay down on her back and tried to catch her breath.

Dean's contribution to the picnic was considerably more interesting than hers. A selection of deli sandwiches, chicken legs and tiny quiches were revealed when he unpacked the various containers. He'd also brought an interesting crunchy salad, a bunch of grapes and a bottle of chilled Orvieto. As he'd packed everything in a cool bag the food was still fresh and appetising.

Ellen's provisions, hastily thrown into the carrier bag, hadn't stood up to the journey very well. The sausage rolls were now a pile of greasy fragments, the cherries had squashed and bled over everything else and the eclairs were unrecognisable and smelt as if the cream had turned.

'Oh dear, I've never been on a picnic before and I'm afraid I'm not very well organised,' she confessed.

'It doesn't matter – I've brought plenty for both of us,' he told her amiably, efficiently removing the cork from her bottle of Sauterne and pouring some into a paper cup.

It was sweet and tepid but Ellen drank it gratefully while she recovered from their walk.

Eventually she felt able to sit up and enjoy the sylvan setting, downing more Sauterne with great enjoyment.

The alcohol on an empty stomach made her wax lyrical about their surroundings, admiring everything with enthusiasm, although she could have done without Dean telling her the Latin names for all the plants and wild flowers.

Hoping to change the subject she asked, 'Can we eat soon? I'm starving.'

He passed her a paper napkin and she bit ravenously into a chicken leg with her small white teeth. The fresh air gave her an even greater appetite than usual and she tucked in enthusiastically.

'That was marvellous,' she sighed eventually, 'but I shouldn't have eaten so much, I put weight on too easily.'

'I like curvaceous women,' he told her lazily, looking admiringly at her voluptuous breasts as they strained against her skimpy black vest. 'They're much sexier than women who're all skin and bone. You're perfect – slender around the waist, nice and rounded everywhere else.'

Ellen was gratified by the compliment and smiled at him sunnily. 'You're also extremely pretty,' he said hoarsely, stretching out a tentative hand to stroke her hair. She nestled her head against his hand like a kitten and, pulling her closer, he kissed her.

Lying back on the old tartan rug Ellen drew him down beside her and they kissed for a long time. He was extremely good at it, his mouth hard but gentle on hers. Through half-closed eyes she could see fingers of sunlight filtering down through the trees, gilding individual leaves and adding an air of unreality to the proceedings.

She was surrounded by unfamiliar but evocative scents in the little glade and together with the wine they went to her head. When Dean sat up and said reluctantly, 'This is making me horny as hell — we'd better stop,' she pulled him back down beside her murmuring, 'Whatever for?'

Excitement was uncurling in her groin and she could feel her creamy juices beginning to seep into her panties as he kissed her again. Being outdoors made her feel so . . . abandoned.

Sitting up, she pulled her tee-shirt over her head, revealing her lacy black bra. He looked at the swelling of her breasts and deep cleavage as if mesmerised.

'Come on,' she urged him. 'I want us to dance naked around the woods.' He looked slightly stunned but obediently began to unbutton his shirt. Within seconds Ellen had stripped off her bra, panties and skirt and began to prance around the clearing.

'Hurry up,' she urged, vanishing behind a tree and then tantalisingly extending one long leg for him to admire. When he approached her she dodged away and ran off, laughing teasingly at him over her shoulder.

He didn't try too hard to catch her at first, the sight of her curvaceous buttocks bouncing up and down as she fled from him was too enjoyable.

Eventually he cornered her against the trunk of a

chestnut tree and held her against it, drinking in the sight of her naked breasts as she pushed her hair back out of her eyes.

'You're absolutely beautiful,' he muttered, passing the palm of his hand over one full breast, his cock standing to attention. She reached out and took it in her hand, squeezing the tip gently then stroking the full length of it.

A trickle of moisture began to run down her thigh from her overflowing pussy and he gulped, watching it for a few seconds before gently parting her legs and pushing his hand into her dripping labia.

His touch set Ellen on fire, she felt as though she'd die if she didn't have him inside her immediately.

'Make love to me,' she begged him urgently.

The head of his cock nudged against the entrance to her wet and welcoming tunnel, then buried itself deep within her. Holding onto his shoulders Ellen jumped up and wound her legs around his waist while Dean placed a hand under each of her buttocks to help support her. Clinging onto his back she met each of his thrusts with one of her own, ecstatically impaled on his plunging rod.

There was no breeze and they were soon running with sweat, the sultry air hanging heavily around them. Faster and faster their bodies moved against each other, the sounds of hot, animal sex filling the small clearing.

When Ellen's climax came she reared up and arched her back, pulling him even deeper into her. He couldn't hold on another moment and, with a hoarse cry which made the birds fly from the trees in a panic, he ejaculated forcibly into her.

INDECENT

They collapsed onto the grass and lay staring up at the sky.

'Are you thinking what I'm thinking?' he asked. In the last few minutes the sky had changed from blue to black, bringing an eerie premature twilight to the woods. At that moment everything was briefly illuminated by a flash of lightning, then there was a deafening crack of thunder and rain began to torrent down on them.

Grabbing Dean's hand Ellen pulled him to his feet and led him in a wild dance around the clearing. Water streamed over her, slicking her hair back from her face and cascading over her breasts. The sight drove him wild with renewed lust and dragging her onto the ground he fastened his mouth onto her breast, spread her legs and thrust into her again.

If anything, this time was even wilder than before as the warm rain beat down on their naked bodies and turned the ground beneath them into a quagmire. Rolling over and over in the mud they used each other shamelessly for mutual pleasure.

When they'd finished and lay panting side by side he propped himself up on one elbow and looking down at her, he burst out laughing.

'You look like you've been mud wrestling,' he exclaimed. 'This afternoon has been about three of my adolescent fantasies rolled into one.'

He pulled her to her feet and helped her hold out her hair so the rain washed the mud from it. When they were both clean again Ellen went to pick up her clothes and had a shock — they'd somehow managed to roll all over them and grind them into the mire.

She tried to rinse them out in the stream and managed to get most of the mud out of her bra and panties but it stuck determinedly to her tee-shirt and skirt.

After slipping on her bra and pants, Ellen unfolded her PVC mac and pulled it on over them, buttoning it up and belting it tightly around her waist. Dean whistled softly.

'That outfit's a wet dream. Let's hope the rain's sent everyone home and we don't bump into anyone.'

Dean had fared better, his clothes were wet but still clean. The rain abated a little but the sky remained ominously black and they decided they'd better return to the car. They squelched in silence through the trees while the rain continued to fall on them in huge fat drops.

They were nearly back at the car when Dean, who was behind Ellen, groaned loudly and dropped what he was carrying. Ellen looked round in concern.

'It's no good,' he said, pushing her up against the trunk of a tree and struggling to undo the buttons on her mac. 'Walking along behind you and watching your gorgeous bum swaying around inside that see-through mac is sending me crazy.'

Ellen was more than happy to have the buttons undone. It was like walking around in her own personal sauna, in fact the inside of the mac was wetter than the outside.

He unclipped the catch of her front-fastening bra and nibbled eagerly at one full breast, while Ellen unzipped his jeans and released his cock. Dragging her panties down around her knees he pushed swiftly inside her again, and screwed her frantically up against the trunk of the dripping tree.

Weak-kneed after this final erotic encounter they eventually made it back to the car — but not before Ellen's outfit had thoroughly shocked an elderly couple sheltering beneath a huge golfing umbrella.

CHAPTER TEN

As far as Jon was concerned, Ellesmere Port was the worst place he'd ever been.

A nightmare journey up the motorway with Ernie at the wheel had been followed by a nightmare day.

They'd left London at around two-thirty a.m. and Jon had closed his eyes and tried to sleep, but it had been impossible with Ernie whistling between his teeth and trying to find something he wanted to listen to on the radio.

They'd stopped at a transport cafe at around five for Ernie to fortify the inner man with a large fry-up. All Jon's inner man wanted to do was to sleep. He couldn't face anything to eat so he sat slouched over a cup of coffee trying not to feel queasy as Ernie consumed vast amounts of greasy food.

The Faranx factory sat on the edge of some bleak marshes overlooking the river Mersey. It had been fine and warm when they'd left London but up here in this industrial northern wasteland it was sheeting with rain and considerably cooler.

A despondent group of men were standing around the factory gates and as the *Daily News* didn't tend to support strikes, the appearance of Jon and Ernie wasn't greeted with much enthusiasm. Jon had to endure fifty minutes of impassioned rhetoric without getting anything much he could use.

Retiring to the car he got on the phone and tried to fix up an interview with one of the management but with no success. No one tried to get past the pickets, there were no angry confrontations and the weather got even worse.

By lunch-time Jon would have insisted they get back on the motorway and head for home if he hadn't feared Vernon's wrath. Over a pint and a stale cheese roll in a nearby pub he bemoaned their fate. Ernie was much more philosophical.

'Come on, man, it's not that bad. I've been in worse places. We can hit town tonight and pull some scrubbers – they'll be bowled over by our southern sophistication and charm.'

'You live in a fantasy world, Ernie. And which particular town did you have in mind? Fifty pounds says there isn't much night life in Ellesmere Port.'

'There's Liverpool just across the river. I hear the scouse women are all red hot.'

Jon groaned and drained his pint.

'In your dreams Ernie, in your dreams.'

The afternoon proved just as fruitless. In the early evening they booked into a cheap motel a few miles away. Jon was adamant that he was going straight to bed and that Ernie was doomed to spend an evening alone.

The photographer was aggrieved.

'It's much easier to pull women if there are two of you – we're an unbeatable team together, man.'

'Ernie, when have we ever pulled two women together?'

'Well, there was that Welsh bint and her mate in Southend that time.'

INDECENT

'Ernie, they were pros! I decided to pass and it cost you thirty quid. I'm off to bed — see you tomorrow.'

Jon's hope for a night's uninterrupted sleep was doomed to disappointment. Not only was his mattress lumpy, but just across the road was the loading bay to another factory where lorries came and went all evening making the floor shake and the windows rattle.

When it began to go dark Jon's room remained brightly lit, as the lights from a massive nearby plant came on and floodlit the area for miles around.

Leaning across and twitching open the curtains to see if the motel had been mysteriously transported into the middle of a football pitch, he blinked at the sight. The illuminated plant looked like a space station from hell and must have been visible from as far away as Birmingham.

At around two he'd just managed to fall into a state of semiconsciousness when there was a loud banging on the door. Pulling the pillow over his head Jon burrowed further down under the purple candlewick bedspread yelling, 'Go away!'

The knocking was relentless and cursing angrily under his breath Jon went to open the door.

Ernie stood on the threshold grinning drunkenly, his arm around a muscular peroxide blonde.

'This is Sharon,' he announced. 'She wants to be a model.'

''Ello,' Sharon greeted him, 'Is 'e reelly a photographer?'

Ernie barged Jon aside and he and Sharon made themselves at home on the end of the bed. Ernie produced a half bottle of whisky and tipped a couple of inches into an empty glass on the formica bedside table.

'Here, have a drink while I tell you what I've found out.'

Resigning himself to the situation Jon pulled on a tee-shirt and took a seat on the room's only chair while Ernie had a swig from the bottle.

'Is 'e reelly a photographer?' persisted Sharon, showing a mouthful of bad teeth as she spoke. ' 'E says 'e can get me work as a model.'

Jon couldn't imagine what type. She was nobody's idea of a looker, and although she had large breasts they were also very low slung – and that was while she was wearing a bra.

'He is a photographer,' he confirmed cautiously, taking a sip of the whisky. Then turning to Ernie, 'So what have you found out that's so important it can't wait until morning?'

'Sharon's brother is the shop steward at Faranx.'

'So?'

'He's been poking the managing director's wife. That's what the strike's really about.'

Jon directed the full wattage of his smile at the inebriated Sharon.

'Why don't you tell me all about it?' he invited her.

Kate paused in the hallway, there was a strange noise coming from Ellen's room.

'Ellen, are you okay?' she called.

Ellen opened the door.

'Yes, I'm fine thanks.'

Looking over her shoulder into the bedroom Kate

asked faintly, 'What . . . what on earth are those?'

On the bed lay a selection of bizarre artefacts. A couple of them were switched on and were bobbing and vibrating around on the quilt emitting low whirring noises.

'Sex aids,' beamed Ellen.

'But, Ellen, I thought the man situation was pretty much on overload.'

Kate had been alarmed when Ellen had arrived back from her picnic on Saturday — wet, mud stained and in a state of undress beneath her mac.

'My goodness,' she'd said faintly. 'Tell me quickly, have you been in an accident or just enjoying a sylvan romp?'

'The latter,' Ellen had returned cheerily, stripping off the dripping mac. 'It was lovely — do you need the bathroom for the next hour or so?'

Now, as Kate stepped into the room to take a closer look at the pulsating gadgets, Ellen giggled.

'Vernon wants me to write an article on sex aids, but I don't know anything about them so I bought these. The only trouble is that none of them come with instructions and I didn't like to ask in the shop so I'm a bit in the dark. What would you do with this do you think?'

She held up something which could have been a small latex candelabra. When Ellen switched it on the branches simultaneously vibrated and rotated. The two women stared at it, puzzled.

'I dread to think,' replied Kate at last in a dazed voice.

'I asked Jon, but he just burst out laughing and walked away. I suppose I'm going to have to interview the manufacturer. I was hoping I wouldn't have to.'

'Well, do let me know when you find out. Shall I open a bottle of wine?'

Ledd had a passion for Mexican food. Liz was less enthusiastic but she did like Margueritas and Tequila Sunrises so she didn't raise any objection when Ledd took her to a Mexican restaurant in Redondo Beach. They sat outside overlooking the marina, with a couple of Ledd's bodyguards at the next table.

Ledd had wanted to bring everybody on the tour but she'd objected so strongly that he'd caved in. Liz didn't like being part of a large group unless she was its focal point. She didn't mind the bodyguards; they were American, spoke only when spoken to and knew their way around the sprawling city. Twice, fans approached Ledd and were efficiently despatched by the minders as soon as they'd been given an autograph.

Liz drank more than she ate, while Ledd gorged himself on tacos, burritos, refried beans and Mexican beer. When they'd finished they took a stroll around the marina on the slatted boardwalks.

Leaning against a railing and looking out over the ocean, Ledd put his arm around her, slipped his hand inside the loose armhole of her top and fondled her breast.

'You've got great tits, doll,' he told her.

'I know. And they're not tits, they're breasts, and if you call me doll again I'll squeeze your balls so hard you'll be gagging on your own semen.'

He looked pained. 'I meant it as a compliment.'
'Well, get the vocabulary right next time.'
But she didn't remove his hand.

Kate arrived at James's flat deliberately early and systematically searched his desk before he arrived to see if she could find any clues to the national scandal she'd overheard him discussing in Barcelona. She didn't really expect to find anything — James was very scrupulous about security — but it was worth a try.

She also played back the messages on his answering machine, but there was nothing of interest on there.

She'd received a parcel in the post that morning and when she opened it she was glad that Ellen had already left for work.

It contained a peep-hole bra, a pair of split-crotch panties and a suspender belt, all in violet satin and edged with black lace.

Now, taking them out of her briefcase she went into James's bedroom and tried them on, adding a pair of her own fishnet stockings.

The transformation from professional woman to tart was fairly dramatic, particularly when she tousled her honey-blonde hair and redid her make-up to darken her eyes and lips.

Standing with her hands on her hips Kate viewed her reflection in the mirror. She thought the outfit was going a bit far, even for James.

Erotically framed by black lace, her nipples thrust their way through the circular holes in the bra cups and jutted temptingly outwards. The open-crotch panties seemed reasonably decent until she parted her legs, then a split appeared in the black lace revealing the inviting pink lips of her honeypot.

She turned this way and that in the mirror regarding herself quizzically — there was no doubt about it, she looked very sexy, very tarty and very available. Lying back on the bed, supported on her elbows, she drew her legs up with the knees together then slowly opened them.

Her pussy did look delicious framed like that, the stiff black lace in direct contrast to the moist pink petals of her labia, the darker pink tip of her clit just visible.

Moving the mirror closer and adjusting the angle, Kate piled a couple of pillows behind her, propped herself up on them and lay back admiring her reflection. With her knees bent and wide apart she tentatively touched her clitoris with one finger. A tingle of sensation shivered through her body and she felt her nipples crinkle and harden.

Languorously she caressed her breasts, then ran her finger along the shaft of her clit and felt herself moisten. Stroking it gently she continued to watch herself — in a strange sort of way it was like watching an erotic video.

She was so absorbed in what she was doing that she didn't hear James's key in the lock. When he appeared in the bedroom a couple of minutes later she barely registered his presence, continuing self-absorbedly to stimulate herself.

He didn't speak, merely sank into a chair and feasted his eyes.

As Kate's pleasure mounted, she noted detachedly

that her cheeks became flushed and her half-closed eyes glittered feverishly beneath her thick dark lashes. James was gazing at her avidly, but she didn't notice him, she was far too intent on her own reflection.

Drawing her knees even further up, Kate could see the pale globes of her bottom with its skimpy covering of violet satin and the darker, more complicated folds of her swollen pink pussy.

Of their own volition her fingers moved faster until she let out a cry and toppled over the edge into a vortex of shaking pleasure.

Unable to restrain himself any longer James tore off his trousers and joined her on the bed, burying his engorged organ up to the hilt in her welcoming wetness. His mouth sought and found one of her provocatively protruding nipples and teased it with his tongue.

Kate had barely come down to earth — just enough in fact to wrap her fishnet stocking-clad legs around his waist — when she felt herself climbing swiftly towards another climax. With a strangled gasp she angled her pelvis for maximum stimulation, then clutched wildly at James's shoulders as her back arched and she came again.

Shuddering and panting, Kate caught a glimpse of them in the mirror, their limbs entwined and both of them moving as if possessed. It was so erotic, particularly when, in a change of tempo, James slowly withdrew until all but the tip of his shaft was visible, then plunged it back into her, before repeating the process.

Unable to help herself Kate came again, leaving

James to reach his own climax a short while later.

Rhett Renton, the country singer, was renting a house high in the Hollywood hills. To Liz's surprise he was very tall, at least six foot three, and even better looking than his photos. She knew how deceptive photos could be and had half expected him to be a foot shorter and nowhere near as attractive in the flesh.

She conducted the interview by the pool from where there was a panoramic view of downtown Los Angeles. They were above the smog line but she could see it hanging over the valley like a brownish pall, smudging outlines and giving everything a sepia tint.

He fixed her a drink, then dropped into the chair opposite hers, stretching out his long denim-clad legs in front of him.

She was relieved to see he wasn't wearing his hat.

He was all good ol' boy southern charm, crinkling his blue eyes at her and leaning forward with practiced good manners to light her cigarettes.

She tried several tacks during the course of the interview to throw him off balance but didn't succeed. He refused to rise to the bait, merely flashing his white teeth and answering her probing and sometimes offensive questions equably.

Towards the end of the interview she asked if she could have a tour of the house. He showed her around, having disclaimed any responsibility for the decor. It was luxuriously if unremarkably furnished but looking around didn't really add anything to her impression of him.

INDECENT

She sounded him out about sexism, racism and jingoism but was unable to trip him up and get him to say anything which showed him in a bad light.

Eventually, she came to her last question, 'Rhett, you don't smoke, you don't drink and you don't do drugs. Do you have any vices?'

'Yes, ma'am. Aah sure do have one,' he drawled, leaning further back in his chair and folding his arms behind his head while he lazily looked her up and down.

'And what's that?' asked Liz. He leaned over and switched her tape recorder off.

'Aah like to fuck like a jack rabbit.'

There was a pause while Liz studied him carefully – my goodness he was sexy. Her toes had been curling and uncurling in her spike-heeled suede shoes since she'd arrived.

'And would you like to fuck me?' she asked after a long drawn out pause.

'Ma'am, it would be my pleasure.'

He uncoiled his tall lean frame from the chair, taking her hand and pulling her to her feet. He led her to the bedroom where he threw himself down on the bed saying, 'It'd be real nice for me if I could watch you undress.'

Nothing loath, Liz peeled off her clothes garment by garment, enjoying the close attention he was paying and the way his deep blue eyes swept appreciatively over her body. When she was down to her black lace teddy she turned this way and that, before slowly undoing the tiny ribbons which kept it fastened. With a whisper it fell to the floor and she picked it up and threw it at him. He buried his face in it for a few moments then got to his feet.

'Now it's your turn cowboy,' she ordered him. He grinned at her, lifting her easily in his strongly muscled arms and placing her on the bed.

'Aah got a better idea honey. Just let me put this on.' He tied a scarf lightly around her eyes, then she heard him walking away. A few minutes later, just as she was wondering if he was coming back, he said, 'Okay, you can take it off now.'

Pulling it off, Liz's jaw dropped at the sight which met her eyes.

Rhett was standing in front of her butt naked except for a large cowboy hat and was sporting one of the biggest hard-ons she'd ever laid eyes on.

Jon was *persona grata* with Vernon again. The story about the Faranx strike made the first page and the obliging Sharon had even supplied a couple of rather blurred photographs taken by her brother of the managing director's wife in abandoned postures.

Jon had modestly refused to take the credit for the story, saying quite truthfully that it was Ernie's scoop. But, as soon as it became clear that the story had come from the shop steward's sister, Vernon had been convinced that only Jon could have charmed it out of her.

A couple of days later, when Jon felt his health and strength had been adequately restored by two nights of unbroken sleep, he decided to go to the club when he'd finished work.

Rather reluctantly he embarked on a work-out in the gym. It wasn't something he particularly enjoyed but he felt he needed to build up his stamina if he was to continue with his investigations into the secret society. The previous week had shown him that he wasn't exactly in peak condition.

The gym was deserted when he went in but he was soon joined by the club's latest instructress, a petite and exotic looking dark girl called Clary. With her slanting dark eyes, tanned olive skin and full red mouth she looked as if she might have Latin or even Arab blood. In fact she came from Penge.

He watched her covertly as he warmed up on the jogging machine. She was doing a series of stretches in front of one of the sections of mirrored wall, her full breasted body bending with a supple grace he knew he'd never be able to achieve in a thousand years.

The tight emerald-green leotard clung seductively to every curve — and there were plenty of them. Her well-developed legs were bare except for a pair of thick socks which came up over her knees.

She bent forwards, briefly placing her hands flat on the ground before straightening up again in a more advanced form of 'touch your toes' than he'd ever seen before. He delighted in the sight of her firm rounded backside sticking in the air then bouncing slightly as she jackknifed upright again. Her leotard fastened between the legs with two small pearl buttons, the stretchy material tautening and putting a strain on them each time she bent forward.

She must have sensed him watching her or spotted him in the mirror because she came over and watched critically for a while as he jogged lethargically on the running machine.

'You've been on that speed since I came in,' she said accusingly. 'You're supposed to keep increasing it.'

Leaning over and giving him a brief and blissful glimpse of her deep cleavage she adjusted the speed. Jon had no choice but to redouble his efforts.

He wished she'd stayed on the other side of the gym leaving him free to admire her from a distance. It was true that the programme he was about to follow wasn't exactly the one Dana had worked out for him. He'd adjusted it to suit himself since he didn't subscribe to the 'push yourself to the limits' theory she was so fond of.

He was just about to slow the machine down and get off when Clary pre-empted him. Reaching across again she turned it up and Jon found himself pounding along at a breakneck rate, his legs going like pistons. He tried to turn it down but she kept her hand over the controls saying, 'Come on! You're not even sweating yet.'

'Stop this thing! Let me get off!' he panted, knowing his face had turned tomato-coloured. In reply she turned it up even further.

'Stop it! I've got a heart condition!' he yelled. She slowed it down then switched it off, looking at his heightened complexion with interest as he slumped to the floor and sat breathing heavily, waiting for his pulse rate to return to normal.

'Do you really have a heart condition?' she enquired sceptically.

'I will have if I run as fast as that again.'

'You need to be properly warmed up before starting with the weights,' she told him severely.

'Otherwise you might pull something.'

Jon decided it wasn't politic to tell her that the weights he was planning to work out with wouldn't have pulled a muscle in a hamster.

Thankfully she went away and resumed her own exercises, leaving him free to go over to the equipment designed to strengthen the leg muscles. He adjusted the weights then, gripping the sides of the seat, he began to push. He saw her glance at him from the other side of the gym and put quite a lot of effort into making it look as if he was working hard.

He thought he was putting on quite a convincing performance – his eyes closed and face contorted. It obviously wasn't convincing enough because she suddenly appeared at his side. To his deep humiliation she leant over and with one small hand pushed the weight he was pretending to strain at with both feet.

'That's the weight we start out of condition, middle-aged women on,' she told him dismissively, adding several more weights as she spoke. 'Pushing that little one won't do you any good at all – here try these.'

To his chagrin, Jon could barely move them. The next half hour was torture as she followed him around the gym; coaxing, cajoling and deriding him as she put him through a gruelling work-out. When he'd finished and lay wheezing and groaning on one of the benches she said brightly, 'Up you get. It's closing time so I need to throw you out and lock up.'

Jon closed his eyes, 'Just a few more minutes,' he pleaded. 'Just until these pains in my chest ease a bit.'

She stood there looking down at him, tapping her foot.

'Well alright, I'll go and see everyone else off the premises then come back.'

By the time she returned Jon was sitting up and, if his breathing wasn't actually back to normal, at least it wasn't still agonisingly painful.

She climbed athletically up the wall bars a couple of feet from where he sat with his eyes still closed.

'Do you know what I like to do sometimes when everyone else has gone home?' he heard her ask.

'I dread to think.'

'I like to do my daily work-out in the nude.'

Jon's eyes flew open. She was facing him, hanging from the wall bars with her hands. She wasn't actually nude but she'd pulled her leotard down to her waist revealing two full orbs the same smooth olive hue as the rest of her body. Her nipples were large, dark brown and flat and seemed to be begging to be sucked and teased into an erect position.

His jaw dropped and stayed that way for a few seconds before he closed his mouth with an audible gulp.

He watched transfixed as she hooked her legs over the top bar and hung upside down. Her breasts were so firm they barely moved as she upended herself. Her eyes were on a level with his as she said, 'Dana says you're great in the sack. Is that true?'

'Er . . . I like to think so.'

'I'm not sure I believe you,' she taunted. 'If you put as little effort into sex as you do into working-out it would be a real non-starter.'

'Sex is a completely different thing,' he protested.

'It's worth making the effort for.'

'Huh! I can't see you standing the pace.'

Stung by having his manhood dismissively impugned, Jon got to his feet and found his face on a level with her groin. Without thinking about it he deftly undid the two tiny buttons, pulling the stretchy material apart and revealing that Clary wasn't wearing any briefs.

Jet black hair curled softly and damply around the hidden entrance to her velvet tunnel and he paused for a moment to savour her arousing musky scent. Parting her outer lips with his fingers, he found the tiny bud of her clitoris and began a delicate assault with his tongue.

For an eternity he lapped, licked and sucked until the bud became a swollen deep red and moisture brimmed around it, bubbling out of her innermost recesses.

She moaned and writhed but he didn't let up until she emitted a piercing shriek and her whole body went rigid as she climaxed.

He felt her fumbling with his shorts, then one of her hands slid inside to emerge triumphantly with his cock. It was his turn to moan as she fastened her mouth around it and, still upside down, began to suck greedily.

Her nipples had stiffened as he'd explored her honeypot with his tongue. Now as she kissed, sucked and nibbled her way along his dick and back again, he caressed her breasts until the swollen nipples jutted out like small thimbles.

Removing his cock reluctantly from her mouth before he could erupt and fill her with his juices, he helped her down from the wall bars and led her over to the vaulting horse.

Laying her over it on her stomach he dragged her leotard off then fondled her gorgeous bum. Full and round, it was one of the juiciest he'd ever handled. He squeezed it gently, as if it were a delectable piece of fruit whose ripeness he was assessing.

Parting the smooth cheeks he couldn't resist pushing his tongue up her again, firmly spreading her legs as she wriggled ecstatically in his grasp.

When she groaned, 'Screw me. Quickly. Now.' He dropped his shorts, kicked them to one side and obliged.

Sliding into her was like the beginning of a ride on a roller coaster. He could only be grateful that the building was empty because her cries of pleasure echoed deafeningly off the walls of the gym.

He forgot his exhaustion in his determination to give her a fuck to remember.

After bringing her to a second climax he scooped her off the horse and, still penetrating her from behind, lay down on his back on an exercise bench. He steadied her with his hands on her hips as she sat up and swung her feet onto the floor.

Sitting astride him she began to rise and fall on his cock. He discovered that he could either watch her smooth skinned buttocks, flexing and relaxing as she rode him, or by lifting his head he could see her reflection in the mirrored wall and admire her bouncing breasts.

Her muscle control was the sort men dream about. She kept him on the brink of ejaculating for what seemed forever, until he couldn't stand it any longer. He grabbed her by the waist and pulled her down hard, pushing himself over the edge into a volcanic eruption.

Turning her head, she looked down at him.

'Now that's what I call a work-out,' she said admiringly.

CHAPTER ELEVEN

He wasn't sure how long he'd been there. It could have been days, it could have been hours. He tried to shift position, but manacled as he was to a metal ring bolted into the wall, there wasn't much room for manoeuvre.

When he'd arrived at this place he'd been stripped and forced to submit to a humiliating body search. Since then they'd kept him chained to the wall, alone except for occasional visits from Elsa, one of the handmaidens.

She had been kind to him, bringing him a flagon of wine and holding it to his lips so he might drink. Small and flaxen-haired, with curving ruby-red lips she seemed to like him.

On the last occasion she'd shyly caressed his naked chest, dropping kisses here and there as she'd worked her way downwards. His only garment was a loincloth and she'd begun to remove it, opening it and staring with delight at what it concealed.

He'd started to swell under her admiring gaze, when suddenly hearing a noise in the corridor outside she'd hurriedly refastened his loincloth and slipped furtively from the room.

The door opened and she came in again, holding a set of keys on a large heavy ring. With her finger to her lips she approached him stealthily and stretching upwards tried one of the keys in the lock of his manacles.

The third key fitted and at last he was free. Tenderly she rubbed his wrists where the metal restraints had chafed them. She smiled at him so sweetly that he put his arms around her, feeling the heat of her young flesh through the thin white dress she wore.

She was naked under the short, loose-fitting garment — that much was obvious. He caressed her firm young haunches, his hands kneading and squeezing while she looked shyly up at him.

He felt his manhood burgeoning and hastily fumbled with the loosely tied piece of cloth. His massive organ reared proudly upwards and he pressed it experimentally against her stomach as he fondled her full, unfettered breasts.

She knelt at his feet and took his iron-hard member into her mouth. The sensation was exquisite, rendered even more so by the way she gazed at him adoringly as she sucked and licked his appreciative organ.

When he knew he could hold back no longer he pulled her to her feet, pushing her face down over the crudely hewn, old table against the wall. Flipping her dress up over her waist he grasped her by the hips then triumphantly thrust his shaft deep within her.

He was on the point of spilling his seed when the massive oak door behind him was flung open. There was an angry cry, then the lash of a whip fell across his shoulders as, unable to stop himself, his hot juices pumped into the young girl.

INDECENT

Two tall, leather-clad women pulled him off the girl, who huddled terrified in a corner of the stone-flagged room. They bent his arms up his back and dragged him to stand in front of the third woman.

If the other women were tall, she was Amazonian, towering several inches over him in her spike-heeled, thigh-length boots.

She raked him with a look of total contempt, tapping the handle of her whip against his shoulder and spoke coldly.

'You have attempted to escape and have assaulted this innocent girl. Prepare for your punishment.'

Liz only intended to go to Sledgehammer's first US concert at the Hollywood Bowl because she was supposed to be covering it for the paper. She made no secret of the fact that she was going reluctantly and that the prospect bored her. She could tell that Ledd was fairly put out by her lack of enthusiasm.

'Why don't you want to come?' he demanded aggrievedly. 'It's going to be a great gig.'

Liz yawned and stubbed out her cigarette.

'It's also going to be hot, crowded and loud. Anyway, I don't particularly like your music.'

He was outraged.

'Well, that's terrific. That really bolsters my confidence to have my lady tell me she doesn't like my music.'

Liz turned over in bed and glared at him.

'Don't be so childish – and I'm not your lady, we just happen to be having a good time together at the moment. Or at least we are when you're not either comatose or sulking.'

Pushing the sheet aside, Ledd went into the bathroom, hurt pride radiating from every pore. Liz got up and went over to the wardrobe. What on earth should she wear for such an occasion?

She actually enjoyed the concert more than she'd anticipated, particularly since she took the precaution of wearing earplugs. Ledd was undeniably hot stuff on stage — strutting around in his leather trousers, his hips grinding suggestively against the mike stand.

When the concert was over they all went to a restaurant which had been taken over for the night. Liz drank several glasses of champagne, picked at her food and became thoroughly bored by all the adulation Ledd was receiving.

There were various other celebrities at the party and she encouraged the attentions of a famous chat-show host. He was rather long in the tooth for her tastes but nevertheless it was better than waiting for Ledd to get rid of the people fawning over him and pay her some attention.

When the chat-show host suggested they leave the party together she agreed and left the restaurant without so much as a backward glance in Ledd's direction. She let her new admirer take her back to his opulent mansion in Laurel Canyon.

She liked the mansion much better than its owner. She insisted on being shown round and wondered, not for the first time, why someone as talented as she was lived in a three-bedroom flat in London instead of somewhere much better suited to her — like this mansion in Laurel Canyon, although she'd prefer Beverly Hills.

INDECENT

He opened a bottle of Moët while she wandered into the master bathroom and inspected the contents of the bathroom cabinet.

Pile ointment. Athlete's foot powder. Laxatives.

She decided she wasn't going to sleep with him — she'd only been half planning to anyway and what she'd found in the bathroom clinched it. When she went back into the bedroom she was startled to find him adjusting his toupee.

That did it.

Accepting the proffered glass of champagne, she told him to call her a taxi and then proceeded to pace moodily around the enormous living room while he tried in vain to find out what he'd done wrong.

When the taxi eventually dropped her at the hotel she stalked up to Ledd's suite, hoping that his entourage had cleared off for the night and that he was ready, waiting and horny.

She certainly was.

Her groin was tingling with expectation as she quietly opened the door. Ledd had been very sexy up on stage. If he hadn't arranged that boring party, which as far as Liz was concerned was just an ego massage, they could have come straight back here and got down to it — that would have been much more to her taste.

Actually Liz loved parties, what she couldn't stand was not being the centre of attention.

She stepped into the room to be faced by the sight of Ledd and a young girl with toffee-coloured hair rolling around naked on the bed.

Liz recognised the girl. One of the roadies had brought her to the party and Ledd had obviously appropriated her. The two of them hastily separated and sat up in bed – the girl nervously pulling the sheet up over her small, pointed breasts.

Liz stood with her hands on her hips for a few moments taking in the scene. Ledd looked half guilty, half triumphant as her eyes met his.

Without saying anything Liz unzipped her tight-fitting black dress and let it fall to the floor, stepping out of it and kicking it carelessly to one side. Underneath she was wearing a transparent, black chiffon teddy, with a matching black chiffon suspender belt and black stockings.

The two of them looked dumbstruck as she slipped the teddy's shoestring straps off her shoulders and let it fall to her waist. She looked superb, naked except for her stockings and suspenders, a froth of gauzy black chiffon around her slender waist.

Easing the teddy down her long legs she stepped out of that in turn and, hips swaying, walked over to the bed, watched by Ledd and the girl.

'Move over,' she ordered them.

The girl was pretty enough in a sullen sort of way, with large brown eyes and a pouting rosebud mouth. She looked as if she was about to argue, but one glance at Liz's expression was enough to make her think better of it. She obediently made room in the bed, then flinched as Liz ripped the sheet off her and threw it on the floor.

Liz took her time about examining the girl's body with her eyes. She was fairly slight with small pert breasts, well-rounded hips and a curvaceous little rump.

Yes, she'd do. It was a while since Liz had taken

part in a threesome and having ascertained that the girl was to her taste she planned to enjoy herself.

Ledd needn't think he was the only one going to have some fun tonight.

Watched by him, she ran her hands in a leisurely way over the hard little breasts which yielded slightly to her touch, then down over the girl's stomach to her thighs, just trailing the tips of her fingers through her silky bush.

The girl made a small sound of protest.

'If you want to play with the grown-ups then it's time you learnt some grown-up games,' Liz told her dismissively.

Parting the girl's thighs she pushed a couple of exploratory fingers between her legs, ignoring her half-stifled gasp. Her fingers came away wet and she thrust them into Ledd's mouth to suck.

Turning casually to the girl Liz said, 'Are you going or staying? I warn you that if you're staying we do this my way.' The girl looked apprehensive but excited at the same time.

'Well?' demanded Liz.

'Stayin'' muttered the girl, staring up at Liz with her big brown eyes.

'What's your name?'

'Jassy.'

'Okay, Jassy, have you ever been down on another woman before?'

Round-eyed Jassy shook her head.

Liz lay down on her back with her head at the bottom of the bed.

'Get busy,' she ordered, opening her legs.

While the girl bent her head tentatively over Liz's

chestnut bush Liz motioned Ledd to move closer. Taking his dick in her hand she squeezed it. Then, opening her lips, she took it in her mouth.

It felt glorious.

She took it deep into her throat and sucked hard, running her tongue along the underside as if tasting a lollipop, while Ledd moaned appreciatively and caressed her breasts. As he did that he watched Jassy, still busy at the other end of the bed, her toffee-coloured hair covering her face as she lapped away at Liz's labia.

When Liz had sucked her fill she released Ledd and twisted languidly away from Jassy. Going down on her hands and knees she had Ledd penetrate her from behind, while Jassy softly nuzzled Ledd's balls and probed at the base of his cock with a searching little tongue. She could tell from Ledd's eager thrusts that he was really into this and she ground her hips backwards into him, urging him on to greater efforts.

Liz always enjoyed being in control and never more so than now. The other two were in her thrall and she knew that there was very little they wouldn't do if she asked them to.

Accordingly, without separating from Ledd, she rolled him onto his back and sat astride him while Jassy lowered herself onto his face. Ledd looked like he'd never had it so good – Liz sitting on his dick and Jassy on his tongue. He thrust away at both ends while the two women used him for their own pleasure.

The rest of the night was lost in a tangle of mouths, limbs and genitals as shuddering climax followed shuddering climax. No part of anyone's body escaped attention and all of them lost sight of just who was doing what to whom as the hours passed.

Some time around dawn Liz awoke sandwiched between Ledd and Jassy. She had her back to Ledd who had an arm curled loosely around her hip, his hand buried between her legs.

Jassy lay on her back on the other side of her and Liz found that she was holding one of the girl's little apple breasts. Instinctively her internal muscles tightened on the couple of fingers which were inside her.

They moved. It felt good.

Reaching behind her she felt for Ledd's cock. Initially soft, it hardened rapidly as she kneaded the head with gentle fingers. As soon as it was hard she removed his hand from her pussy and substituted his dick, wriggling herself backwards onto it until it was completely inside her.

Half-awake, he began to move with her until Jassy woke up too and, turning sleepily towards Liz, fastened her small mouth over one of the older woman's milk-chocolate-coloured nipples and began to suck.

Vernon emerged from his room and made his way through the busy office to Ellen's desk. He eyed her breasts lasciviously.

'Ellen, my dear, I'm about to give you the cushiest assignment of your young career. I trust you'll be suitably appreciative.'

Ellen looked up expectantly.

'We've had a tip off that our new Minister for Health, Ian Stanstead, is about to enjoy a dirty weekend with a nubile young model at a country house hotel in the Cotswolds. All you have to do is get the dirt. Talk to one or both of them if you can, talk to the chambermaid, talk to everyone and come back with a good story.'

The new Minister for Health had been ill-judged enough to antagonise Ross Talbot, the paper's owner, when they'd met at a dinner party given by a mutual acquaintance.

Ross Talbot was not a man to antagonise lightly. A couple of reporters had been told to investigate the Minister's private life and discovered that he had just embarked on a discreet liaison with a twenty-year-old glamour model.

Ian Stanstead had also recently made a speech in which he'd said that the spread of Aids was due solely to a lack of self-control. He'd indicated that if people stayed in a monogamous relationship instead of behaving irresponsibly, then the problem could easily be eradicated. It was a very long speech and dealt with various areas of public health, but Ross Talbot made sure that only that aspect was reported on the front page.

'A weekend in the Cotswolds – how lovely.' Ellen beamed happily up at her editor.

Vernon threw a glossy hotel brochure down on her desk.

'That's where you'll be staying. Book a double room. Take Ernie and pretend to be a honeymoon couple.'

Ellen's delight turned to dismay. Behind Vernon's

back she saw Ernie grinning at her, showing a mouthful of mossy teeth. He smacked his lips silently, then made an obscene rutting movement with his groin.

Vernon walked off down the office and Ellen hastily scrambled to her feet and hurried after him. Following him into his room she closed the door behind them.

Her initial reaction had been to beg him not to send Ernie with her, on the grounds that there was no one she'd less like to spend the weekend in a double room with. In the time it took her to follow Vernon down the office she decided to abandon this approach. Vernon expected his staff to put up with any discomfort, unpleasantness or inconvenience to get the job done. Instead she decided on another tack.

'Vernon, could we possibly talk about this?' she asked, smiling prettily.

'Certainly, my dear. I suppose it would be too much to expect that Ernie could get some compromising photographs, however we can but hope. As long as he gets some showing them together.'

'Do you think perhaps that having Ernie stay at the hotel is such a good idea?' began Ellen hesitantly. 'He's a good photographer but you know what he can be like. What if he gooses the waitress or something? Or insults one of the other guests? Getting us thrown out isn't going to help get a story.'

Vernon pursed his lips and moved the paperweight on his desk half an inch to one side.

'Wouldn't it be better if I went with someone like Jon,' she continued. 'You know how charming he can be. If anyone can get information out of the chambermaids or anyone else, he can. Between us I'm sure we could get a really good story. If I go with Ernie he'll end up offending everyone and it'll be a disaster.'

'I take your point,' said Vernon slowly.

'Ernie could stay in some bed and breakfast place nearby and we could keep in touch by mobile phone to let him know when there's a photo opportunity,' she finished.

'Hmm, alright then, go up with Jon. And Ellen . . .' he ran his eyes over her lustfully.

'Yes?'

'Your taste in clothes is charming, quite charming. But for this weekend could you wear something plainer? You do rather attract attention in your er . . . colourful clothes. Dress like a demure young bride on her honeymoon.'

Ellen was flamboyantly clad in a short, canary-yellow cotton dress worn under a vivid-green jacket. There was a two inch split in the side seam of the dress and a button hanging off the jacket.

'I'll go through my wardrobe tonight and see what I have,' she assured him.

'Send Jon in if you can find him. I'll tell him about the treat he has in store. In fact, maybe I ought to cover this one myself – a weekend in the country with a lovely young thing like you would do me the world of good.'

He bared his teeth at her and Ellen's heart sank. Vernon would be nearly as bad as Ernie – though less of a social embarrassment. But she didn't relish the prospect of spending the weekend fighting either of them off. It would be much more relaxed with Jon, he was so successful with women that he was unlikely to waste time trying to persuade an unwilling one.

Luckily Vernon didn't seem to be serious about the idea.

'Perhaps not,' he sighed. 'Send the laddie in and I'll make his day.'

After Vernon's comments on suitable clothing, Ellen turned up at the office the following day wearing an old sprigged cotton Laura Ashley dress. Wearing it, virtually any other female would have looked demure.

Ellen looked like jailbait.

The dress made her look about fourteen and the combination of that, her curvaceous figure and innocent face was a potent mix.

In Vernon's office both Vernon and Jon stared at her puzzled.

'She can't dress like that,' Jon commented at last. 'The management will call the police thinking I'm a child molester.'

'Don't you have anything... dowdy?' enquired Vernon. Ellen shook her head.

Kate was called in to offer her advice.

'You could put Ellen in a sack and she'd look sexy,' was her opinion. 'If you want her to look pretty but inconspicuous I'd suggest grey or black. No short skirts and nothing tight or fitted.'

Both Jon and Vernon stared at her hopefully.

'I could probably lend her something of mine,' she suggested. 'I'm a few inches taller so my clothes would be longer on her.'

Ernie was furious when he discovered that Jon was staying at the hotel with Ellen in his place.

'You could have been sharing a room with a real man,' he pointed out, scratching his armpit. 'What's wrong with me, that's what I'd like to know?'

'What isn't?' retorted Ellen. 'Jon has so many girlfriends he'll be grateful for a couple of nights off. You, on the other hand, would spend all your time trying to grope me rather than concentrating on the job at hand. We will be working after all,' she ended virtuously.

'So I'm supposed to spend a lonely evening in a poxy bed-and-breakfast place while you two live high off the hog – it's not fair,' moaned Ernie.

Jon joined them at that moment.

'You'd hate it, Ernie,' he assured him. 'You'd have to wear a jacket and tie, the food would all be messed about with and they'd expect you to get it straight from your plate into your mouth rather than via the front of your shirt. You'll be much happier having a meat pie in a nice cosy pub, ogling the barmaid.'

For the journey Ellen wore a grey linen dress she'd borrowed from Kate. She'd wanted to pull the waist in with a wide leather belt but Kate had forbidden her to. She still managed to look sexy.

Glancing at her as they made the journey up the crowded motorway in his MX5, Jon hoped that sharing a double room with Ellen wasn't going to try his self-control.

INDECENT

When Vernon had told him about it, the idea of a weekend in the Cotswolds had seemed very attractive. It also indicated that he was back in favour with his boss. The story about the strike in the Faranx factory in Ellesmere Port had redeemed him to a certain extent in Vernon's eyes. He'd also struck lucky on another couple of assignments.

He'd had to put his investigation into the mysterious secret society on hold while he assiduously pursued the two stories – with the result that he hadn't actually had sex for what seemed like quite a while.

The weather was warm, his libido was high and he was going to have to spend two nights in the same room as the luscious Lolita. He wished rather belatedly that he'd seen one of his casual girlfriends the night before. The weekend suddenly seemed fraught with difficulty. He reminded himself that Dana was back in a few days – he'd have to wait until then.

Ellen was peacefully eating a bag of liquorice allsorts.

'Could you just check the map and tell me which exit we need?' he asked her.

After wrestling with the unfolded map for a couple of minutes she said, 'The next one. Then it's only about ten miles. Isn't it great getting to do this? Oh, and before I forget...'

She took a box of confetti out of her bag leaving several pieces behind. Carefully she pushed a tiny white paper bell in her hair then sprinkled some more confetti around the car. 'Mustn't overdo it,' she murmured, stuffing the box into the glove compartment and returning to her bag of liquorice allsorts.

The Lynton Hall Hotel stood in its own extensive grounds among the rolling meadows of the Gloucestershire countryside. Built from honey-coloured Cotswold stone and bathed in golden sunlight it looked like the ideal place to spend a summer weekend.

'Oh, it's lovely!' exclaimed Ellen as they pulled up outside. 'It'll be strange pretending we're on our honeymoon, won't it?'

Jon grinned. 'I've had to pretend much stranger things than that before now.'

A porter carried their bags in and, after they'd registered, showed them to their room. Jon was relieved that it was on the first floor and didn't have a fire escape directly outside it. Had that been the case he wouldn't have put it past Ernie to lurk outside the window in the hope of getting compromising photos of the two of them in addition to the ones he was supposed to get.

Spacious and sunny, the room was attractively furnished in shades of green and rose pink. Ellen danced around admiring everything, watched indulgently by the porter as Jon searched his pockets for a tip.

'What shall we do first – unpack or explore?' she asked him.

'How about going down for some coffee and seeing if there's any sign of our unfortunate quarry and his paramour?'

They had coffee at a table on the terrace overlooking the driveway. They were the only ones

INDECENT

there and they discussed various strategies in low voices.

When they'd finished, Ellen sat in the sun keeping watch, while Jon strolled around the building and rejoined her a few minutes later. Several more guests arrived but there was no sign of Ian Stanstead.

'Let's go up to the room,' suggested Ellen. 'I could use a bath and we can take it in turns to watch from the window.' Once in the bedroom Jon sat on the window seat while Ellen unpacked her case.

'What do you think?' She held up an ivory-satin nightdress with thigh length splits up both sides and a plunging neckline.

'Very pretty,' replied Jon faintly, wondering how many cold showers he was going to have to take over the course of the weekend.

'Kate lent it to me. I'm not actually going to wear it, I'd probably tear it or something. She just thought I should have one to leave lying around if we're supposed to be on our honeymoon.'

Jon hoped fervently that she wasn't planning to sleep in the nude.

'Do you mind if I have first bath?' she asked.

'No, go ahead.'

Ellen lingered in a scented bubble bath thoroughly enjoying herself. She was just taking the tops off all the complimentary toilet products and trying them when there was a tap on the door.

'I think they've arrived,' called Jon, 'I'll go down and see.'

He went down to reception and pretended to study the leaflets about local places of interest until the new arrivals had checked in. Then he followed them at a discreet distance when the porter led them up to their room.

He walked back into the bedroom just as Ellen emerged wrapped in a fluffy white bath towel, with her dark hair half pinned up, half tumbling onto her shoulders.

'They've just arrived and by a stroke of luck they're in the next room,' he told her, going over to the window and looking resolutely out.

'Oh good. Does that mean we listen at the wall with glasses to our ears?'

Their mobile phone went at that moment.

'Guess who,' muttered Jon picking it up. 'Hi, Ernie. No Ellen's fully dressed and putting her hair in rollers ... They've just arrived. Chances are they'll have drinks on the terrace before dinner — you should be able to get some good shots from the trees ... I haven't a clue what they'll be wearing but I'll phone you back as soon as I see them in their evening finery.'

He kept his back turned until he heard Ellen return to the bathroom.

When at last she emerged she looked radiant in a black off-the-shoulder evening dress.

'This is Kate's, too. It's got a designer label and everything. Isn't it classy?' She twirled around in front of him. It was also very sexy.

'It suits you. I'm going to take a shower. Do you want to go down and I'll meet you on the terrace?'

'Oh no, I think we should go down together if we're supposed to be on our honeymoon.' She pouted at him teasingly. 'We're only just married and you're trying to get rid of me already.'

Ellen explored the mini-bar while she was waiting and poured herself a Cinzano and ginger ale. Settling down on the window seat she flicked through a magazine until Jon was ready.

She clung to his arm as they went downstairs, smiling up at him winsomely.

'I think I'm going to be good at this,' she murmured. 'I'll be so convincing that even you'll start to believe we're on our honeymoon.'

Jon hoped not.

They sat on the terrace and ordered drinks. Ellen glanced round at the other people.

'Are they here?'

'Yes, over by the balustrade.' Ellen watched the couple for a few moments.

'I wouldn't have recognised him,' she said puzzled, 'and I studied several photos before we left. What's he done to himself — other than the clothes?'

The Minister for Health usually wore nondescript grey single-breasted suits with a white shirt and dark tie. Tonight he was resplendent in a double-breasted beige suit, a bright turquoise shirt and a flamboyant tie.

'He's changed his hair,' said Jon. 'It's usually slicked sideways with gel, now it's all fluffed forward.'

'And he's wearing different glasses — they're usually square with black rims,' observed Ellen. For his weekend of relaxation Ian Stanstead had donned a pair of round horn-rims. She giggled suddenly. 'They're pinching his nose, he keeps pushing them upwards.'

'They've booked in as Mr and Mrs Johnson,' Jon told her. 'How very imaginative.'

The Minister's companion was a stunning blonde with a magnificent bosom which kept threatening to spill out of her tight scarlet dress. Her mass of bright gold hair was teased out over her shoulders and looked as if it had been sprayed so firmly into place that it would withstand a force nine gale.

'I'll go and phone Ernie and tell him which couple they are,' murmured Ellen. 'The red dress will make them easy to spot. Is he lurking among the trees do you think?'

'He's probably watching us through the telephoto lens looking for signs of post-coital activity even as we speak.'

'Do you think so?' Ellen coiled her bare arms around Jon's neck and kissed him. He responded automatically, feeling her full soft lips on his. His stomach lurched with lust as he was enveloped in a wave of warm seductive perfume.

She stood up.

'I do hope he saw that. He's been a complete pain in the neck this week, following me round the office being disgusting – or rather, even more disgusting than usual.'

She set off towards the door then turned to give Jon a gay little wave which he knew was really intended for Ernie. Jon took out a handkerchief and mopped his suddenly sweating brow, then took a cooling gulp of his drink.

When Ellen was nearly back at their room she saw a chambermaid in the corridor and was struck by inspiration. Hastily sliding the room key back into her bag she went up to the woman, smiling.

'I've forgotten my key,' she said, indicating the door to the Minister's room. 'Do you think you could let me in or do I have to go back downstairs?'

'No, I can let you in,' returned the chambermaid, obligingly producing a set of keys. Ellen smiled her thanks then went into the bedroom and closed the door behind her.

After glancing round for a few moments she examined the door. The lock was a simple Yale and she put it on the latch, then left the room, closing the door behind her on its old-fashioned catch. The chambermaid was still in the corridor and she nodded to her before returning to the terrace.

Slipping into her seat she said, 'I've just done something clever.'

Jon felt a frisson of alarm.

'What?'

'Come with me and I'll show you.'

Taking his hand she pulled him to his feet. He followed her upstairs. Luckily, the chambermaid was nowhere in sight as she opened the door to the Minister's room. Dragging him behind her she slipped inside.

'Ellen! This isn't such a good idea,' he exclaimed. 'They could come back upstairs at any minute.' Ellen was already flicking through a pile of papers on the dressing table.

'No, they won't,' she assured him. 'They're having pre-dinner drinks and next they'll have dinner — we've got ages. Don't just stand there, Jon — go through their suitcases.'

Jon groaned but obeyed. There was nothing of real

interest there, although he noted that the Minister bought his underwear at M & S and the glamour model had brought along several sets of frilly lingerie which he wouldn't have minded seeing her in himself.

He joined Ellen where she was busy looking through the clothes hanging in the wardrobe.

'There's nothing of any use to us — come on let's get out of here,' he urged her.

'I'll just . . .'

They both froze at the sound of voices in the corridor. The voices got nearer. Then, to their horror, they heard them right outside the door.

A key turned in the lock.

CHAPTER TWELVE

Jon grabbed Ellen's wrist and dragged her into the wardrobe, pulling the door shut behind them. They stood pressed against each other in the darkness hardly daring to breathe, the sound of voices now much louder as their owners entered the room.

Jon became aware of a thin finger of light penetrating the gloom and realised that there was a crack in the panel of the antique wardrobe door. He peered through it and felt Ellen's hair tickling his chin as she did the same just below him.

Ian Stanstead and his blonde companion were standing by the bed apparently arguing about whether to have sex or not.

'Why can't it wait until after we've eaten?' she asked sulkily. The Minister ran his hands over her naked shoulders.

'Because I can't wait that long,' he breathed hoarsely. 'It's your own fault for wearing that dress. Come on, Karen, it won't take long.'

This wasn't an argument that Jon would personally have used to persuade a woman into bed. Karen, however, seemed prepared to acquiesce.

'I don't know why we couldn't do it before I got ready,' she grumbled as her lover buried his head between her breasts, kissing them noisily.

He emerged long enough to say, 'I was tired after the drive.'

'Just don't mess up my hair and make-up, that's all,' she admonished him. He pulled the front of her dress down revealing a pair of splendid breasts with dark pink nipples.

Jon knew it was a bad idea to continue watching, not from any natural delicacy but because it was guaranteed to arouse him.

But he couldn't help himself.

The Minister bent down and began to push Karen's tight red dress up her thighs, eventually revealing a matching scarlet suspender belt and panties. Hooking his thumbs in the sides of the panties, he dragged them down her legs. When he tried to push her backwards onto the bed she protested, 'No! Not like that – you'll spoil my hair.'

He looked momentarily irritated and demanded, 'How then?'

Turning around she bent forward over the high, old-fashioned bed. Jon sucked in his breath at the sight of her gorgeous rounded backside, a fuzz of very dark pubic hair peeping out from between the smooth globes of her buttocks.

He felt Ellen give a little involuntary wiggle against him and wished she hadn't. He was standing with his chest pressed against her back. She was wearing high-heeled shoes and as his knees were bent to facilitate peering through the crack, her bottom was on a level with his groin.

He was already hard but the wiggle made him grow harder. He hoped Ellen couldn't feel it. He tried to edge away but it was so cramped in the confined space of the wardrobe that it was impossible.

Ian Stanstead unzipped his trousers and jammed himself up against the girl, penetrating her immediately. Jon noted that he hadn't taken the precaution of donning a sheath.

Fastening his hands onto her breasts he laboured away, his trousers around his ankles, while Jon and Ellen watched breathlessly.

Jon didn't think much of his technique. There'd been barely any foreplay and all he was doing now was thrusting in and out of her.

Karen began to moan and move against her lover, throwing her head back and arching her spine. Jon wondered whether she really was becoming aroused or if she'd just decided she'd better show some enthusiasm for the proceedings.

Whichever it was, he wished she'd stop it — it was turning him on too much.

He could smell Ellen's perfume and feel the warmth of her curvaceous body pressed against him. He knew his erection was growing and was unable to stop himself from leaning even closer so it was pushed hard against her backside.

As if of its own volition one of his hands closed on her hip. He knew he only had to slide it upwards and forwards and he'd be able to caress her luscious breasts, tease them and stroke them until the nipples hardened . . .

He was still watching the couple bent over the bed but his attention had been distracted by the delectable body so close to his own. It was reclaimed when the Minister suddenly let out a strangled cry and pumped away even faster, his eyes bulging and the veins standing out on his neck.

The couple disentangled themselves, took it in turns to use the bathroom, then thankfully left the bedroom.

Jon and Ellen remained wedged against each other in the wardrobe until Ellen whispered in a choked voice, 'Do you think it's safe to come out?'

Mustering all his self-control, Jon managed to say, 'I should think so.'

Ellen cautiously opened the wardrobe door and they staggered shakily out. Jon stuck his head round the bedroom door into the corridor and, seeing that the coast was clear, grabbed Ellen's hand and pulled her outside. A few seconds later they were in the safety of their own room.

Ellen collapsed onto the bed — her blue eyes like saucers — while Jon fought a strong desire to join her there and put his not inconsiderable powers of seduction to good use. He was just hesitating when the mobile phone went. Operating on autopilot, he picked it up.

'What are you two doing up there?' demanded Ernie. 'You're poking her aren't you, Wright?'

'Only in your imagination, Ernie,' he managed to say. He moved over to the window. 'The couple you need to photo have just appeared on the terrace. She's in a red dress. Try and get them in an intimate moment.' He knew that would get on Ernie's nerves.

'What, rather than waiting until she's blowing her nose do you mean? Or, even better, when one of them's gone to the bog,' he snapped. 'Do me a favour and let me take the photos.' The call was abruptly terminated.

Jon returned his attention to Ellen who was still looking stunned.

'Ellen, are you okay?' he asked.

She looked at him through glazed eyes.

'I've never seen anyone having sex before,' she admitted. 'It's made me feel really strange.' Jon went over to the mini-bar.

'What we need is a drink.' After placing a sweet Martini in her hand he retired to the window seat. Ellen took a couple of gulps then asked, 'What if they'd wanted something from the wardrobe and found us there?'

'Luckily they didn't, but it was a bit of a close call. I was terrified one of us would sneeze or something.'

Actually no such thought had crossed his mind at the time, but he felt it would be a good idea to get the conversation off sex and onto a more prosaic track. Ellen however was not to be diverted.

'He wasn't very good at it, was he? He didn't kiss her or anything. In fact he didn't seem at all bothered whether she enjoyed herself or not.'

Jon considered several replies but none of them seemed appropriate. She continued, 'He was nearly as bad as Si—' then stopped abruptly, blushing.

'If you're feeling okay maybe we'd better get down there and see if we can eavesdrop on their conversation,' suggested Jon. 'And, anyway, surely you're hungry by now, Ellen? It's a long time since that bag of liquorice allsorts.'

Ellen drained her glass.

'Now you come to mention it, I was looking at the

menu earlier. It's full of really yummy things.'

Kate was having an early night.

Alone in her flat, she brushed her glossy dark blonde hair in front of the mirror. She was wearing a short chiffon nightie in pale turquoise which fastened down the front with three sets of ribbons. Under it was a matching pair of frilly little briefs, also fastened with ribbons.

The transparent chiffon veiled but didn't conceal the firm orbs of her breasts or the darker circles of her nipples. As she moved around the room the nightie swung out around the tops of her thighs, the fine fabric whispering erotically in the silence.

She climbed into bed and switched off the lamp. It wasn't yet dark but only a glimmer of light penetrated the thick curtains. She tried to drift off to sleep but it eluded her.

A faint scraping sound in the hallway made her start. Holding her breath she wondered if she'd imagined it. No, there it was again.

She heard the creak of a floorboard, nearer this time, and sat up in bed, her heart pounding. There was the unmistakable sound of her bedroom door opening and a shadowy figure stood there in the dim light.

Silently swinging her legs off the bed on the side away from him, she tried to stand up but her legs felt wobbly. He stepped into the room and she sensed rather than saw his head turn in her direction.

Managing at last to get to her feet, she stood with her back against the wall and stealthily began to move along it. When he came further into the room she made a dash for the door.

He was too quick for her.

He grabbed her round the waist and they struggled together without a sound except for their erratic breathing. She tried to break free but he was much stronger than she was. His arms felt like iron bands as he lifted her off the ground and lowered her onto the bed.

She fought him frantically, but he managed to pinion her wrists above her head and trap her lower body beneath his. Wrenching one hand free she struck out, catching him a hard blow on the shoulder.

He grunted in shock, then leant sideways and grabbed one of her stockings from the bedside chair. He half knelt, half lay astride her as he wound it around her wrists, then bent her arms back above her head and secured her hands to the headboard.

As Kate twisted and writhed beneath him she felt the hardness of what was undoubtedly a huge erection pressing into her groin. Abruptly she stopped struggling – it would probably only arouse him more.

He'd left the bedroom door ajar and a shaft of light from the hallway lit the room enough for her to see his shadowy figure looming above her in the darkness.

Without warning his hands closed on the front of her chiffon nightdress. With a savage yank he ripped it open, tearing the fine material and exposing her naked breasts.

Kate gasped and then gasped again as the palm of his hand grazed over her puckered nipple. His hand felt dry and warm as it traced the contour of her breast, then closed over it firmly. His other hand glided over her flat stomach, then smoothed over her hip, pausing for a moment to linger on one of the tiny bows which kept her panties fastened.

Unable to help herself, she tried to twist her hips beneath him and throw him off. Her attempt was unsuccessful. He leant forward bringing more weight to bear on her trapped legs, his hard-on pushing further into her mound.

He continued to explore her upper body with his hands, smoothing over every inch of her skin, touching her intimately. He shifted position so he was half lying on her, his erection through his trousers now rubbing hard against the thin fabric of her panties.

She moved her hips hoping to dislodge the hardness pressing so intrusively against her, but he wedged a knee between her legs and prised them apart. She heard the sound of his zip going down and he fumbled a few moments with his clothing. Then she felt the throbbing heat of his manhood pushing up against the entrance to her honeypot.

She strained at her bonds, frantically bucking her hips but he bore down on her and she felt his cock probing its way between her outer lips. There was still a thin film of chiffon between them and she felt the bows on the sides of the panties digging into her hips as slowly, almost imperceptibly, he slipped further into her, stretching the fine fabric to its limit.

He could penetrate no further, although he tried fruitlessly for a few more moments. He slipped out of her and forced her legs wide apart. Kneeling between them he fondled her chiffon covered bush, massaging her hard with the palm of his hand. She felt damp there as the fingers moved slowly between her legs and paused, stroking her over the silky material.

Kate gasped and wriggled then let out a cry as, without warning, he grasped the front of her panties and wrenched them from her, ripping them in the process. Grabbing her by the hips he half lifted her off the bed, then he was inside her, filling her up, leaving no room for anything but savage sexual desire.

He thrust in and out of her hungrily, a raging heat possessing them both while her hips ground upwards into his as he fucked her relentlessly. The heat in her groin spread through her body and she could feel the prickle of perspiration between her breasts. He angled his thrusts for maximum clitoral stimulation and she felt the world slipping away from her as with a series of breathless, gasping shudders she climaxed.

While she was still shaking with pleasure he made three last forceful thrusts, then came himself with a choking inarticulate cry.

He collapsed onto her, breathing hard for a while, then he spoke for the first time, 'Are you alright, darling?'

'I will be when you've untied me.' He obligingly undid the stocking then gently rubbed her wrists. 'That's better,' she murmured. 'You wretch, James. When you gave me this nightie yesterday you didn't tell I was only going to get to wear it once before you ripped it to shreds.'

He chuckled softly, then leant over and kissed her.

'I'll buy you another,' he promised.

Jon and Ellen had a drink on the terrace, still slightly stunned after what they'd witnessed from the wardrobe.

When the waiter escorted them into the restaurant, he led the way to a table on the other side of the room from their quarry. Ellen fluttered her eyelashes winsomely.

'Do you think we could have that table over there?' she asked, indicating the one next to Ian and Karen.

'Certainly, Madam,' he returned obligingly. He presented them both with huge menus then left them alone to make their choice.

Ellen pored over hers with total concentration. Vernon had warned them to eat and drink frugally but Ellen had no intention of starving herself to meet that particular directive.

After they'd ordered, the waiter enquired, 'And the wine – perhaps Madam would like some champagne?'

'No thank you,' she returned cheerfully, knowing that meant someone had spotted the confetti. 'It's too dry for me.'

'Perhaps a bottle of Asti Spumante?' he asked solicitously.

Jon was in mid-perusal of the wine list. He'd been thinking of a bottle of claret, but Ellen looked so pleased by the suggestion of something sweet and sparkling that he nodded. He didn't like the stuff

INDECENT

himself but it was probably better if he kept a clear head.

The couple at the next table didn't talk much, so Ellen chatted gaily away while she enjoyed her meal.

'This is all so lovely,' she commented, draining her third glass of wine.

Jon was busy thinking what beautiful shoulders she had and how the tops of her creamy breasts looked so inviting rising from the low-cut front of Kate's expensive black evening dress. There was a rosy glow to her smooth skin and her round blue eyes shone as she related the story of one of her blind dates.

He'd always thought she was attractive, but tonight she seemed like the most lusciously desirable female he'd ever encountered and later they'd be sharing the same bed...

He came back down to earth as she asked him, 'Are you having a pudding? Ooh, they've got crêpe suzettes *and* chocolate mousse. I can't decide which I'd rather have.' In the end she had both, eating one while the waiter flambéed the other.

Jon refused a pudding and drank his coffee rather morosely, heartily wishing he was back in his flat in London. How could he bear to spend the night in the same bed and not try to screw her? But he knew she'd suggested he come instead of Ernie because she hadn't wanted to spend the weekend fighting off unwanted advances. She'd even told him ingenuously that she felt safe with him.

Gloomily he watched her spooning down the last morsel of crêpe suzette, then she leaned back contentedly in her chair smiling beatifically.

The couple at the next table had finished eating too and at last began an interesting conversation. It appeared that the shapely Karen had aspirations towards being an actress and that the Minister had promised to arrange a screen test with a friend of his in the film industry. No date had yet been set and she seemed to find this annoying.

'You promised, Ian,' she insisted. 'In fact you've been promising for weeks. What's the hold-up this time?'

She was talking more loudly than he was and they were unable to hear his reply. Whatever it was it didn't appear to placate her and she pushed her chair back abruptly saying, 'I'm going to powder my nose.'

Ellen waited a few moments then followed her. Karen was in one of the cubicles when she entered the chintzy toilets, but she soon emerged and joined Ellen at the mirror. Ellen tried not to think about the fact that a couple of hours earlier she'd been crouched in a wardrobe watching this woman being screwed rather ineptly from behind.

Instead she smiled at her.

'Did you enjoy your meal?' she asked. 'Mine was delicious.'

'Yes thanks. You must have enjoyed yours, I noticed you had two sweets.' She patted her hips. 'I wouldn't dare have even one or it'd go straight there.'

'Me too, I'll have to starve myself for a week to compensate for being so greedy.' They both attended to their make-up in silence for a few moments. Ellen

INDECENT

had left a few flakes of confetti in her bag in anticipation of such an occasion. She allowed a couple of them to drift down onto the surface of the vanity unit. The other woman wasn't slow to notice.

'Ooh, you're on your honeymoon.' Ellen lowered her lashes and tried to look embarrassed.

'Yes we are, but we're trying to keep it a secret,' she murmured untruthfully.

'You lucky thing. Your fella's really good-looking. I noticed him while we were eating. He obviously can't wait to get you upstairs. He was undressing you with his eyes.'

'Was he?' she asked startled. Then remembering the purpose of this conversation, 'Is that your husband you're with?'

'No.' Karen looked glumly at her reflection in the mirror. 'He's someone else's at the moment actually. But we will be getting married as soon as he can get a divorce,' she added lamely, as if regretting her frankness.

I'll bet, thought Ellen. Aloud she said, 'Are you staying here long?'

'Just until Sunday.' Karen closed her bag with a snap. 'Better get back – bye.'

When Ellen returned to the table the couple had gone so she swiftly related her conversation to Jon, omitting the reference to him undressing her with his eyes.

'He'd be furious if he knew she was being so indiscreet to a total stranger,' grinned Jon. 'I think they've gone into the bar, shall we follow them?'

A pianist was playing some smoky jazz in the dimly lit bar and one couple were dancing close together on the tiny dance floor. They were unable to get close enough to hear the conversation between the Minister and his girlfriend as the tables were too far apart, but they appeared to be arguing again.

When Karen marched determinedly onto the dance floor followed by her clearly reluctant lover, Ellen grabbed Jon's hand.

'Come on, we might be able to hear what they're saying.'

Jon stayed in his seat alarmed to think what might happen if they danced close together. It had been difficult enough losing his earlier erection.

'I'm too full,' he protested weakly. A passing waiter stared at him disbelievingly. Ellen giggled.

'He thinks you're being churlish – and so do I. After all we are on our honeymoon.'

Jon groaned.

'Ellen, I think there's something we should talk about.'

'Later. Look, Jon, they're having a really heated argument. We've just got to find out what it's about.'

Reluctantly he allowed her to pull him to his feet and they joined the others on the dance floor. She wound her arms around his neck while he tried to keep their lower bodies as far apart as possible. No easy matter.

They manoeuvred themselves close to the other couple and listened hard. Karen, it appeared, was finding the evening dull and wanted to set off in search of night life. The Right Honourable Member, however, wanted to go up to bed. Presumably, thought Jon, so he could do something dishonourable with his member.

INDECENT

Jon's sympathies were with the other man. He closed his eyes and wondered if he could manage to leave the hotel without anyone noticing and go and doss down with Ernie, however repellent the idea and even if Ernie did snore.

Or he could sleep in the car. Anything was better than tossing and turning next to Ellen as she slept peacefully and provocatively beside him. Perhaps she'd be nude, or in a flimsy little nightdress...

The couple left the dance floor, the Minister leading a sullen-looking Karen away by the hand. Jon and Ellen watched them go, dancing their way to the other side of the floor to see if they went upstairs. They did.

'Looks like he got his way,' commented Jon. 'Let's go and have another drink.' Ellen pulled him closer, her breasts flattened against his chest. He could feel the hard points of her nipples as she moved against him.

'Let's just dance for a while, I'm really enjoying myself.' She gazed kittenishly upwards at him. He could tell by her slightly unfocused gaze that she was feeling the effect of the pre-dinner drinks, five glasses of Asti Spumante and two Cointreaus she'd consumed.

Firmly, he unwound her arms from around his neck and led her back to the table saying, 'I need another drink.'

'Shall we go back out to the terrace then?' asked Ellen. 'It's hot in here.'

The evening was cool and sweetly scented. Ellen broke a flower from a climbing rose which swarmed up the lichen-covered wall near to their table and inhaled deeply. The night was full of unfamiliar sounds to those accustomed to the rumble of traffic. Something among the trees let out a high-pitched primaeval cry, making Ellen jump.

'That's probably Ernie,' she giggled.

A waiter was clearing the table next to them as Ellen said, 'Shall we go up to bed?'

She took his hand between both hers and, leaning forward, kissed him softly on the mouth. Jon pulled away as soon as he felt he decently could, but not before he'd registered the urgent tugging in his groin which signified that his dick was sitting up and taking notice — a state it had been in pretty much all evening.

'You go up and get ready — I'll be up shortly.'

She kissed him again then swayed provocatively off across the terrace, her high heels clicking on the worn flagstones. The waiter was too well trained to gaze after her overtly lustfully, but Jon felt the man's envy enveloping him almost palpably.

If only he knew, he thought moodily.

He sat there and had another drink, aware that the waiter wondered why he was hanging about down here when Ellen was waiting for him upstairs. When he felt that to stay any longer would cause comment he drained his glass of cognac and left the terrace.

'Goodnight, sir,' called the waiter, so did the porter on reception. He knew that both of them would probably have sold their souls to be in his place that night, whereas he would gladly have swapped with them.

He tapped on the door when he arrived upstairs,

the last thing he wanted to do was catch Ellen in a state of undress.

It was worse than that.

She was stretched out on the bed in a vampish pose wearing nothing except Kate's diaphanous nightdress. She was on her side, propped up on an elbow, one shapely leg exposed up to the hip through the split in the side of the flimsy garment.

Jon stood there transfixed, his mouth suddenly dry.

'What are you doing in that?' he asked hoarsely. It took more self-control than he'd ever had to exert in his life not to throw himself onto her and do what he'd been wanting to do all evening. Several times.

She fluttered her eyelashes at him coquettishly.

'What a churlish thing to say to your bride on your wedding night.' A half empty glass beside her on the bedside table and a slight slurring of speech indicated that she was even tipsier than previously. 'I thought you might like to see me in it.'

Jon would have preferred to see her out of it. His hands thrust deep in his pockets and clenched themselves into fists of frustration as he managed to say casually, 'Ellen, I think you've had one too many. Why don't you put something else on, get under the covers and go to sleep? I'm going to take a shower.'

A lacy black suspender belt and a pair of sheer black stockings were thrown over the back of an armchair, seeming to mock him in his frustration.

He strode into the bathroom, stripped off and stood under an icy shower for as long as he could bear it, wrestling with his conscience. This was unusual in itself, Jon wasn't usually troubled by such niceties. Had it been virtually any other woman tucked up in bed in the next room he wouldn't have hesitated to make a determined pass at her.

But there was something about Ellen which made him feel reluctantly chivalrous. Maybe it was because she looked so young. He wasn't sure. He felt that if he railroaded her into having sex with him now when she'd patently had too much to drink, he'd feel like a complete shit — like he'd stolen a lollipop from a child.

When he emerged Ellen was tucked up in bed wearing an outsize black tee-shirt. He fervently hoped that she was also wearing panties.

'Just sit up a moment,' he instructed her, his face set. She did so obediently, watching puzzled as he dragged the old-fashioned bolster from beneath the downy pillows and arranged it down the centre of the bed.

'Wha . . . what are you doing?' she asked bemusedly.

'What I'm doing is trying to stop myself jumping on you the moment I get between the sheets,' he told her grimly. He threw his dressing gown onto a chair and climbed into bed in his briefs, keeping his back turned so she couldn't see the erection even an icy shower had been unable to subdue.

He lay on his back staring resolutely at the ceiling. Ellen sat up and looked over the bolster at him.

'But I want you to jump on me,' she wailed, 'I've been wanting you to all night. Don't you want to make love to me?' Jon lay motionless for a few seconds, then in reply grabbed the bolster and hurled it to the floor. She might hate herself — and possibly him — in the morning but that was just too bad.

No man alive could be expected to turn down an invitation like that.

'I wish you'd mentioned it earlier,' he muttered, reaching across and pulling her into his arms.

She snuggled up against his chest as he wound a hand in her hair, tipped her head back and kissed her deeply, sliding his tongue between her parted lips.

She responded eagerly.

He slipped a hand beneath her voluminous tee-shirt savouring the warmth of her smooth flesh. He found one of her heavy breasts and inhaled sharply at the pleasure of at last getting to fondle it.

She felt wonderful — yielding, scented and very willing.

He stroked her breasts but the tee-shirt kept getting in the way. Reaching downwards he murmured, 'Let's get this off.'

With a sexy little wriggle, she helped him pull it over her head then threw it carelessly onto the floor.

She lay on her back in the large double bed, the light from the bedside lamp falling across her chest and revealing two of the most perfect breasts he'd ever seen, shell-pink nipples pointing sharply upwards.

Bending his head and impatiently pushing a lock of dark hair out of his eyes, he coiled his tongue around one nipple. Licking and circling his way around the tip, he teased it with his tongue until it stood out from the smooth globe of her breast like a small, ripe raspberry. He turned his attention to its twin, pulling it into his mouth and sucking gently with an insistent tugging motion.

She moaned softly beneath him and he felt her hands stroking their way down his back, exploring every bump of his vertebrae. His cock was straining against his briefs, the elastic digging painfully into him. Moving away from her he stripped them off, sighing with relief as his hard-on sprang freely upwards.

Throwing the sheet back, he saw she was wearing a seductive pair of black lace panties. He peeled them down her legs with a practised movement revealing the silken down of her bush. She parted her legs invitingly and he bent his head between them burying his face in her damp, female-scented warmth.

Jon always considered that some of his happiest moments were spent with his tongue between a woman's legs. He knew some men who didn't like it, who claimed not to like the taste or the hot, sharp scent of female arousal.

He loved it.

He lapped, licked and probed his way around her honeypot, exploring every intricate fold he could reach with his tongue. She wriggled and squirmed beneath him emitting little mewing noises of pleasure.

He just couldn't wait any longer.

Dragging himself up on his elbows he positioned himself to enter her.

He felt her fingers brush over his dick, then her

hand closed firmly over it guiding him to exactly the right place. Sliding easily into her warm, tight and very wet little pussy he felt a renewed flood of hot moisture envelop him.

As he established a slow, seductive rhythm he briefly offered up grateful and heartfelt thanks to Vernon.

CHAPTER THIRTEEN

San Francisco. Arguably the most beautiful city in the world. Standing at the window of her suite with its panoramic views across the bay, Liz asked herself again why she lived in London.

Not that she'd actually want to live in San Francisco — too many of the men were gay and the climate wasn't very good. But it was a wonderful city to visit if you lived in Los Angeles. In a way it was more like an east coast or European city, but cleaner and with a buzz of energy she'd never found in Europe.

Ledd was in his own suite sleeping off the valium needed for the plane journey. With great forethought she'd taken possession of his tablets the day before the flight and only allowed him to take five milligrams. She knew that left to his own devices he'd take enough to sedate an elephant and she wanted him sentient and functioning.

She'd effectively distracted him on the way to the airport by going down on him in the limo. Once on the plane she'd made him remove his leather jacket and put it over his lap, then spent most of the hour-long flight fondling his dick and telling him in a low voice what they'd do together once they were in San Francisco.

It had been fairly successful — he'd at least

remained conscious. They'd arrived at lunch-time and he'd acquiesced to her suggestion that he sleep it off ready for a night on the town.

She was interviewing the actor, macho man Chet Wyndham that afternoon. He was on a location shoot in the city and she'd arranged to interview him in his trailer. Sitting at the table by the window Liz reluctantly tore her eyes from the view and looked instead at his photo.

Short and muscular with a beaten up face, he was an action-man actor. She studied the photo carefully. Definitely not her type. Liz liked her men lean and good-looking, she wasn't keen on overdeveloped muscles. She just hoped she could get a good column out of her interview with him.

She commandeered Ledd's limo to take her to the car park where Chet's trailer was temporarily located while some street scenes were being shot.

Every time the car crested one of the many hills there was a whole new view of the city spread out in front of her. While they were stopped at a red light she sat there feeling as if the view had been laid on especially for her.

She could see right down over the business area where the elongated triangle of the Transamerica building stood out from the more traditional architecture of the other skyscrapers. Beyond that the Golden Gate bridge spanned the bay, glinting in the sunlight above the intense blue of the ocean.

It made her feel dissatisfied, she wanted some of this, why couldn't she have it?

She was glad she had taken the limo when she arrived and was told Chet was learning his lines and wouldn't be able to see her until later – his publicist wouldn't commit herself to exactly when.

Hanging around a windy car park wasn't Liz's idea of a good time so she returned to the car, settled herself comfortably in the leather seat and began to draft out a hatchet job. The car was well stocked with drinks and snacks so she opened a bottle of white wine and lit a cigarette to help fuel her creativity.

Eventually, after a wait of over an hour, Liz was conducted into the presence of the actor. The first thing that struck her was the smell. What on earth was it? Someone had obviously been spraying some air freshener around, but beneath that was the fetid odour of what smelt like sweaty socks.

Chet Wyndham, she saw to her delight, was even shorter than she'd been led to believe. About five foot two in his stocking feet. Talking of which... that smell was definitely coming from his socks.

Taking a seat, Liz began her interview. Chet was totally devoid of charm and made no attempt to answer her questions in anything other than monosyllables. This didn't phase her, her features were often based more on her observations than on the interview itself.

He was wearing a ratty old tee-shirt and a pair of camouflage trousers. Sharp-eyed as always, she noticed that he was already running to fat despite his much-hyped musculature.

He was obviously impatient for the interview to be over but she wasn't about to let him off the hook until she was ready. When her next question indicated that he wasn't attractive to women, only to men, he flushed an unpleasant shade of beetroot.

'Are you saying I'm gay?' he demanded angrily.

Then before she could reply he unzipped his trousers and produced a short, thick, very red penis. The unpleasant smell in the room became stronger.

'I can get it up for anything in a skirt,' he told her. 'Even a stuck-up bitch like you. Sit on this and I'll show you whether I'm gay or not.'

Liz glanced at it with distaste.

'No, thank you. Now just one last question. How long have you had a personal hygiene problem?'

Ledd was still asleep when she arrived back at the hotel. The familiar itch was gnawing at her groin. She considered waking him up but decided that if she wanted him on form tonight the longer she left him to sleep the better.

Returning to her own suite she ordered a pot of coffee from room service and began to write her feature. When the coffee arrived she glanced briefly at the waiter, then liking what she saw let her gaze linger on him longer. He was tall and slim, looked about nineteen and had the sort of boyish features she always went for.

'Well now,' she purred as he placed the tray on the table in front of her, 'you're the best-looking man I've seen since I arrived in the city. I suppose you're gay?'

He grinned at her showing his perfect white teeth. When he spoke his voice had an attractive southern twang.

'No, ma'am. I'm the all-American red-blooded boy.'

INDECENT

Liz poured herself a cup of coffee then perched on the edge of the table to sip it, letting her short skirt ride up her shapely thighs.

'Are you now?' she enquired interestedly. 'Then what are you doing in San Francisco?'

'I'm here because I heard there was a shortage of us old-fashioned boys who prefer women.'

Hmm, this was interesting.

'And do the ladies reward you well for your services?'

He looked shocked and a little offended.

'I don't do it for money, ma'am. I just like to enjoy myself.'

Liz uncrossed her stockinged legs, then crossed them again.

'Would you like to enjoy yourself now?' she asked softly.

When Ellen woke up the next morning she had a raging thirst. Reaching for the glass on the bedside table she took a gulp then nearly spat it out. Cointreau didn't taste as good first thing in the morning as it did last thing at night.

Climbing unsteadily out of bed she went into the bathroom and drank a glass of water, sitting on the edge of the bath while she mentally reviewed the events of the night before.

Oh dear, she hadn't really intended to sleep with Jon. But after a couple of drinks her resolve not to do it with anyone from work had evaporated. She'd always found him attractive and never more so than last night.

Watching the couple next door screwing had been

a strange but arousing experience. She wasn't sure whether it was that which sparked off the demanding heat in her groin, or kissing Jon on the terrace, or possibly both.

Prior to the weekend she'd just been looking forward to enjoying a weekend in a luxury hotel at the paper's expense. Sometime over dinner she'd decided she wanted Jon to make love to her.

Jon always dressed well, unusual in itself for a journalist. Yesterday evening he had been wearing a light-coloured linen suit which he looked good in. His freshly washed dark hair flopped over his brow in the most engaging way and she had it on good authority that his slim, long-fingered hands knew their way around the female erogenous zones.

It was too good an opportunity to miss.

She had to admit that last night had been outstanding, even among her recent pleasurable experiences. The memory of it made her shiver with lust and press her thighs together. She could feel her clit swelling as she briefly relived some of the highlights and was unable to stop herself opening her legs and bearing down on the cold marble surface of the bath surround.

She suddenly caught sight of her reflection in one of the mirrored walls and was horrified. Imperfectly removed eye make-up was streaked below her eyes and her hair was a limp mass of wildly tangled curls. Better take some remedial action before Jon saw her again.

After cleaning her teeth she stepped under the shower and lathered her hair. The most important thing was not to let Ernie know, otherwise it would be all round the paper. Jon himself she knew was discreet. It was always Ernie who told everyone how long he'd sat around in a parked car waiting for his colleague's reappearance.

She was just rinsing soap out of her eyes when the shower cubicle door slid open behind her and she felt herself pulled backwards against a tall, hard body.

'You've missed a bit,' he said, reaching for the soap.

An hour later Ellen sat on the edge of the bed wrapped in a thick snowy towel, her damp hair tumbling around her shoulders. She dialled Ernie's number on the mobile phone.

'Hi, Ernie, it's Ellen. Is Jon with you by any chance? No? He must be with that redheaded receptionist then. I hope he manages to make it back up here without anyone noticing or it'll look a bit odd.'

In the act of pulling a tee-shirt down over his shoulders Jon stifled a burst of laughter.

'Honestly, Ernie, he was like a dog on heat hovering around her yesterday evening. He spent more time leaning over the reception desk than he did with me. Then when we got back up to the room he said, "See you tomorrow," and vanished.'

There was a pause and she pulled a face at whatever Ernie was saying before she continued, 'The worst thing is that I'm absolutely starving and I can hardly go down to breakfast on my own if we're supposed to be a honeymoon couple. Oh, just hold on a minute . . . Jon, where have you been? We've nearly missed breakfast. Talk to you later, Ernie.'

Over her large cooked breakfast, the size and content of which made Jon shudder, Ellen asked, 'What shall we do today?'

Jon was toying rather unenthusiastically with a croissant – he didn't usually eat anything until lunch-time.

'We can do whatever you'd like to do. Explore some of the surrounding countryside perhaps, then have lunch at a pub somewhere.' He looked at her lustfully. 'Maybe come back here and spend the afternoon in bed. The possibilities are endless.'

Buttering her third slice of toast then spreading it liberally with marmalade Ellen asked, 'Do you think we're going to be able to shake Ernie for the day? I don't think I can face his customary lewd insinuations and he's bound to want to do whatever we're doing.'

'Not if I have anything to do with it. I'll give him a call when we get back upstairs.'

Jon told Ernie that the Minister and his girlfriend were planning a picnic, and if their conversation of the evening before was anything to go by were intending to have carnal knowledge of each other on some grassy bank. Could Ernie manage to get photos?

'I could hear him dribbling with anticipation,' commented Jon as he put the phone down. 'Now all we have to do is tell him when they're leaving so he can tail them and the day's our own. There's nothing much we can do ourselves until tonight after all.'

Jon lay on his back with his hands behind his head enjoying the novel sensation of having his dick

INDECENT

sprinkled with sweet sherry.

Sitting astride his chest with her knees on the bed and her back to him, Ellen concentrated single-mindedly on the task at hand. When his member had been doused liberally enough to meet with her satisfaction she bent forward, wriggled the tip of her tongue under his balls and began licking.

As she bent forward, her bottom rose in the air giving him a close-up view of the petal-pink folds of her female parts. Removing his hands from behind his head he cupped her curvaceous little rump and gently separated her buttocks even further so that she was completely exposed to his gaze.

He could see the bud of her clitoris, darker pink than the surrounding intricate folds of her honeypot, and there was a creamy slick of moisture over the whole area which indicated that he wasn't the only one enjoying himself.

Having licked up every drop of the sherry from around Jon's balls, Ellen turned her attention to his cock. Her tongue flickered this way and that, licking its way around his rock-hard column, like a contented cat lapping cream.

Jon couldn't ever remember having a woman with such a capacity for sensual pleasure. She practically purred whenever he touched her, opening herself up to him and exhibiting an enthusiastic enjoyment for the more esoteric aspects of sex.

But in other ways she was such an innocent. He'd introduced her to several new pleasures and was surprised to discover she'd never tried them before.

She continued to wind her tongue around his cock

while he groaned and tried not to shift around on the bed too much. With one hand he began to trace the crease between the cheeks of her bottom. He followed it downwards, circling the rosy, puckered indentation of her anus with the tip of his forefinger. Moving further downwards he brushed lightly over the first wispy fronds of her bush, then his forefinger reached the slippery outer lips of her sex.

He stroked his way around the area, delicately probing her hidden recesses and sending uncontrollable shivers of pleasure through her. She became wetter as he slid one finger inside her, moving it this way and that to caress the internal walls of her hidden cavern. His thumb found her clit and began to stimulate it just as she took the tip of his cock between her parted lips.

Having licked up all the sherry she began to suck away, applying a heart-stopping erotic suction with her full lips. He moaned involuntarily as she worked more and more of him inside her mouth until he could feel the end of his cock wedged up against the back of her throat.

Grasping her by the hips he pulled her backwards and inserted the tip of his tongue into her. While she slid his dick in and out of her mouth he sucked away at her clit.

She began to gasp loudly then her body went rigid as she climaxed, pushing her pussy hard against him. His face pleasurably buried in Ellen's private parts, it only took a few more moments of ministrations from her persuasive mouth before he came. The force of his orgasm was so great that his cock sprang out of her mouth and his hot liquid spurted up over her full breasts, exciting him all the more.

A while later Ellen lay at right angles to him, her head on his stomach while she lazily examined his cock. Running her finger over the thick, plum-like head she murmured ingenuously, 'It's very big Jon, especially around the tip. And I particularly like the way this little ridge runs down behind the head.' She ran her fingernail gently along the length of it then turned her face towards him, 'Or am I being too personal? If I'm embarrassing you just say so.'

He smiled at her.

'There isn't a man with a heartbeat who doesn't enjoy having his dick admired. You can keep it up all afternoon as far as I'm concern—'

The bedside telephone chose that moment to ring. They'd taken the precaution of switching off the mobile phone but hadn't expected any calls on the hotel phone.

It was the receptionist.

'Mr Wright? You have a visitor – a Mr Holdgate. Shall I send him up?'

'No!' exclaimed Jon hastily. 'Would someone show him onto the terrace please. I'll be down in a few minutes.'

'Shit,' he said as he put the phone down. 'Ernie's downstairs.'

'Oh no! What time is it?' Jon sat up and reached for his watch from the bedside table.

'Five o' clock. Damn bloody Ernie to hell. I'd better get down there before he comes banging on the door.'

Dropping a kiss on her shoulder, Jon strode into the bathroom and stepped under the shower, being careful to keep his hair dry. As he came out Ellen went in. She was still under there when he was ready to go.

'I'll join you in a few minutes,' she called over the sound of the running water. 'Say I've gone out for a walk. I'll go out the back way and circle round. Oh and Jon . . . will you order me some afternoon tea please?'

Ernie was hot and disgruntled.

'They don't serve drinks to non-residents,' he said resentfully, 'and I'm gasping for a pint.'

Jon beckoned to the hovering waiter.

'Did you get any photos?' he asked as soon as the man was out of earshot.

'Naw. It was a bleeding wild-goose chase. The nearest they got to stripping off was when she took her sunglasses off. One of the fittest bints I've ever seen mind you — stacked, man, absolutely stacked.'

An arousing memory of Karen bending over the bed with her generous breasts hanging out of her dress assailed Jon as Ernie continued to complain.

'They spent most of the day driving round the countryside. I've seen enough poxy fields and trees today to last me the rest of my life. I left them looking round some shithole called Broadway. They'd obviously decided not to have a quickie in the woods after all. They seemed to be arguing most of the time anyway.'

Reflecting that the peace and beauty of the Cotswolds scenery was apparently wasted on his colleague, Jon wished Ellen would put in an appearance.

'Where's Ellen?' demanded Ernie, as if reading his mind.

'Gone for a walk.'

'What have you been up to you dirty bastard?' continued the photographer. 'She said you were off poking some red haired receptionist last night. What's the matter with you, man? Why didn't you get your leg over Lolita while you had the chance?'

'Unlike you, Ernie, some of us think that a certain amount of cooperation on the woman's part helps things along,' he returned mildly. 'Ellen wasn't interested.'

Thankfully, at that moment Ellen emerged from the trees on the far side of the lawn. She strolled across the grass carrying an armful of wild flowers. Jon had to admire her little start of surprise, followed by a cheerful wave as she seemed to spot them for the first time.

He beckoned the waiter and ordered afternoon tea.

'Hi, Ernie,' she greeted the photographer. 'Did you get the photos?' Jon had to endure Ernie's tale of woe again as Ellen tucked into her scones. When Ernie had finished complaining he fixed Ellen with a lascivious leer.

'What's this I hear about you turning super-dick here down? That must have been a first for him. What was all that snogging on the terrace about then? That's prick-teasing in my book.'

Ellen spooned some more cream onto a scone.

'A woman blowing her nose in the same room is prick-teasing to hear you talk, Ernie. Jon and I were just acting out our role as a honeymoon couple.

Unlike you, Jon doesn't think that a kiss means sex is automatically on the agenda. In fact, Ernie, I suspect that a woman just talking to you makes you think sex is on offer — despite the overwhelming evidence to the contrary.'

Ernie downed the last of his pint, belched and wiped his mouth with the back of his hand.

'You needn't be lonely tonight, Lolita. Smuggle me into your room and I'll give you the seeing-to of a lifetime.'

Ellen grimaced and swallowed the last morsel of scone.

'You're putting me off my tea,' she complained. 'Anyway it's time you were going, Jon and I have work to do.'

Ernie stood up and prepared to take his leave.

'You don't know what you're missing.'

'Yes and I'd prefer to keep it that way. Bye, Ernie.'

'They aren't enjoying their weekend very much are they?' asked Ellen in a low voice as they lingered over coffee.

The Minister and his girlfriend had barely exchanged a word over dinner. He looked resentful and she looked sullen.

'Unlike us,' returned Jon, stroking her bare shoulders where they rose enticingly from a cream dress with a tight-boned bodice. It was something else she'd borrowed from Kate. Slightly too tight, the dress pushed her satin-skinned breasts upwards, endowing her with an even deeper cleavage than usual.

As soon as they'd arrived back inside the bedroom

after Ernie had left, they'd fallen on each other breathlessly and had only reluctantly emerged over two hours later to continue their observation of the other couple.

There was a low-voiced altercation going on between the Minister and Karen. Suddenly Karen leapt to her feet and dashed off in the direction of the Ladies.

'Now's my big chance,' murmured Ellen, picking up her bag and following.

Karen was dabbing at her eyes in the mirror.

'Hi,' Ellen greeted her. 'How are you?'

'Okay, I suppose. I won't ask how you are — I saw the way you looked at each other over dinner. It must be wonderful to be so in love.' She took out a peach-coloured lipstick and applied a liberal coating to her wide mouth.

'Aren't you in love?' asked Ellen innocently.

Karen's face crumpled.

'I thought we were but now I'm not so sure. Everything seems to be going wrong this weekend.' She fished out a tissue and blew her nose. 'We must be having a lover's tiff, I suppose.'

'We have them all the time,' Ellen assured her. 'What's yours about?'

'Oh, you know. The future. Where we're going, if you see what I mean.'

Ellen did see what she meant. Unfortunately before she could delve further, the door opened and another woman came in. Karen ran a brush over her hair, gave Ellen a wan smile and left the room.

'She seems pretty much at breaking point,' Ellen told Jon when they'd moved to a secluded table in the bar. 'I think if we get her on her own tomorrow she'll talk to us. She's really fed up with him.' The unhappy couple had already retired upstairs.

'Okay. Let's get up early and lie in wait. A confrontation with the Minister may be on the cards too, depending on what happens. And . . .'

'And what?'

'And if we're going to get up early I think we'd better get an early night.'

She drew his head down and kissed him lingeringly, her tongue probing provocatively into his mouth. Jon pulled her to her feet.

'Unless you want me to push you down on the table and have my evil way with you right now, I think we'd better go upstairs.'

It was with great reluctance that they got out of bed the following morning after spending most of the night in various forms of satisfying sexual activity. Just before they left the room Jon pulled Ellen into his arms.

'We've got to check out by twelve. What do you think the chances are of another session before we leave?' he asked softly.

'Fairly good,' returned Ellen demurely, 'but I suppose it depends on the state of play between the lovebirds next door.'

They passed the Minister on their way down to breakfast. On his way back upstairs, he pushed past them with a face like thunder. In the restaurant they found Karen in floods of tears with a couple of waitresses hovering uncertainly nearby.

They looked deeply relieved when Ellen and Jon

joined her at the table. Ellen put her arm round the other girl's shoulders.

'What's the matter? Have you had another argument?'

'No, it's much worse than that,' the girl sobbed.

'It can't be that bad,' said Ellen soothingly. 'Why don't you tell us about it.'

Karen did.

She was pregnant.

The Minister didn't want to know.

At the start of their relationship he'd told her he was leaving his wife and that they'd get married as soon as he was divorced, but the weeks had passed and he hadn't done so. Yesterday she'd tried to force the issue but he'd become angry and refused to discuss it. She hadn't wanted to admit she was pregnant until he'd separated from his wife, but that morning in desperation she'd told him.

'He said it wasn't his!' she wailed. 'But it is! There hasn't been anyone else and he always refused to wear a johnny. He said it spoiled it for him.'

She blew her nose noisily.

'He's just dumped me. He told me never to try and contact him or he'd tell everyone I was a whore and he'd paid me. Paid me! That's a laugh! I've never met anyone tighter with money — he never wanted to take me out anywhere. And he's not even going to drive me back to London. Now how am I going to get home? I haven't any money with me. And how am I going to be able to support a baby on my own? He earns plenty of money — he's an MP.'

Ellen and Jon exchanged speaking glances over her head. At that moment Jon saw the Minister looking as if the hounds of hell were on his heels, dashing along the driveway towards the car park with his suitcase in his hand.

'I think maybe we can help you,' he assured her.

They let Karen continue to believe that they were on their honeymoon, but admitted to being journalists. In her current overemotional state she readily agreed to sell them the exclusive story.

Over several pots of coffee, and in Ellen's case a large plate of toast, she told them the whole story, including some wonderfully titillating details about the Minister's sexual preferences.

Early on in the proceedings, Jon went to summon Ernie to come and take some photos.

'Don't put in an appearance until lunch-time,' Jon warned him. 'I told her you were driving up from London. Oh and Ernie, the Right Honourable Member has buggered off and left her stranded and we're in the MX5, so will you be able to give her a lift?'

'I'll give her a lift alright – on the end of my pr—'

'I know it'll mean changing the habit of a lifetime but try not to behave like a complete dickhead, we need to keep her sweet for a while. This one will run and run.'

It took all morning to coax the full story out of Karen and they had to check out of the room without getting a chance to tear each other's clothes off again. On the drive home Jon bemoaned the fact at length and made it quite clear that as far as he was concerned they owed each other at least one more interlude.

Ellen eventually arrived back at Kate's flat

around nine. She'd gone into work to write up the story while Jon, with Ernie in tow, went round to confront Ian Stanstead and get a statement.

It would make the front page tomorrow.

Kate was out so she had a bath then settled down on the sofa with a plate of sandwiches to watch TV. The bell went at around ten o'clock – it was Jon with the suitcase which she'd left in his car. He followed her into the sitting room and accepted a drink.

'Vernon will be awarding us gold stars for this one,' Jon predicted, his eyes lingering on the spot where her dressing gown gaped open as she bent forward to pour his whisky. 'In fact I'm thinking of awarding a few gold stars myself,' he continued.

He caught her wrist and pulled her onto his knee, his hand sliding up her naked thigh.

'What for?' she asked innocently.

'For the most fantastic legs.' His other hand found its way into the front of her dressing gown. 'And the most luscious breasts.'

Her dressing gown fell open and he buried his head between her breasts, kissing his way down her cleavage.

'We have some unfinished business,' he murmured.

'Do we?' she asked breathlessly.

'You know we do.'

He rolled his palm over her nipple, which immediately stood to attention in response to the lazy caress. Her head fell back and he kissed her throat, slipping her dressing gown off her shoulders as he did so. She pulled it back up.

'Not here.'

'Where then?' Standing up she took his hand, holding her dressing gown closed with the other.

'This way.'

They were just walking down the hall when Kate came in through the front door. Ellen hastily fastened her dressing gown.

'Hi, did you get the story?'

'We certainly did,' Ellen confirmed happily. 'We're going to be teacher's pets tomorrow.'

'Were you just arriving or leaving, Jon?'

Jon looked enquiringly at Ellen.

'Leaving,' she said regretfully. She saw him to the door while Kate vanished into her bedroom.

'The walls are paper thin,' she whispered. He bent down and kissed her hard on the lips.

'Okay, but it's still unfinished business as far as I'm concerned. See you tomorrow, Lolita.'

Ellen returned to the sitting room where Kate joined her a few minutes later.

'So how was the last of the red hot lovers on a scale from one to ten?'

Ellen widened her eyes innocently.

'Whatever makes you think that I'd know?'

'Ellen you're more transparent than a sheet of plate glass. You've had the pleasure of more than his company this weekend — it's written all over you. And it looked very much like my arrival interrupted a repeat performance.'

Ellen smiled dreamily.

'It was a wonderful weekend,' she admitted.

CHAPTER FOURTEEN

The dozen men in the room were kneeling side by side in a line. They were all naked, blindfolded and in varying states of sexual arousal. Four leather-clad women prowled up and down the line, their high-heeled boots making a staccato tapping noise on the stone-flagged floor.

One woman carried a riding crop, another a whip, the third a cane and the last one a leather belt. The kneeling men never knew what was coming next. Sometimes it was a blow, sometimes a caress.

One of the men felt the welcome moist warmth of a woman's mouth gliding up and down his cock then sucking it insistently. He began to relax, his head dropping backwards as his arousal mounted. Now her tongue coiled itself around the tip, flickering and licking lasciviously. He let out a groan of pleasure which was suddenly changed to a yelp of pain as the leather belt landed squarely on his buttocks.

Another man felt a leather-gloved hand stroking the back of his thighs, then it moved between his legs to caress his balls. He shuddered ecstatically as gentle fingertips feathered around the base of his shaft, then began to work their way upwards. He was just opening his legs further to give the hand greater access when he felt the stinging flick of a whip across his cock.

Whenever they came to this place the men never knew what to expect — it was different every time.

They only knew that in the course of a few short hours they would experience both heaven and hell.

Ledd liked Fisherman's Wharf. After hearing about it from one of the bodyguards he insisted they pay it a visit that evening. Liz on the other hand wanted to dine at one of the restaurants in the Ghirardelli centre where they could eat overlooking the bay. In the end they agreed to do both.

They made an incongruous couple. Ledd a leather-clad teenager with a face like a depraved angel, his arm thrown casually around Liz, elegant and soignée in her short silk dress and high-heeled shoes.

They wandered around mingling with the crowds, the two bodyguards just behind them.

'It's just like Margate,' he said enthusiastically.

'I wouldn't know.'

'C'mon doll — you must have been to Margate.'

'Certainly not. My family holidayed in the Dordogne.'

Ledd paused in front of a ghost train, a happy smile on his usually sullen features.

'Let's take a ride.'

'Don't be ridiculous.'

He bent down and muttered something in her ear. A couple of minutes later they were climbing into one of the small cars. Liz glanced round and saw the two large bodyguards getting impassively into the car behind. She lost sight of them when their own car cranked slowly through the doors into the pitch blackness beyond.

Ledd was galvanised into immediate action. She heard the sound of his zip going down then his hands closed on her waist.

'Okay, Liz, get ready for the ride of a lifetime.'

Nothing loath, Liz stepped astride him, grasped his shoulders and lowered herself towards his waiting cock. It slipped easily past the loose crotch of her satin camiknickers to bury itself eagerly in her hot, throbbing sex.

Ledd's hands found her breasts as she pushed urgently downwards. Their groans of mutual satisfaction were drowned in the screams issuing from other passengers. The excitement of the ghost train's special effects were wasted on them as they enjoyed a ride of their own.

A sudden flash of fake lightening gave Liz a brief glimpse over Ledd's shoulder of the bodyguards a dozen yards behind. She hoped they hadn't seen her and registered the fact that she was sitting astride Ledd rather than next to him. On the other hand, who gave a stuff?

The sex was fast and furious, the excitement heightened by the fact that they didn't know how soon they'd find themselves precipitated back into the daylight.

Fearing that the ride would finish before he did Ledd slipped his hands beneath Liz's buttocks, giving greater force to her movements.

Matters had just reached an intensely satisfying conclusion when their car began to slow down. Liz just managed to disengage herself and resume her seat beside Ledd before the car swung out into the fresh evening air.

Kate paused for a minute by Ellen's desk, raising her voice to make herself heard over the sound of ringing phones and other raised voices.

'I keep forgetting to ask you — how's the flat-hunting going?'

'It's not really at the moment,' said Ellen guiltily. It had been over a fortnight since she'd been to look at one.

'This isn't a hint,' Kate assured her. 'It's just that a one-bedroom flat in my building has become vacant — the previous tenant did a midnight move. If you're interested you'll have to act fast before it's advertised.'

'I'm interested,' confirmed Ellen.

'Fine, I'll just get you the number.'

Kate walked off down the office just as Jon sauntered up and perched on the edge of Ellen's desk with his hands in his pockets.

'Morning, Lolita,' he greeted her casually.

'Morning,' she returned, busying herself with a pile of papers and not looking up.

It was the Wednesday after their weekend in the Cotswolds and Jon was beginning to think Ellen was avoiding him. On Monday they'd both been away from the office on different stories and when he'd phoned the flat in the evening Kate had told him Ellen was out. On Tuesday he'd suggested lunch or a drink after work, but she'd been evasive.

Now she kept her head down and he got the distinct impression that she wished he'd go away.

INDECENT

'Are you doing anything tonight?' he asked her. 'I thought we might go out for a meal.' She glanced up briefly.

'I'm doing something actually.'

'How about tomorrow, then?' he persisted. At that moment Vernon appeared.

'Ellen my dear, can you come into my office for a moment please?'

Ellen flashed a vague smile over her shoulder at Jon as she followed Vernon down the office, leaving him feeling faintly puzzled. Was she avoiding him and if so why?

She was out of the office for the rest of the day so he didn't get a chance to pursue the matter.

When he arrived home in the early evening there was a letter from Dana waiting for him. He wasn't particularly surprised to read that she wasn't coming back to England in the foreseeable future. She told him she'd met and fallen for the Greek owner of a hotel and leisure complex. She was going to run the health club for him and had already moved into his apartment.

Jon took it philosophically. He'd never been the only man in Dana's life and recently he seemed to have spent most of his time in her company terrified out of his wits for one reason or another.

And, anyway, since the weekend the only thing he'd been able to think about was Ellen.

The bell rang at that moment and when he answered the door he wasn't particularly pleased to see Ernie. For a fleeting moment he'd hoped it might be Ellen.

'What do you want?' he asked ungraciously as the

photographer barged his way in without waiting for an invitation.

'We've got to get up to Milton Keynes man,' Ernie told him. 'There's been a major train crash — hundreds dead and so on. You'd just left the office when it came in so Vernon told me to pick you up and get up there.'

Jon groaned out loud, he'd been looking forward to a couple of beers and a quiet evening and he wanted to try phoning Ellen again. In any case, he hated reporting accidents, it wasn't usually his area but several of the paper's staff were on holiday at the moment.

He went into the bedroom to get his jacket and when he came out he found Ernie reading Dana's letter.

'Hey, one of your bints has ditched you!' gloated the photographer. 'That must be a first. Which one's Dana?'

Briefly Jon contemplated thumping his colleague but rejected the idea as not being worth the trouble. Instead he asked mildly, 'Are we going, or would you like to read my shopping list too?'

Ernie dropped the letter and led the way out of the flat chortling. As they walked out to the car he said, 'Dana. Isn't she the redhead who works at that posh health club? The one with bazookas like . . .'

Tuning Ernie out Jon thought that he really ought to buy a Walkman to wear on these occasions.

Ellen liked the flat which had just fallen vacant and signed the lease on the spot. It would be nice to have her own place, even though she'd enjoyed staying with Kate. She could move in at the weekend by simply packing her cases and carrying them down a couple of floors.

As she bathed that evening she thought about Jon. He'd made it clear that he wanted them to get together again for more of the fantastic sex they'd enjoyed at the weekend.

She was very tempted.

It was the best sex she'd ever had, even including the various encounters of the last few weeks. Just the memory of it made her nipples harden as she dreamily soaped them. But if she saw much more of Jon on an intimate level he might become a habit she wouldn't want to give up.

And if they started seeing a lot of each other he might get like Simon, always finding fault with her and criticising her clothes. No, it was a much better idea to keep last weekend as a wonderful memory.

What a pity sex wasn't always as good as that. It made her wish she hadn't stayed with Simon so long because her recent experiences had shown her that he was absolutely lousy in bed. They'd always done exactly the same things in the same order and the occasional time that she'd tried to introduce a variation he'd been angry with her.

Jon on the other hand seemed to have an inexhaustible sexual repertoire. She suspected they'd only scratched the surface of the pleasurable things they could try together.

Sighing, Ellen stretched one of her shapely legs out of the water and began to sponge it. Oh well, she had another blind date on Saturday – but she had to admit she wasn't particularly looking forward to it.

Liz was fuming. As if it wasn't bad enough that Ledd was out of action for a while every time they flew, he was also jittery just before each appearance. She hadn't been with him just before the Los Angeles gig so it was news to her.

It was the San Francisco concert that evening and around six she'd gone down the hallway to his suite. For once he was alone and obviously trying to decide what to wear. He greeted her in a preoccupied manner and continued to rifle through his wardrobe.

Stretching out sinuously on the bed she said imperiously, 'Stop doing that. I want to fuck.' She was taken aback when, without looking round, he muttered, 'Later, Liz, I'm too strung out at the moment.'

'What the hell does that mean?' she demanded dangerously.

'It means that the only thing on my mind at the moment is the concert. We'll do it later, okay?'

'No, it's not okay.'

Considerably put out, Liz stalked out of the room and returned to her own suite. She ordered a drink from room service hoping it would be the waiter whose services she'd availed herself of before.

It wasn't.

The man who brought her cocktail looked like a small acned rodent and was no use to her at all. She'd have to find somebody else.

Ledd was surprised when she joined him in the limo later.

'Didn't think you'd want to come,' he mumbled.

'Oh, I wouldn't miss it for anything,' she assured him.

While the support band were on she prowled around backstage sipping a glass of iced vodka, carefully appraising all the men. She eventually decided on one of the support band's roadies and engaged him in conversation. He was respectful, flattered and very attractive. Of course he could still be gay.

She moved nearer, bending forward for him to light her cigarette and giving him a close-up of her cleavage. His reaction was gratifying and indicated that he was very definitely heterosexual.

Forty minutes later Sledgehammer swept onto the stage and launched into their first number. Backstage at exactly the same time Liz bent over an amp, dropped her satin camiknickers and opened her legs invitingly. The young roadie couldn't believe his luck. He was getting to shaft Ledd Lomas's lady just behind the stage where the singer was giving it his all in front of a massive crowd.

The roadie gave it his all too.

Rising to the occasion he thrust eagerly inside her and, while the sound of the band echoed around them, began moving vigorously in and out.

She had the most gorgeous bum he'd ever seen — firm, well-rounded and tapering to a narrow waist. His balls made a slapping sound against her buttocks with each thrust and he fondled her breasts as he screwed her, teasing her hard nipples with the palm of his hand.

If he'd anticipated a quick fuck he was in for a surprise. At the end of the first number Liz stood upright and let him slip out of her. Elegantly she lay on her back on the amp, knees apart, legs bent. It was at just the right height for him to penetrate her without bending his own knees.

At the end of every song she made him change position until he was too exhausted to screw her any more. He'd come twice and lay slumped on the floor watching her as she masturbated herself to a final climax during the encore.

It was the most exciting thing he'd ever seen as she lay back her legs apart, her closely clipped bush the same chestnut as her hair. Her scarlet-tipped fingers moved against her clit to the same rhythm of Sledgehammer's last number and she climaxed to the sound of wild applause from the audience.

When she'd finished she pulled her camiknickers back up her long legs then pulled a mirror out of her bag to check her appearance. Stepping over the roadie's recumbent body in her high-heeled, scarlet suede shoes she waved a casual goodbye and walked off.

Jon and Ernie were standing by the drinks machine when Ellen sashayed past them, flashing a faint smile at Jon. Both men turned to watch her walk the length of the office.

It was a cool and blustery day and she was wearing a cream angora dress which was moulded to her figure like a second skin. It stopped several inches above the knee and although the neckline was fairly modest her generous breasts pushed against the soft wool in a manner guaranteed to overwhelm the most jaundiced male.

INDECENT

But it was her back view which made Jon and Ernie suspend their conversation. Her buttocks twitched beguilingly against each other under the clinging fabric, the cleft between them clearly defined.

Ernie exhaled feelingly.

'Like jelly on springs, man. Wouldn't you just like to get your prick between those arse cheeks and . . .'

In essence it was pretty much what Jon was thinking but hearing Ernie verbalise it so crudely suddenly made him angry.

'Shut your fucking stupid mouth, Ernie!' he snapped furiously and set off in pursuit of Ellen while the photographer stared after him, his jaw dropping in surprise.

Jon caught up with her by the lifts.

'Ellen, I want to talk to you. How about a drink at lunch-time?'

Ellen pressed the lift button urgently.

'I'm sorry, Jon, I'm doing something.' Jon glanced upwards and saw that the lift was almost at their floor. Grabbing a startled Ellen by the arm he pulled her into the storeroom, closing the door behind them and standing with his back to it.

'Why are you avoiding me?' he demanded. She flushed slightly.

'I'm not.'

'Oh yes you are. Why? I thought we had a great couple of days together last weekend so why will you suddenly not give me the time of day?' Ellen stared uncertainly up at him.

'Jon, I'm on my way to interview someone.'

In the confined space of the storeroom he could

smell her perfume. Instinctively he moved closer so he could feel the heat of her body, then as she didn't move away he put his arms around her, bent his head and kissed her.

The sexual charge between them was so strong that within seconds Jon was rock hard and Ellen's groin felt molten. He felt her breasts pressed against his chest and her hips moving against his as she wound her arms around his neck and kissed him back.

He stroked his way down her spine thinking she felt like a kitten in the fluffy angora dress. His hands moved downwards to cup the globes of her backside, pulling her harder against him.

She wriggled arousingly as he slipped a hand up her dress to caress the soft couple of inches of bare thigh between her panties and stocking top. She opened her legs for him and arched her back, sighing with pleasure as he began to massage her with the palm of his hand. He could feel the crotch of her panties dampening as he rubbed harder and he could hear her breath coming in little gasps.

The door suddenly opened and Kate stepped into the room carrying an armful of files. They hastily separated as she regarded them quizzically.

'Shall I come back later?' she enquired.

Flustered, Ellen smoothed her dress down over her thighs. 'I'm late. I've got to go,' she muttered, then fled from the room.

Jon returned to the office only to be waylaid by Ernie.

'Vernon wants to see us. There's a bomb gone off in . . .' He broke off for a moment then demanded,

INDECENT

'What's that on your jacket?'

Glancing down, Jon saw that his dark jacket was covered in cream fluff from Ellen's dress. He could only be thankful that he was wearing jeans. If he'd been in dark trousers it would have been all over his groin as well. 'You've been giving Ellen one,' accused Ernie triumphantly.

'Don't be so bloody asinine, Ernie,' he growled. 'She brushed past me going through the door. Now I'm covered in bits. Where has this bomb gone off? I wish Dave was back – I hate covering carnage.'

He strode off towards Vernon's room ineffectually brushing at the front of his jacket.

Ellen's blind date on Friday evening was with a Hampstead art restorer. He'd suggested they attend a party given by a friend of his and as Ellen liked parties she'd happily acquiesced to the idea.

She'd had to put up with some teasing from Kate about being found in an embrace in the storeroom with Jon, particularly when she'd asked Kate to say she was out if he rang, which he did several times. Their paths hadn't crossed at work since Wednesday, giving Ellen time to remind herself sternly that their interlude had been strictly a one-off.

Unfortunately she couldn't stop dwelling on it so she hoped the party would be a welcome distraction.

'Who's the lucky man tonight?' asked Kate, as Ellen emerged from her bedroom in a tight, emerald-green silk dress. The dress had a high neckline at the front but swooped down to the waist at the back.

Ellen was wearing it with black high-heeled shoes and black seamed stockings and looked absolutely stunning.

'His name's Daniel and he's taking me to a party,' Ellen informed her, cramming a bottle of perfume into her already overflowing bag. 'I just hope it's a good one.'

'Ernie told me today and I quote, "Jon's been ditched by that fit redhaired bint he's been shagging for the last few months." Do you know anything about it?'

'No, I don't,' Ellen returned truthfully, dragging a brush through her hair. She hoped fervently that it wasn't anything to do with their weekend together. The bell went at that moment. 'That'll be my minicab. See you tomorrow.'

To Ellen's horror, the party turned out to be in honour of a lady harpist who was to give two recitals in the course of the evening. Everyone else there was in formal evening dress and Daniel turned out to be a crashing intellectual snob of mind-numbing magnitude. She had to concede he was quite good-looking in a leonine sort of way, but she felt her eyes glazing whenever he talked to her.

Ignoring his faintly disapproving glances she drank as much wine as she could get her hands on, shamelessly waylaying all passing waiters and wondering whether she could escape before the recital started.

She wasn't so lucky and was forced to endure forty-five minutes of what to her was sheer torture as the lady harpist gave it her all. Daniel patently found her attractive but for some reason she wasn't interested. She didn't know why, but when his hand rested on her bare back she found it repellent.

Maybe it was because she hadn't drunk enough.

Grabbing another drink, she made an effort to join in the conversation. She was standing with a group of people and thought quite honestly they might as well have been talking Greek as they discussed classical music. The women all seemed to be staring at her disapprovingly and the men lustfully. When she cheerfully admitted that she didn't know Bach from Brahms both sexes united in looking at her condescendingly.

Daniel commenced a covert fondling of her hip which made her feel intensely irritated. Spotting a waiter circulating with a tray of food, she murmured an excuse and left the group. As she made her way across the room she wondered gloomily whether she had enough material for her last article on blind dates, or whether she should stay and subject herself to more excruciating boredom.

She grabbed something from the waiter's proffered tray and was just in the process of cramming it into her mouth when to her surprise she spotted Jon on the other side of the room.

A middle-aged woman with strong patrician features was hanging onto his arm and he had a politely inscrutable expression on his face which she knew meant he was as bored as she was.

He spotted her at the same moment and a few seconds later was by her side, just as she realised that whatever it was she was eating was absolutely disgusting.

Spitting it unceremoniously into a tissue she took

a long swig of her drink, trying to obliterate the horrible taste.

'Raw fish and seaweed roulade,' Jon explained. 'A Japanese delicacy.'

'They should stick to hi-fis and cars,' she complained, gulping down the rest of her drink. 'What on earth are you doing here?'

'Working. Trying to get some information out of my companion. Unsuccessfully so far.'

When Jon had been unable to get in touch with Ellen he'd decided to put his evening to good use by seeing yet another of his old flames and trying to find out anything he could about the secret society.

He'd enjoyed a brief but satisfying affair with Anna Stewart while she was separated from her husband a couple of years ago and she'd seemed delighted to hear from him when he'd phoned her. She'd suggested he accompany her to a party. He'd agreed, then like Ellen found himself doomed to spend an evening being bored into a coma.

'This is my last blind date,' said Ellen mournfully. Then she wailed, 'Oh Jon, I don't think I can stand another hour of that woman playing a harp. It's the worst party I've ever been to.'

'Let's leave,' suggested Jon promptly.

'Dare we?' she asked hopefully.

'Of course we dare. Go and tell your date that you feel ill and I'm taking you home and I'll tell mine the same thing. See you by the door in a couple of minutes.'

Shortly afterwards they were ensconced in a booth in a cosy bistro just down the road. Ellen pored thankfully over the menu and found it a huge relief to be in the company of someone she felt comfortable with, doing something she enjoyed doing.

When Jon put his arm around her shoulders she snuggled up to him, for the moment completely forgetting her resolution not to see him again. Jon plied her shamelessly with food and alcohol, well aware of what a mellowing effect this tended to have on her.

When they left the bistro after the meal Jon waved down a taxi and gave his address.

'No, Jon, I can't,' protested Ellen as she climbed in. 'I'm moving flats tomorrow.'

He pulled her into his arms and dropped several kisses on her neck, his breath warm against her ear as he murmured, 'You and I have some unfinished business. Don't you remember?'

Ellen felt a languorous tingling in her groin as the memory of several erotic scenarios they'd enjoyed together last weekend presented themselves.

'Mmm,' she sighed as his warm hand began to glide over her bare back, sending hot shivers of lust through her. 'Maybe we do.'

Forty minutes later they lay panting side by side on the carpet in Jon's sitting room. Ellen had become so aroused during the taxi ride that as soon as they'd stepped through the door she'd pulled Jon onto the floor and commenced tearing his clothes off.

Her green dress was bunched around her waist leaving her full breasts bare, the nipples dark pink and jutting sharply upwards. Her black satin panties were hanging from a door handle and one of her stockings had come adrift from its suspender and had unrolled itself down to her knee.

She sighed voluptuously as Jon rolled onto his side and began to caress her stomach, smoothing over the curve of her hip then down her thigh.

'I wonder how the party's going?' he asked lazily, sliding the tips of his fingers under the top of the stocking which was still attached to its suspenders. Her thigh felt soft and warm as he stroked it. Ellen shuddered.

'I dread to think. Thank goodness I've got rid of the taste of that raw fish, now all I can taste is you. Talking of which . . .'

Gracefully shifting position she bent her dark head over Jon's groin so her curls tickled his thighs. Then, slowly and seductively, she took him into her mouth again.

When Ellen awoke the following morning curled up next to Jon in his large double bed, her first impulse was to dress silently then leave.

Oh dear, she'd done it again — and after all her good intentions too.

Turning her head she studied him briefly while he slept. She noticed for the first time what long eyelashes he had, almost as long as hers. The sheet had tangled around his waist leaving his lean, lightly tanned chest bare. She ran her hand gently down it then withdrew it quickly as she saw his cock stir beneath the sheet.

She knew she ought to go, but where the pleasures of the flesh were concerned Ellen had always been weak-willed. Perhaps just one more time . . .

Going into the bathroom she took a quick shower then padded naked into the kitchen. The sink was stacked with unwashed dishes so she rinsed a couple of plates and rummaged through the drawers looking for a tea towel. She came across a navy-blue-and-white-striped cook's apron, still in its unopened packet and deduced it was an unwanted Christmas or birthday present. She tied it on then set about making coffee and toast.

Jon's early-morning erection strained excitedly against the soft cotton of the sheet when he opened his eyes and saw Ellen in the apron. Her luscious breasts were only partially covered by the bib front and one nipple peeped perkily out above the top. When she bent down to place the tray on the bed her taut, rounded backside stuck out provocatively below the tie around her waist.

Instantly wide awake, he sat up against the pillows and ran a hand through his tousled dark hair.

'I think I must have died and gone to heaven,' he remarked. 'Are you an angel?'

Ellen giggled and curled up on the bed next to him, her other nipple popping out from behind the apron as she did so. He stretched out a hand to caress it, rubbing his thumb over the point until it hardened appreciatively.

They ate their toast without tasting it. When they'd finished Jon went into the bathroom and Ellen picked up the tray and returned it to the kitchen. She was just bending over the fridge to put the milk away when Jon appeared behind her, running his hands over her rounded hips and curvaceous rump.

She shut the fridge door and turned round, putting

her arms around his waist and rubbing her breasts seductively against his bare chest.

'I'll have to be going soon,' she murmured.

'Not yet,' he returned, putting his hands on her waist and sitting her on top of the kitchen unit. She leant back on her elbows while he lifted the apron up to her waist and parted her thighs. His tongue felt warm and slightly rough as he circled her clitoris, flickering lightly over it while sheer animal lust spiralled upwards from her groin bringing a warm flush to her face.

She groaned and wriggled forward on the kitchen surface, pushing her private parts harder against his mouth. He probed, licked and sucked until she was reduced to a writhing mass of quivering limbs, her head thrown back and her eyes closed.

Raising his head at last he slipped his hands under her backside and slid her towards him. She cried out when he entered her, locking her legs around his waist as he forged onwards and upwards until he couldn't go any further. After withdrawing slowly he thrust into her again with a rocking motion, feeling her warm juices bubbling welcomingly around his iron-hard cock.

Again and again she took the full length of him until they were both breathless and perspiring. Pulling out of her Jon muttered, 'Turn over.'

She flipped onto her stomach and reached behind her, helping guide him back between her widely parted thighs, grinding her bottom into his groin as he shafted her forcefully from behind.

Eventually they staggered into the bedroom on shaking legs and collapsed onto the bed.

'I really do have to go,' said Ellen regretfully, then began to squirm with renewed excitement as Jon slipped his hand between her legs again.

The phone went at that moment.

Jon ignored it for a while but it was right by the bed and continued to ring insistently. Picking it up with his other hand he snapped, 'Yes! ... Oh hi, Vernon.'

He was silent for a few moments and Ellen could hear the sound of Vernon's voice at the other end then Jon said, 'Can't someone else go? I've seen enough carnage this week to last me a lifetime. What about...'

Whatever Vernon said next it resulted in Jon eventually growling, 'Yes. Okay. Okay. Ten minutes.'

Ceasing his erotic manipulation of her clit he lay back on the bed and threw an arm over his eyes.

'Guess who's just drawn the short straw for covering a plane crash at Gatwick? When's Dave back? And where the hell's Matt been for the last few days? Sorry, Ellen, I've got to go.'

He kissed her lingeringly, then vanished into the bathroom for a hasty shower.

CHAPTER FIFTEEN

Ellen's move into her new flat was soon accomplished. Technically it was an unfurnished flat, but she'd been able to buy some of the last tenant's furniture from the landlord who was keen to sell it to try and recover the arrears of rent.

While she unpacked her crumpled clothes and hung them in the closet she thought about the previous evening. She knew she'd exhibited all the self-control of a three year old by going to bed with Jon again after being so determined not to.

But he was so devastatingly good at sex.

He only had to touch her and her body went into pre-coital overdrive, making immediate enthusiastic preparations to accommodate him. In fact, he only had to stand near enough for her to catch a whiff of his cologne and her stomach started to churn with excitement and her groin to throb with longing.

She was going to have to avoid being alone with him in future if she was going to stick to her resolve not to go to bed with him again.

She was in the shower when the bell went and, thinking it was Kate, she wrapped herself in a towel and went to answer the door.

Jon stood there holding two takeaway pizzas and a bottle of Asti Spumante.

The towel was only a hand towel and did a totally inadequate job of covering her. Jon grinned as his eyes roved over her body.

'I see I've picked a good moment.'

'Jon . . .' faltered Ellen, trying unsuccessfully to keep the towel up. 'What are you doing here?' she ended lamely.

'I've brought you a flat-warming supper. May I come in or shall we eat it in the hallway? There are two men coming this way, incidentally.'

Ellen stepped hastily back into her flat and Jon promptly followed her and closed the door behind him. The towel fell to the floor at that moment and before she could pick it up she found his arms around her and her damp body pressed against the full length of his.

Of their own volition her arms coiled around his neck, and she said weakly, 'You've got to leave. We can't keep doing this.'

'Mmm, why not? Shall I come and wash your back? And your front? And your . . .'

On Sunday evening James arrived at Kate's flat following a weekend spent in his constituency. After extensive enquiries she was no nearer to finding out more about the mysterious secret society — a situation which she was finding increasingly frustrating.

When James arrived he asked if he could use the phone, then stood there waiting for her to leave the room. She went out leaving the door open a crack, then wandered into the kitchen for a few moments. As soon as she heard him speaking she crept back

INDECENT

down the hallway and stood outside the door listening. She'd started doing this on a regular basis, but to date had overheard nothing of any interest.

Tonight she was in luck.

After several minutes of conversation she heard him say, 'Yes I've got the video. Damning, absolutely damning. I don't know what they could have been thinking about . . . Yes, I'll put it in the safe tomorrow. I would never have thought it of . . . Yes I think we should — urgently.'

As the conversation wound up she went into her bedroom and closed the door, thinking fast.

A few minutes later James was delighted to see her enter the sitting room wearing a skimpy ivory-coloured teddy, a matching suspender belt, a pair of cream silk stockings and high-heeled shoes.

He put his glass of whisky down and rose to his feet as Kate leant against the door in a provocative pose, running one hand suggestively over her full breasts.

'Tonight we're doing it my way,' she told him huskily.

'And what's your way?' he asked interestedly, striding across the room and fastening his mouth on the swell of one full, creamy breast. In reply she took him by the hand and led him to her bedroom.

'Don't say anything,' she murmured. 'Just do what I tell you to.'

She removed all his clothes, dropping a kiss onto his magnificent erection as she released it from the confines of his underwear. He protested when she tied his wrists to the headboard; James liked to be the one in control.

Well, for once he wasn't going to be.

When she'd secured him to the bed she blindfolded him with a scarf, effectively impairing his hearing as well as his vision.

'I'm not sure I like this,' he complained.

'You're going to love it,' she assured him. 'Back in a minute.'

'Kate!' he called after her. 'Where are you going?'

She didn't reply. Picking up his jacket she left the room, closing the door behind her. Once in the sitting room she pulled his keys out of the pocket and swiftly unlocked his briefcase. Inside were a couple of bound documents, a sheaf of miscellaneous papers and a video. Placing the video in her VCR she set it running. A couple of minutes later she sank to the floor in front of the TV, her eyes wide, her mouth open.

She really couldn't believe it as she watched various leading figures from the British establishment either disporting themselves with girls in flimsy clothing, or receiving punishment at the hands of leather-clad women with whips.

Prominent members didn't *begin* to cover it.

Rewinding the tape, Kate inserted a blank cassette in the other slot and began to make a copy. Then she hastily skimmed through the papers, photocopying the relevant ones on her fax copier.

When she heard James calling plaintively from the bedroom she thought she'd better put in an appearance while the tape was being dubbed.

Grabbing a bottle of baby oil from the bathroom she went to rejoin him.

He stopped complaining when she began to massage baby oil into his dick, kneading and squeezing it gently as she did so. She took a long time over it, until the full length was hard, glistening and obviously more than ready for action.

Leaning forward Kate pulled the scarf from his eyes, then slipped the teddy down to her waist, baring her full, ripe breasts. She knew that James was particularly turned on by the visual aspects of sex and wanted him to fully appreciate the next part.

Picking up the bottle of oil she trickled some between her breasts and with slow, sensual movements began to rub it in. She heard James swallow, then his deep voice charged with excitement said urgently, 'Untie me, darling. I want to help you with that.'

Pulling on his bonds he tried to free himself, urging her again to untie him, but Kate was deaf to his pleas. She leant over him, clasped his cock in the slippery channel between her breasts and began to move up and down. His breathing became ragged as she broke her rhythmic movements to stimulate the tip of his penis with one provocatively swollen nipple.

The end of his dick looked like a juicy, dark red plum and Kate had to exert a lot of self-control not to slip it between her legs and use it for her own gratification. Instead, she continued to slide it up and down between her full breasts while James panted and strained against his bonds.

With a sudden strangled groan he erupted like a geyser, spurting hot liquid over her breasts, where it mingled with the baby oil and ran down towards her stomach.

He lay there gasping. Then, as she began to massage the liquid into her skin, he exclaimed, 'Don't – I can't stand it!'

'You're going to have to stand a lot more than that,' she assured him tantalisingly, leaning forward to retie the scarf over his eyes.

A couple of hours later she kissed him a passionate, lingering goodbye in the hallway then saw him out of the flat. She'd kept him tied to the bed for most of the evening and his wrists were red and sore where he'd strained against his bonds.

At one stage in the proceedings she'd left him on his own while she checked the copy she'd made of the video, replaced the original in his briefcase and returned his jacket and keys to the bedroom.

She knew that James had been very excited by the scenario in the bedroom, but was also frustrated because he hadn't been in control. It had been very exciting for her too. Particularly when she'd climbed astride him and used his cock to stimulate her to orgasm, before bearing down and allowing him to penetrate her deeply and satisfyingly.

Sometimes she thought that sexually she let James take control too often. It wasn't that she didn't find it extremely arousing – she invariably did. But she enjoyed keeping him off balance and surprising him sometimes – like tonight and the time she'd exposed herself to him at the press briefing.

Best of all, in addition to the sex, she now had a lot of vital information about the secret society, including irrefutable proof of its existence.

All in all it had been quite an evening.

Liz flew back down to Los Angeles to conduct her third interview. On the way she worked on the first in a series of articles about life on the road with Sledgehammer.

It was a completely spurious account.

Somewhat to her irritation, both the band and the rest of Ledd's entourage seemed to lead pretty blameless lives. In fact, between gigs they seemed to spend most of their time sightseeing, taking photos and buying souvenirs. It definitely wasn't what she'd hoped for.

Certainly, some of them picked up girls and partied after a gig, but that was about it. Other than the occasional joint she'd seen no sign of drugs, there were no wrecked hotel rooms and no drunken brawls.

As this was undoubtedly not what Vernon wanted, Liz unconcernedly set about fabricating tales of excess and debauchery.

After she'd checked into her hotel she took out her file on the politician she was scheduled to interview. Joe Quentin was forty-two, extremely charismatic and a hot tip for the White House. From a wealthy Californian family he was based in Los Angeles but kept houses in several other parts of the country.

Studying his photo, Liz couldn't help but admit

that he was a very attractive man — much too old for her of course, but nevertheless attractive.

She was annoyed to receive a phone call from one of his aides postponing their meeting at four o'clock. She was somewhat mollified to hear that the senator would very much like her to come to dinner and, if she was agreeable, would send a car for her at seven. Liz was more than happy to accept. She couldn't get enough of American gracious living and she was certain that the senator lived very graciously.

The house in Bel Air was magnificent.

So was Joe Quentin.

Although Liz had seen him on television she was unprepared for the force of his charm when she met him in person.

At six foot three he towered over her. Dark-haired and lightly tanned, he had the bluest eyes she'd ever seen. When he smiled he showed even white teeth and his eyes crinkled up in the most engaging manner. He was saved from being too handsome by a crooked broken nose which added a rakishness to his otherwise perfect appearance.

He was wearing casual clothing which only served to emphasise the spread of his shoulders and the taut, muscular curve of his buttocks. Liz was surprised to feel a shiver of the intense lust she usually only experienced for men twenty years his junior.

He led the way to a terrace overlooking the pool and helped her into her chair at a beautifully set table. Taking a mental note of the expensive crystal glasses and silverware she felt another surge of dissatisfaction with her own lifestyle in London.

INDECENT

Although she commanded a high salary it didn't begin to compare with wealth on this scale.

She'd dressed up for the occasion in a cream silk dress with a short, tight skirt. The neckline wasn't particularly low but she wasn't wearing anything underneath it above the waist and the darker circles of her milk-chocolate nipples were just visible through the fine fabric.

She knew that Joe Quentin had noticed by a barely perceptible flicker of the eyes. She had to admit that he was good. He didn't leer or ogle her, but subtly he let it come across that he found her desirable. She would have put money on it that he had an identical effect on every woman he came into contact with, attractive or not.

After pouring her a glass of champagne he sat back in the chair opposite her in a relaxed posture.

'I warn you that you only have thirty minutes for direct questions,' he told her. 'After that dinner will arrive and I'm much too frightened of my chef to delay it.'

'Can't we continue the interview over dinner?' she enquired.

'Certainly not. That's when I want to find out all about you. In any case, the food will be much too good for you to concentrate on trying to find out my weak spots.'

He grinned at her engagingly and Liz found herself smiling back.

'Why don't you make it easy for me and tell me what they are upfront,' she challenged him.

'I still cry when I watch *Dumbo*. Don't you?'

Liz had never cried over a film in her life but she

found herself saying, 'Sometimes.'

The thirty minutes was over far too soon. Joe Quentin was a very experienced interviewee and she thought that unless he gave something away over dinner she'd be casting around for a peg to hang the story on.

He was right about the food. She savoured every moment of the dinner eaten under a rapidly darkening Californian sky. Just before it went dark a series of spotlights came on in the grounds, illuminating the pool and picking out clusters of shrubs and flowers. The staff were efficient and discreet, appearing silently at the appropriate moments but generally remaining unobtrusive.

He drew her out about herself, asking intelligent questions about her career and achievements. He also made it diplomatically clear that he was aware that in England she was queen of the tabloids and infamous for her hatchet jobs. She was impressed that he'd taken the trouble to find out.

Over coffee he leant back in his chair and asked her quizzically, 'So, how will I feature? Smug and fatuous? Ruthlessly ambitious? Rich and spoilt?'

She leant back herself, her small, high breasts thrusting hard against the bodice of her dress.

'Maybe, maybe not.'

'Can we consider business over for the day now? What I'd really like to do is dance you round the terrace in the pale moonlight.'

He injected just enough humour into the declaration to redeem it from being corny. Liz suppressed a snort of derisive laughter but nevertheless made no objection when he helped her from her chair and took her in his arms. There had been soft music playing in the background all evening — a touch Liz considered schmaltzy in the extreme. But there was nothing schmaltzy about the erection she soon felt pressing against her stomach.

He kissed her softly and she felt her pelvic muscles tighten with lust as she kissed him back.

Ten minutes later she was flat on her back on the diving board, wearing only her stockings and suspender belt as they screwed vigorously under a midnight-blue velvet sky.

The sprung diving board juddered beneath them as he plunged into her again and again, urging her to spread her legs wider to accommodate him.

And there was a lot to accommodate.

With her legs wrapped around his waist Liz moved beneath him, crying out with pleasure at each thrust, mewing with delight as he teased her nipples with his tongue.

She didn't know how it happened, but just as she climaxed she found herself flying through the air, still joined at the groin to the senator. The next second they'd separated and she hit the water in the pool and went under before she even had time to shriek.

She panicked for a moment then felt herself dragged back up to the surface and helped to the side by Joe, who looked as shocked as she felt.

'Well, that's a first,' he told her as she wrung out her streaming hair. 'You must be one exciting lady. We were going at it so strongly that the diving board flipped us into the water. Are you okay?'

Turning round Liz swam down to the shallow end,

climbed out and sat on the side of the pool. He followed her and asked again, 'Are you okay?'

Opening her wet, stocking-clad legs and pulling his head between them Liz murmured, 'I will be in a minute.'

Jon stopped by Kate's desk.

'Have you seen Ellen?' he asked.

Jon was a baffled man. Ellen was avoiding him again and he just couldn't work out why. They'd had a great time together at the weekend and now she was back to being elusive.

'Not this morning,' Kate returned. Vernon appeared by Jon's side.

'Kate, do you have a minute?' Kate nodded and followed him down the office leaving Jon leaning against her desk. His eyes lighted aimlessly on the screen of her VDU, then he blinked hard and looked again. A few seconds later he sat down at her desk and began to read through the file she was obviously just putting on disc.

Someone else was onto the secret society.

When Kate reappeared and saw him reading through the material she was compiling she was annoyed.

'What the hell do you think you're doing?' she demanded.

'I'm working on the same story,' he told her wryly. Then, as she let out an exclamation of annoyance, 'What do you say we work on it together? I've got information you don't have and vice versa.'

'As you seem to have just read through mine, I

don't seem to have much choice,' she pointed out acidly.

'Sorry, Kate. I know we keep our stories confidential, but I was just so surprised to see your screen reflecting what I was thinking about.'

'I thought you were thinking about Ellen.'

'That too,' he admitted. 'Kate, I don't suppose you have any idea why she's avoiding me?'

'None at all. So pull up a chair and tell me everything you know about this particular juicy scandal.'

An hour later they sat and watched Kate's copy of the damning video.

'Strong stuff,' commented Jon.

'Strong indeed,' agreed Kate. 'And what a lot of familiar faces.' Jon suddenly sat forward in his chair.

'Talking of which – just run that bit again. Now freeze frame . . . no, back a bit.'

They both stared at the couple in the picture. 'I know that girl,' he said thoughtfully. 'She works at the health club.'

The girl in question was a petite brunette with a lush figure and gamine face. He'd seen her around but had never actually spoken to her. 'She's called Tessa, I think.'

'Do you think she'll talk to us?' asked Kate.

'Well, she's more likely to than his worship there,' said Jon watching the on-screen antics of a well-known High Court judge. 'It's certainly worth a try. In fact, I'll get right down there now. Do you want to come?'

'I certainly do. Although I'll let you do the talking

since you have such a way with women. Give her the full voltage of your charm and let's see if we can establish her price.'

They were in luck, Tessa was just finishing her shift. Initially she refused to go for a drink with them, saying she had an appointment at the hairdressers, but when Jon indicated there might be something in it for her, she acquiesced.

She was an attractive girl, small but shapely; her figure kept in excellent condition by daily work-outs at the gym. She'd thrown a jacket and a pair of jeans on over her leotard, which clung so closely to her breasts that Jon's mouth went dry and briefly he forgot what he planned to say next.

Once the three of them were ensconced in a nearby bar he gave himself a mental shake and came right to the point.

'We're journalists from the *Daily News*. We're just about to break the story of the secret society we know you've worked for. If you'll talk to us about it, we'll make it well worth your while.'

Tessa didn't look particularly disconcerted.

'I knew it was only a matter of time. Still, the money came in useful. What are you offering, just out of interest?' Jon named a figure. She looked thoughtful.

'It's not enough. You're dealing with some powerful men here. I'd need sufficient to live abroad for a couple of years and some sort of assurance that no one would ever know I'd talked to you. And if it ever went to trial, under no circumstances would I be a witness in court.' She drained her glass of wine.

Indicating the empty glass, Kate interjected, 'Another drink?'

Tessa smiled at her.

'No thanks. I've got to go. I'll think about your offer and let you know my price.' Picking up her bag she accepted Jon's proffered card and left the bar.

'She was very cool, considering the circumstances,' commented Kate.

'She's obviously thought it through in advance,' said Jon. 'Okay, let's consider our next move while we're waiting for her to get back to us. Are you sure you don't know why Ellen's avoiding me?'

CHAPTER SIXTEEN

Tessa got back to Jon and Kate the following day and agreed to meet them in the same bar to discuss her price.

'She's going to be expensive,' predicted Kate.

'We can do the story without her if we have to,' said Jon, 'but getting an eyewitness account would be so much more effective.'

'Not to mention obtaining names, dates and details of whatever else they all got up to, as well as the golden moments we already have captured on video.'

They'd made a comprehensive list of all the men present that they'd been able to recognise. Kate had immediately spotted James's cousin Dickie wearing only a tie and an expression of drunken rapture as he was spanked by a formidable-looking blonde in a leather basque.

Kate wondered idly what Dickie's wife, Vanessa, would have to say to him when it all came out, but it was always possible that she already knew.

Tessa kept them waiting for half an hour, during which time Jon brooded about Ellen. She was out at Heathrow airport testing security by seeing how many off-limits areas she could penetrate.

He'd managed to speak to her by phone the night before but only briefly. She'd told him she was just about to go out and that her minicab was waiting and had said goodbye before he'd managed to really say anything.

Tessa arrived at that moment looking extremely attractive in a tight cream skirt which buttoned up the front and which revealed a lot of her shapely thighs. She was wearing it with a close-fitting black top which Jon suspected was a leotard. He hoped it wasn't, he'd much rather imagine her in a pair of frilly black panties with a ...

He was jolted out of his erotic reverie by Kate who kicked him sharply under the table.

'Sorry, what was that?' he asked.

'Tessa was just asking for a written guarantee of anonymity,' said Kate smoothly. 'I don't think that'll be a problem will it?'

'Er, no it won't,' agreed Jon pulling himself together. 'So, what's your price Tessa?' He gave her the benefit of his most charming boyish smile.

'I was thinking it was something which needs discussing at length — perhaps over dinner,' murmured Tessa. Kate shot Jon an ironical look.

'That's no problem,' he assured Tessa, looking at her legs again and thinking that there were worse ways to earn a living than being a journalist.

He might be currently besotted with Ellen but he was certain he could rise to the occasion with Tessa if the job demanded it.

'Where would you like to go? I'll book a table for two and we can take it from there,' he told her, assiduously topping up her glass from the bottle of wine on the table.

Tessa met his eyes.

'I didn't mean you,' she said. 'I meant your colleague.' Both Kate and Jon stared at her. 'I prefer women,' she explained simply.

Kate looked dumbfounded. Jon took a gulp of his wine but it went down the wrong way and he coughed.

The silence threatened to become embarrassing and, as Kate was patently speechless, Jon said, 'I'm sure that will be fine with Kate. Can she call you later to arrange the details?'

Tessa nodded then rose to her feet.

'This evening then, just the two of us. I'll be looking forward to it,' she said to Kate, giving her a look which Jon could only describe as lascivious, before leaving the bar.

Kate emptied the last splash from the bottle of wine into her glass then said faintly, 'Get another bottle will you please, Jon?'

He went obediently to the bar.

'Do you know what you've just committed me to in such a cavalier fashion?' she demanded. Jon grinned at her.

'A night of carnal delights, I should imagine. What's the problem?'

'What do you mean, what's the problem? Now what am I supposed to do?'

'Lie back and enjoy it?'

'That's easy for you to say.'

'I was quite prepared to sacrifice my own fair white body,' he protested. 'Come to that, what about my ego? It's just taken a hammering. How do you think it makes me feel, that the fragrant Tessa has rejected my virile charms in favour of your more womanly ones?'

Kate was silent for a while, before eventually saying, 'I don't think I can do it.'

'Why on earth not? She's a very attractive girl. I was ready to jump at the chance myself.'

'So I noticed. But strange as it may seem to you, Jon, my experience to date has been limited to members of the opposite sex.'

'Just have a few drinks and let her make the running. You might find it a pleasant change.'

'I'll bet you wouldn't take such a sanguine view if the potential informant was a bruising great trucker who wanted a night with you,' Kate said sourly.

'Probably not,' he agreed cheerfully. 'Just one thing . . .'

'What?'

'Can I watch?'

Liz slammed the phone down abruptly. Ledd could be a real pain in the backside sometimes. He'd just demanded that she fly up to Seattle that afternoon to join him and had become petulant when she'd told him crisply that it wasn't possible.

Liz had absolutely no intention of leaving Los Angeles in the immediate future.

She and Joe Quentin were virtually inseparable at the moment and she was loving every moment of it. Power clung to him like an invisible cloak. Wherever they went people fawned over him – the best table in any restaurant was automatically his, as were the best seats virtually anywhere.

Liz absolutely revelled in it. The thought of returning to dreary London and the squalid offices of the *Daily News* was totally unappealing.

INDECENT

She'd received a fax that morning from Vernon asking when she'd be back, but hadn't bothered to reply.

Picking up a bottle of scarlet nail polish she shook it vigorously then began to paint her nails.

Joe was taking her to a party in Beverly Hills that evening and she wanted to look her best. She didn't know how long he'd remain interested in her, but if she had anything to do with it, it would be indefinitely.

It was with some trepidation that Kate took her seat in the restaurant that evening. She asked to go straight to her table and immediately ordered a bottle of champagne. What the hell — the paper was paying.

She hadn't known what to wear but, on Jon's advice, dressed as if for a date with a man. Her smoke-blue silk jacket had a plunging neckline and was worn with a tight black skirt. Slit up to midthigh, the skirt showed off most of her long legs as she walked — a fact which hadn't gone unnoticed by the male diners in the restaurant.

Underneath she was wearing a lacy, dark grey bra with matching panties and suspender belt.

Kate couldn't remember the last time she'd felt so nervous. It was all very well Jon making a joke out of it but what did you actually *do* with another woman?

At that moment she saw Tessa being led to their table by the waiter. The other woman leant across and kissed her on the cheek — her cloud of dark hair an attractive contrast to Kate's blondeness.

Tessa was wearing a deep red dress which left her shoulders bare and clung to her like a second skin. Her body was truly superb and it unsettled Kate to know that later that evening she would, in all probability, be kissing and caressing it.

'Shall we get business out of the way first?' asked Tessa, sipping her glass of champagne.

'Certainly,' said Kate with a coolness she was far from feeling. It didn't take long. Tessa's price and terms were high but Kate knew she could agree to them. They arranged that she'd tell her story to both Kate and Jon tomorrow, ready to make the headlines the following day.

Once it had all been agreed Kate was at a loss and couldn't think of anything else to say.

'Relax,' purred Tessa, obviously sensing how tense she was. Reaching out she stroked her arm.

'I've never been with another woman before,' blurted out Kate.

'Then you're in for a pleasant surprise. Enjoy your meal, sweetie. What happens later will be great for both of us. Wouldn't all these men just love it if they knew?' returned Tessa wickedly, looking around the crowded restaurant.

'Jon wanted to watch.'

'Don't they all?'

Kate spun out the meal as long as she decently could, but all too soon it was time to call for the bill.

Tessa lived in a spacious bedsitter in Camden Town. The room was comfortably furnished and through an open door Kate could see that it had its own adjoining bathroom.

INDECENT

The other thing she registered was that there was a large mirror set in the ceiling over the bed.

She sat nervously on the edge of a chair while Tessa put some soft music on the stereo and dimmed the lights. Kate had been in similar scenarios many times before – but never with another woman.

Tessa led Kate over to the bed and pulled her down onto it. Slowly she began to stroke her hair, then leant forward and kissed her lightly on the lips.

Kate was very aware of Tessa's exotic perfume enveloping both of them and of how soft her lips were. It felt alien to be having sexual contact with someone whose body was as slender and yielding as her own. She was accustomed to James's hard, masculine body, the slight abrasive stubble on his chin and his strong arms around her.

Tessa stroked her neck and shoulders, before gently urging her to lie down on the bed and commencing a soothing, relaxing massage of her back. Imperceptibly Kate felt the tension ebbing from her body to be replaced by a vague sense of wellbeing.

'Why don't I take these things off so they don't get creased?' the dark girl asked huskily, indicating Kate's silk jacket and skirt. Kate dutifully sat up and allowed her to remove them. 'You're beautiful,' murmured Tessa, kissing Kate's collarbone delicately and laying her down on the bed again – this time on her back.

While Kate watched, Tessa removed her deep red dress. Underneath she wore only a pair of the palest pink camiknickers with a matching suspender belt and ivory coloured stockings. She had beautifully firm, rounded breasts with pert little nipples. Kate had a sudden vision of herself with her mouth closed firmly over one, sucking and tasting. She was taken aback to feel the first faint stirring of desire.

Joining her on the bed again Tessa said, 'Look,' and indicated their reflection in the mirror on the ceiling. Kate had to admit they made an aesthetically pleasing picture lying side by side.

'We don't have to do anything you don't like,' Tessa told her softly, then leant across and began to caress her breasts over the lacy grey bra. It was actually very erotic to watch in the mirror.

Tessa stroked her as if they had all the time in the world. Kate was aware of a feeling of languorous pleasure stealing over her and made no objection when Tessa unclipped her bra and ran a hand over her bare breasts. The nipples immediately hardened in response to the caress, then Tessa bent her dark head and took one in her mouth.

She stroked Kate's stomach as she did so, then slipped one hand between her legs. Her touch was feather light, barely perceptible in fact. Kate found herself parting her thighs and wishing that Tessa would intensify the caress. Her clit throbbed with the need for greater stimulation and she pressed herself against the other girl's hand.

Tessa's fingers sought and found the swelling of her clitoris and concentrated her attention there, until the grey lacy fabric of her panties began to dampen.

Kate moaned softly, then slowly and hesitantly reached up and placed her hand over one of Tessa's breasts. It felt very strange, but good too, particularly when the nipple stiffened appreciatively. Suddenly they were in each other's arms, stroking, caressing and kissing each other as their mutual desire mounted.

When Tessa made a move to remove Kate's panties, Kate raised her bottom from the bed to help her, then let out a muted exclamation of delight when she felt the other girl's cool fingers slipping into her well-lubricated interior and exploring it gently.

Tessa touched her just the way she wanted to be touched and she gave herself up to it, watching them both in the mirror as her arousal mounted. It was a slow, sensual process and when her climax came it was in long-drawn-out waves of heady pleasure, leaving her gasping weakly in its eddying wake.

Twice more Tessa brought her to orgasm before Kate said weakly, 'Your turn now.'

Bending over her, she removed Tessa's pink silk camiknickers. To her surprise, she found that the other girl had removed her pubic hair, leaving her mound completely bare. It was strange to be exploring the slippery folds of another woman's private parts, but it was also very exciting.

'Tell me if I'm not doing it the way you like it,' she murmured, her forefinger circling the swollen bud of Tessa's clit.

'You're doing fine,' said Tessa breathlessly, her pelvis rotating as Kate commenced a gently rhythmic stimulation of her most sensitive point. She came very quickly, arching her back and closing her thighs tightly over Kate's hand.

Kate waited for her to recover then turned her

over and stroked her small, rounded buttocks, before bending down and softly biting one. She could smell the musky tang of Tessa's personal scent, heady and arousing in itself. Parting the other girl's legs she bent her head between them, then paused briefly.

'You don't have to,' she heard Tessa murmur.

'I want to,' she found herself replying.

With the tip of her tongue she licked tentatively at Tessa's labia. Sharp and salty at the same time, the taste wasn't like anything she'd ever experienced before. She continued with her oral exploration, thinking that this was what it must be like for James. She'd never realised before how complex all those folds were and how difficult it must be for a man to navigate his way through them without some sort of guidance.

She at least knew what she liked herself and used the knowledge to try to give Tessa the maximum pleasure.

A couple of hours later the two women lay in each others arms, perspiring and sated.

'I've got a very large bath,' Tessa breathed in her ear. 'Shall we take one together?' It sounded like heaven to Kate.

Slowly she removed her stockings and suspender belt and followed Tessa into the bathroom. They lay among the scented bubbles languidly soaping each other's slender limbs, then made love again in the warm water.

As she lazily cupped her hand over Tessa's bare mound and worked up a rich creamy lather, Kate wondered what James would think if she told him about it.

INDECENT

* * *

The unmasking of the secret society had Vernon almost ecstatic with triumphant glee.

'Well done, my dear!' he exclaimed, taking the opportunity to press a wet kiss on Kate's cheek. 'Well done, laddie!' he said to Jon, slapping him painfully across the back.

The paper had to run extra editions and Ross Talbot stopped by the *Daily News* offices himself. He didn't actually offer any congratulations, but he was marginally less bombastic than usual. It was the first time Vernon had ever had a meeting with him which hadn't resulted in indigestion.

The editor broke the habit of a lifetime and offered both Kate and Jon a drink, then the three of them watched the video again in Vernon's office.

There was a tap at the door and Ellen appeared. She'd spent the last couple of days at Heathrow and had come into the office straight from there. Her clothes were crumpled, her make-up smudged and her hair in tangles — nevertheless she exuded an endearing sexiness which both Jon and Vernon found irresistible.

'Ellen, my dear!' Vernon greeted her exuberantly. 'Come in and have a drink.'

'I saw the headlines on a newsstand at the airport,' she said. 'I've got a good story for you about airport security Vernon, but it pales in comparison to this. Is this the incriminating video?'

'It certainly is — hot stuff, isn't it? Ernie's already run off a copy for home use,' Jon told her, then giving in to temptation pulled her into his arms and kissed her. She responded passionately, then remembered where she was and belatedly disentangled herself.

She turned her attention back to the figures on the screen, then blushed when she saw what was happening there. She was glad no one had ever suggested doing that with her. While they watched they were all lost in their own thoughts.

Ellen wished she was in bed with Jon.

Jon wished he was in bed with Ellen.

Kate wondered if James would like it if she shaved her pubic hair off.

Vernon wished that Liz was back and wanted a very big favour.

When the video finished Ellen stretched and yawned.

'I'll get my copy in then I need to go home and change. I've been in these clothes for forty-eight hours.'

'Take the rest of the day off,' said Vernon magnanimously.

Liz was standing on the terrace of Joe Quentin's mansion smoking a cigarette, her beautiful predatory face triumphant, her eyes half closed against the smoke. She looked out over the beautifully tended grounds and felt a heady surge of exultation.

It was within her grasp now.

Joe Quentin had just offered her the editorship of one of Los Angeles' most influential daily newspapers, at four times her current salary.

It was the opportunity of a lifetime.

She'd be a vital part of the political machinery, instrumental in furthering Joe's career and at the same time her own. Joe was also, at least for the moment, besotted with her and she intended to keep it that way.

Liz had never in her life seriously considered marriage, but she was considering it now. All this could be hers, the power, the prestige and possibly one day the White House.

But that was looking ahead. For now she intended to build her career here on the West Coast where she'd always felt at home. And even if she didn't marry Joe, she'd have an enviable lifestyle in a glorious climate, with an endless supply of bronzed Californian boys to keep her happy.

Her aquamarine eyes glittered as she mentally composed a letter of resignation to Vernon. Or maybe she should fly back and do it in person, as soon as she'd signed her contract here.

Lifting her glass Liz drank a silent toast to her new life.

Ellen had fallen into bed as soon as she arrived back at her flat and slept until eight o'clock in the evening.

While she slept she slipped from one disturbing erotic dream to another, each more arousing than the last. Jon featured strongly in all of them and in one particular scenario he did something so sexy that when she did wake up, she was panting with frustrated desire.

Standing under a cool shower she tried to think about something else but it was no good. There was a hot, urgent throbbing between her legs and she felt edgy and flushed.

As she dressed she thought about all the reasons

why she shouldn't do what she was planning to do.

It was hopeless.

Ellen's body was clamouring for the sort of satisfaction which, at the moment, she felt only Jon could give her.

Grabbing a bottle of wine and a large bunch of seedless grapes — both moving-in presents from Kate — she thrust them into a carrier bag and left the flat.

When Jon answered the door he was surprised but delighted to see Ellen standing there.

He was even more delighted when she suddenly threw open the light cream trenchcoat she was wearing. Underneath, she was clad in only a black silk basque, tiny black panties and black seamed stockings. She stood there in her high-heeled shoes with her luscious breasts threatening to spill out over the top of the tight-fitting bodice, smiling at him invitingly.

Jon felt his automatic physical response so strongly that he half expected his zip to give way under the strain. His mouth went dry and he tried unsuccessfully to speak.

There was a movement in the hallway behind Jon and to her absolute horror Ellen saw Ernie emerge from the sitting room. His jaw dropped, then his mouth worked spasmodically for a few moments before he managed to exclaim triumphantly, 'You randy sod, Wright! You *are* poking Ellen!'

He leered at her knowingly and she hastily closed the trenchcoat, knotting the belt firmly around her waist.

'How about a threesome, Lolita?' he suggested

hopefully. 'It'd be the best night of your young life.'

Wheeling round, Jon grabbed Ernie by the collar and pushed him back against the wall.

'You're going now, Ernie,' he told him amiably, 'and if a word of this gets around the office I'll tell everyone about that time in Bristol – I still have the negative – then I'll bang your head against the wall until your brain has rearranged itself into some semblance of intelligent life.'

A few moments later, after Ernie had been pushed out of the door, Ellen asked apprehensively, 'Do you think he'll keep quiet?'

'It would be breaking the habit of a lifetime, I admit. On the other hand, he knows that if I pin a copy of a certain photo on the office wall, he'll never be able to show his face in there again. Anyway, enough about Ernie . . .' His hands went to the belt of her mac. ' . . . where were we before we were so rudely interrupted?'

An hour later, propped up against a pile of pillows on Jon's bed, Ellen tentatively told him about her dream. They were both dishevelled and breathless and Jon had just opened the bottle of wine Ellen had brought. It was immediately obvious that he found her dream as arousing as she had.

'Do you want me to go out and get some grapes now?' he enquired, running his hand lazily over the curve of her hip.

'I brought some with me,' she admitted demurely. 'I put them in the fridge while you were in the bathroom.'

Jon pushed a pillow under her backside and arranged her to his satisfaction, so she was half reclining with her legs spread and her knees bent.

Pulling a large juicy grape from the bunch, he gently inserted it into Ellen's honeypot. She shivered with delight when she felt the fruit's yielding coolness against her pussy lips. With her head back and her eyes half closed she moved her pelvis against his hand as he inserted another.

When there were three grapes inside her he popped one into her mouth and watched as she bit into it. Ellen felt the sweet juice spurting out and moaned in anticipation.

Three more grapes followed the first ones into her honeypot. Then Jon set about the immensely pleasurable task of retrieving them.

One of them must have burst its skin because, when he plunged his tongue into her, he could taste it. Licking and probing, he managed to get his tongue around a grape and scoop it out, biting triumphantly into its sweetness. While Ellen wriggled ecstatically he removed them one at a time.

'I can't stand it,' she moaned.

'You'll have to,' he told her. 'There's still one to go.'

By the time the last grape had been removed Ellen was writhing around on the bed, incoherent with pleasure, the pillow beneath her backside sticky with juices. Reaching out she pulled Jon down on top of her and wound her legs around his waist.

'Screw me,' she moaned imploringly. Jon slid obligingly into her, penetrating as far as he could, then slowly withdrew. Ellen squeezed with her internal muscles, trying to keep him inside her, but he pulled out until only the tip of his cock was still making contact.

INDECENT

He thrust slowly into her again while she relaxed internally to make his entrance as easy as possible. They made love at this leisurely pace for several minutes, with Ellen relaxing on every up stroke and tightening her muscles on every down stroke.

But she was too impatient for it to be that way for long.

Soon she was urging him on to greater efforts, her legs locked tightly around his waist, her dark hair spilling out over his pillow as her head thrashed wildly from side to side.

At last she felt the delicious hot spurting inside her and arched her back with a little cry as the first of several dizzying waves of pleasure broke over her.

Late in the evening they lay there in the light of the bedside lamp among a twisted tangle of damp sheets.

'I wonder what Ernie's doing now?' said Ellen teasingly.

'Probably thinking about what we're doing,' returned Jon.

'What a horrible thought.'

'Or watching his copy of the notorious video for the twenty-third time.'

'Even worse.'

She glanced at the clock.

'It's nearly midnight. I'd better be going.'

Jon propped himself up on one elbow and looked down at her.

'Why don't you stay the night?'

Ellen looked evasive then said determinedly, 'This was just a one-off Jon. We can't carry on like this.'

Reaching out Jon slipped a hand between her thighs.

'Really?' he asked softly. 'How about like this?' Against her will Ellen found herself opening her legs wider and settling back among the pillows.

'Maybe,' she gasped at last, winding her arms around his neck and pulling him down beside her.

Headline Delta Erotic Survey

In order to provide the kind of books you like to read - and to qualify for a free erotic novel of the Editor's choice - we would appreciate it if you would complete the following survey and send your answers, together with any further comments, to:

Headline Book Publishing
FREEPOST 9 (WD 4984)
London
W1E 7BE

1. Are you male or female?
2. Age? Under 20 / 20 to 30 / 30 to 40 / 40 to 50 / 50 to 60 / 60 to 70 / over
3. At what age did you leave full-time education?
4. Where do you live? (Main geographical area)
5. Are you a regular erotic book buyer / a regular book buyer in general / both?
6. How much approximately do you spend a year on erotic books / on books in general?
7. How did you come by this book?
7a. If you bought it, did you purchase from: a national bookchain / a high street store / a newsagent / a motorway station / an airport / a railway station / other........
8. Do you find erotic books easy / hard to come by?
8a. Do you find Headline Delta erotic books easy / hard to come by?
9. Which are the best / worst erotic books you have ever read?
9a. Which are the best / worst Headline Delta erotic books you have ever read?
10. Within the erotic genre there are many periods, subjects and literary styles. Which of the following do you prefer:
10a. (period) historical / Victorian / C20th / contemporary / future?
10b. (subject) nuns / whores & whorehouses / Continental frolics / s&m / vampires / modern realism / escapist fantasy / science fiction?

10c. (styles) hardboiled / humorous / hardcore / ironic / romantic / realistic?

10d. Are there any other ingredients that particularly appeal to you?

11. We try to create a cover appearance that is suitable for each title. Do you consider them to be successful?

12. Would you prefer them to be less explicit / more explicit?

13. We would be interested to hear of your other reading habits. What other types of books do you read?

14. Who are your favourite authors?

15. Which newspapers do you read?

16. Which magazines?

17. Do you have any other comments or suggestions to make?

If you would like to receive a free erotic novel of the Editor's choice (available only to UK residents), together with an up-to-date listing of Headline Delta titles, please supply your name and address:

Name..

Address...

....

....

More Erotic Fiction from Headline:

JOHNNY ANGELO
GROUPIES
RED-HOT DAYS IN THE SUMMER OF SEX

SUMMER IN THE CITY

It's London in the summer of 1966 in the heady days of sex and drugs and rock and roll. And for the members of The Getaways, the country's hottest new group, the most important of these is sex!

There's Tony, the lead guitar, whose speciality is charming dolly birds out of their minidresses in the back of his E-Type. David, the bass player, is a sucker for the more sophisticated woman – like the manager's kinky wife. The rhythm guitarist, Sly, will pull anything for a laugh – and he doesn't care who's watching. Then there's Jud the drummer, the innocent of the group. But now he's surrounded by fans with long legs, short skirts and wicked ideas, innocence is a vanishing commodity...

More erotic entertainment from Headline:
HIGH JINKS HALL   AMOUR AMOUR
LUST ON THE LOOSE   EXPOSED
FONDLE ALL OVER   AMATEUR NIGHTS

FICTION/EROTICA   0 7472 4091 4

A selection of Erotica from Headline

FONDLE ON TOP	Nadia Adamant	£4.99 ☐
EROS AT PLAY	Anonymous	£4.99 ☐
THE GIRLS' BOARDING SCHOOL	Anonymous	£4.99 ☐
HOTEL D'AMOUR	Anonymous	£4.99 ☐
A MAN WITH THREE MAIDS	Anonymous	£4.99 ☐
RELUCTANT LUST	Lesley Asquith	£4.50 ☐
SEX AND MRS SAXON	Lesley Asquith	£4.50 ☐
THE BLUE LANTERN	Nick Bancroft	£4.99 ☐
AMATEUR NIGHTS	Becky Bell	£4.99 ☐
BIANCA	Maria Caprio	£4.50 ☐
THE GIRLS OF LAZY DAISY'S	Faye Rossignol	£4.50 ☐

All Headline books are available at your local bookshop or newsagent, or can be ordered direct from the publisher. Just tick the titles you want and fill in the form below. Prices and availability subject to change without notice.

Headline Book Publishing PLC, Cash Sales Department, Bookpoint, 39 Milton Park, Abingdon, OXON, OX14 4TD, UK. If you have a credit card you may order by telephone — 0235 831700.

Please enclose a cheque or postal order made payable to Bookpoint Ltd to the value of the cover price and allow the following for postage and packing:
UK & BFPO: £1.00 for the first book, 50p for the second book and 30p for each additional book ordered up to a maximum charge of £3.00.
OVERSEAS & EIRE: £2.00 for the first book, £1.00 for the second book and 50p for each additional book.

Name ....

Address ....

....

....

If you would prefer to pay by credit card, please complete:
Please debit my Visa/Access/Diner's Card/American Express (delete as applicable) card no:

Signature ....Expiry Date ....